"Why are you still married?" Trevor asked.

"I don't want to talk about that. I just am and will probably go on being married unless I can sort out one big problem."

"Let me help you with the problem."

Caitlin shook her head.

"I don't understand why you're holding back," he said.

Caitlin was here again, close, yet as far away as she'd ever been since she left him before. That much he understood very well.

"Remember our place on the cliffs?" she asked.

"You know I remember."

"What comes back the clearest, Trevor?"

He was only human and he'd gone over those times again and again, embellishing each little encounter. "This." Leaning toward her, he gathered both her hands into one of his. "Next step is yours."

"Shut up," she said, so softly he wasn't sure he'd heard correctly. "Shut up and kiss me. Then don't say another word before you take me home."

Also available from MIRA Books and
STELLA CAMERON

MOONTIDE
UNDERCURRENTS
ALL SMILES

Watch for STELLA CAMERON's
newest historical romance

7B

March 2001

Stella Cameron

ONCE AND FOR
Always

MIRA

ISBN 1-55166-580-8

ONCE AND FOR ALWAYS

Visit us at www.mirabooks.com

Printed in U.S.A.

In memory of Selina Lloyd-Worth,
my mother

TENBY, or *Dinbych-y-Pysgod* in Welsh:

"You may travel the world over, but you will find nothing more beautiful: it is so restful, so colorful and so unspoilt."
—Augustus John, artist

Prologue

TENBY, or *Dinbych-y-Pysgod* in Welsh:

"You may travel the world over, but you will find
nothing more beautiful: it is so restful, so colorful
and so unspoilt."

—Augustus John, artist

He was the quietest eighteen-year-old boy she'd ever
met. At least, he was quiet around her. She'd seen him
being pretty rowdy with his friends.

"Do you like being in Wales?" he asked. "It must be
a lot different from America."

Caitlin looked up at him. He stared at the ocean. "I do
like it here," she said. "It's different and that's exciting."
Every day this week he'd followed her from school and
asked in his soft Welsh voice if he could walk her home.
And each day she'd said yes, her heart thumping, a funny
tingling in her arms and legs.

He shoved his hands into the pockets of his jeans and
kicked at rocks underfoot. She liked the way he dressed,

casually but more tidily than most of the boys in the local school. And she liked him being tall because she was, too.

"How long will you stay in Tenby?"

"Until it's time to start school in Los Angeles in the fall. I wish I could be here longer, but I need to be back in the States for my senior year of high school."

"Why did you come?"

Anyone else would have asked these questions when they'd first met. Not Trevor Morgan. Until today he'd barely said two words to her. Their afternoon walks had been carried out in silence until he said goodbye at the gate to her grandparents' yard. Now the strained set of his fine features, his big hunched shoulders, the occasional sidelong shift of his serious gray eyes let her know that he'd probably rehearsed what he wanted to say a dozen times and agonized again and again, trying to get started.

They carried on along the cliffs toward her grandparents' house, which lay north of the bustling fishing and resort town of Tenby on the southwest coast of Wales. Just as Trevor had suggested, everything here was foreign to Caitlin, but with each day, Los Angeles felt farther away and less real.

Trevor stopped walking and faced the sea. "Would you like to sit down for a bit?"

No eighteen-year-old boy back home would be so diffident, so uncomfortable around a girl who interested him. Caitlin was very sure she interested Trevor.

"Yes. There's a hollow over there. Right at the edge of the cliff. We'll be mostly under the wind."

Wordlessly he took her hand and guided her through wildly rustling scrub grass into a sandy bowl above a sheer drop to the chrysolite-green water. As soon as she sat cross-legged on the coarse sand he let her go and dropped down beside her.

"Only another week before school's out," he remarked.

"Mmm. A month hasn't really been long enough to get much of a feel for the differences between the curriculum here and back home. But I've got an idea school's a little tougher here, and I'm looking forward to the summer vacation."

"What will you do?" Now he looked directly at her. His eyes were a steely gray, like the ocean below them on a cloudy day. "I mean what will you do in the holidays?"

"I haven't really thought about it too much. Help my grandparents around the house, I suppose. And come out here to walk. Maybe sail a little if I can rent a boat. And swim, of course."

"I've got a sailboat."

Instantly he became red and poked holes in the sand with a long forefinger.

She mustn't laugh or he'd think she was amused at him rather than delighted. "Is that an invitation?"

"I suppose so."

"Then thank you. I'll look forward to it. Do you like to swim—when you're not playing that awful rugby, that is?"

"Rugger isn't awful. It's a great game."

"If you say so." She wouldn't tell him that the only reason she'd gone out to the school playing field to watch the team practice the strange rough game was that she wanted to see him. He was as noisy as his teammates out there—yelling and pushing, playing a sport she didn't understand, although it reminded her of American football.

"We won't be playing rugger in the summer," Trevor said.

"Does that mean you might want to come swimming then?"

"With you?"

She was the one with the reputation for reticence. The tables were being turned here, and she enjoyed the sense of power. "Yes, with me. You take me sailing because you've got a boat, and I'll take you swimming because I can swim."

"I can swim, too."

They laughed and Caitlin felt him relax a little.

"Your family runs that big tavern in town, don't they?"

He nodded and stuck a blade of grass between square even teeth. "The White Knight. Only it's called a pub in this country, not a tavern. My grandfather ran it before my dad took over."

"And one day I suppose it'll be your turn."

"No." He sounded adamant. "Not me. I want to go to school in London and become an accountant."

Before she could make the mistake of saying that being an accountant sounded boring, a gull swooped in, squawked, flapped its wings furiously at the sight of Trevor and Caitlin and swept away again. The dried grass around them smelled sweet, the salty aroma from the sea, warm.

Trevor leaned forward and his striped T-shirt stretched over his broad back. "Where did you get a name like Caitlin? It's Irish, isn't it? Caitlin Rhys. They don't match. You said your father grew up here and you can't get much more Welsh than Rhys."

When he said her name it sounded different—lilting, nice—not flat the way she was used to hearing it. She glanced at his strong tanned arms, his straight brown hair tossed this way and that in the breeze. "My grandmother came from Ireland. Her mother's name was Caitlin, so that's where my name comes from. I guess that's where I got the red hair, too, just like Dad. They call him Red.''

"I've never seen him. Does he have blue eyes like you, too?"

"Yes." Her stomach felt jumpy. Just as she'd been watching him, noticing everything about him, he must have been doing the same with her.

"They say in town that your father's a big film producer in Hollywood and your mother's Eileen Allen the actress."

"That's right." She didn't want to talk about all that. Here everything was quieter, more down-to-earth, and much as she loved her parents, she'd rather not think about the make-believe life she often felt she lived.

"Will you be an actress like your mother? You'd look lovely in the pictures."

She couldn't see his face, but his cough made her certain he was blushing again. "I don't want to act. I want to go into design clothing or something. I'm not sure what."

"I see." The way he said it suggested he didn't see at all. "You live in Hollywood, they say. I can't even imagine that. It's something out of the pictures to me."

"It wouldn't be if you went there. It's ordinary. But actually I live in Beverly Hills. That's close to Hollywood though."

"What's it like to have lots of money and live in a big house with a pool and servants and…?" He closed his mouth. "That's rude to ask personal questions. I'm sorry."

"It's okay. And living that way is okay, too, only it's better here."

He scooted around until he faced her. "You mean that?"

"Yep. This is the first time I can remember when I've felt free. You shouldn't have to wait until you're seventeen to feel free."

Trevor let sand slip through his fingers before he replied. "I like you, Caitlin Rhys. I'd like to swim and sail a lot with you."

She leaned over and folded her hands over his. "I'd like that, too," she told him.

He sighed, keeping his eyes on their hands until the silence made Caitlin nervous. She swallowed and swallowed again, waiting for him to say something. He didn't.

"Trevor," she said when she couldn't be quiet any longer, "look at me." When he did she leaned forward and touched her mouth to his. She felt him jolt. He pulled back, his eyes startled, then put a hand on each of her shoulders.

He'd never kissed or been kissed by a girl before, Caitlin realized. The idea thrilled her. She returned his gaze, thinking how firm yet gentle his mouth had felt.

The next kiss was better, a lot better. With Caitlin's guidance, Trevor learned quickly.

The sun was much lower when he finally walked her the rest of the way home.

"Do you have to go back?"

"You know I do."

Trevor held her so fiercely she could hardly breathe. "Tell them you won't. Tell them you'd rather go to school here."

August was drawing to a close but the sun beat down into their little hollow above the ocean with more intensity than it had all summer. Caitlin shifted until she could kiss

Trevor's neck. Her insides hurt, and her throat and her eyes stung.

"Tell them." He shook her slightly and rested his cheek on her hair. "Come October, I'll be in school in London. But it's not so far, and we can see each other there or here whenever I can get the money."

He was old-fashioned. Throughout the weeks of vacation he'd refused to allow her to pay for as much as a candy bar, and she'd let him spend the money he earned helping his father, because she wouldn't risk hurting his ego.

"Caitlin, will you stop with the silence and say something?" When he was anxious he sounded even more Welsh than usual.

She wanted to stay right where she was forever. But in some ways she saw what had to be more clearly than Trevor. "I must go home to my parents. You know how your mother and father would miss you if you went away and then said you didn't want to go home to them."

"That's different. I'm the only kid they've got."

Caitlin shook her head. "You aren't thinking. *I'm* the only child my folks have. But that isn't the point. I don't want to go, Trevor, but I *have* to."

"I love you," he said, and she knew he was crying.

Her own tears began. "I love you, too. And I'm going to write to you every week. I promise. Every week."

He sniffed and held her away to see her face. She would go, just as she said she must. Somehow he had to imprint in his mind the way she looked: her tall almost frail body, her long red hair, shot through with sunlight now, her slender face that showed barely a trace of tan...her blue, blue eyes.

"Will you write to me, Trevor?"

"Yes," he whispered. "I'll write every week, twice a

week. And one day we'll be together again. Promise me that, *cari*.''

He'd called her *cari* many times before she'd asked what it meant and he'd told her it was Welsh for *love*. Now his heart hurt with the love he felt for her.

''We'll be together again,'' she said. Her cheeks were wet and he kissed salt tears.

''Forever?'' he asked. ''Tell me we'll never stop loving each other and one day we'll find a way to be with each other forever?''

''Forever and for always,'' she said. ''I promise.''

1

As Caitlin had noted a week ago, on the evening she'd arrived back in Tenby, the town had changed very little in nineteen years. Her uncle, Thomas Rhys, had picked her and Mary up at Heathrow Airport in London and driven them to Wales. As they'd entered the outskirts of the medieval walled town she'd held her breath, expecting to be disappointed, to wish she'd stayed away and kept her memories. But it all looked the same: winding narrow streets, Regency houses in the center of town and along the perimeter of the old fishing harbor and, standing stark on its seaward knoll, the ruined Norman castle.

Tonight, at her uncle's insistence, she'd left her daughter at home and ventured out for the first time since her arrival. Enough carrying on like a hermit up there on her cliff, he'd told her. Coming to Wales for a rest and a quiet place to work for a few months was all very well, but "young things" needed to get about a bit.

"Now then, Caitlin, are you and Mary getting settled in that old cottage?"

Thomas was a big man, as big as her father had been and with the same shock of curly hair, once bright red but white now that he neared seventy-five.

"Pretty much," she told him. "Mary and I have scrubbed and painted all week. She loves it. It's like playing house, she says. This is the first time she's ever been

able to do things like paint walls. Back in..." Caitlin
stopped. Back in L.A., she'd almost said, but that was a
subject to be avoided. "Mary's going to do well here. I'm
sure of it."

From the window of Thomas's old green Morris, Caitlin watched the moored boats jostling in the harbor. Leaving Los Angeles and coming here for a winter would
prove a good decision. It had to. At first she'd worried
about uprooting fifteen-year-old Mary, but now her
daughter was more animated and carefree than Caitlin remembered her in years. If the animation could only last....

"Mary's a good-looking little thing," Thomas said.
"With that blond hair she reminds me of your mother
when she was younger. Red used to say that. She didn't
get the brown eyes from Eileen, though. And she's too
thin, like..." Thomas closed and pursed his lips.

Like David, Caitlin thought, and sighed. David Mc-
Bride was very evident in their daughter's appearance, but
not in her character. Mary was as thoughtful of others as
David was self-centered, as gentle as he was hard.

Thomas cleared his throat. He'd visited Los Angeles
several times and his dislike for her husband had been
obvious. "Red and Eileen were always so close," he said
of her parents. "She must miss him."

"Yes, she does. They were married a long time." It
still hurt to think that her beloved, incorrigible father was
dead. He'd been a force wherever he went, moving like
a purposeful whirlwind through every situation. "Mary
adored Dad, as well. The last two years have been hard
for her and for Mother. Me, too."

Thomas turned the Morris from Warren onto White
Lion Street. He drove with his whole body, as if shifting
his weight would help direct the car. "Of course it's hard
on you," he agreed. He might have added that his only

brother had meant more to him than anyone else in the world, including his parents. "Have you made a decision about finalizing... That's none of my business, none of my business indeed." He frowned. "That Mary of yours is bright, too, the way you were at her age."

Caitlin knew he'd been about to make a reference to David and their suspended marriage. Although he'd never said as much, she was sure Thomas shared the opinion of many that it was time she turned her longstanding legal separation into a divorce. She was glad not to discuss the subject. She made herself smile. "You didn't meet me until I was seventeen. And I suppose you mean I got dumber as I got older?"

He looked at her blankly and didn't answer. Humor wasn't Thomas's long suit. A bachelor who'd lived with his parents until first his mother, then his father died, he was a man of few words and very serious. He'd been a schoolteacher for thirty years, and Caitlin wondered how he'd coped with generation after generation of Tenby's eleven-year-olds.

"School started a month ago," Thomas said suddenly as if she'd transmitted an idea. "Is Mary enrolled? Time she got started."

"I know, but I haven't had much time yet. It took me all of September to get organized to come, and somehow I didn't get around to writing about Mary's schooling. I just assumed she'd go where I did when I was here before and that all I'd have to do was get her there. I can't believe we're into October already."

"I'll go and see the principal for you," he stated. "Jon Ellis is a friend of mine. He'll see the girl's properly placed and keep an eye on her. I'll do it tomorrow."

Caitlin slipped down in the seat. "I'd appreciate that.

I'm hoping this break will be good for her. Things have been tough, Thomas.''

He glanced at her, nodded and returned his attention to the road. They turned left at the Norton and rumbled past a row of tall, flat-fronted terraced houses—red brick, gray concrete-faced, blue, yellow or whitewashed, most with an apexed roof and attic windows topping the three-or four-story structures.

Thomas steered the car into a narrower street. It was familiar but Caitlin didn't remember the name. ''Where are we going?''

''Pub,'' Thomas said in a tone that suggested she ought to know. ''Time you got yourself a local, like any other self-respecting Welshman.''

She thought about mentioning that she was neither Welsh nor a man, but decided the effort would be wasted. Thomas had a way of behaving as if the rest of the world outside Wales didn't exist, a trait he'd inherited from his parents, her grandparents. Caitlin remembered, as she had so often during this week, her Welsh grandparents and the summer she'd spent with them. It made her sad to recall that she'd only seen them once more after that, in Los Angeles where they'd been clearly uncomfortable, and now they were both dead.

At the next corner Thomas made another of his racing leans and slowed from fifteen to five miles an hour to enter the courtyard of a large whitewashed pub. Caitlin looked up at the swinging sign on its ornate black pole and her stomach made a slow revolution.

The White Knight.

Her skin turned a little cold before she sat upright and told herself how foolish she was. Before coming back to Wales, she had thought briefly of Trevor Morgan. There had even been moments when she'd wondered how it would feel to see him again. But Trevor was in London, following his star and being an accountant, just as he'd planned. She knew that much from the few letters they'd sent back and forth before Trevor lost interest and his correspondence stopped. Trevor's father might still be landlord of The White Knight, but he wouldn't even know her.

The bar Thomas led her to was crammed with Friday night celebrators. She followed her uncle's broad back through the crowd to a spot near a crooked stone fireplace, where brass pots and kettles suspended on hooks reflected the flames.

Acrid cigarette smoke stung Caitlin's eyes and laced every breath she took. Still, she liked the cozy atmosphere and was grateful for refuge from the chilly air outside.

"What'll it be?" Thomas, normally soft-spoken, bellowed over the din.

"Manhattan, please," Caitlin said automatically and turned her attention to an elderly looking parrot. Its cage hung from a bar embedded in a stone wall, and he surveyed the jumble of laughing people with one large and slowly blinking eye. The other eye he kept closed.

Thomas, returning to tap her shoulder, broke her staring match with the green and orange bird. "You put sweet vermouth in one of those things you drink, don't you?"

Caitlin nodded. "Yes, that's right."

He scratched his beaked nose. "Trevor asked if it's rye that goes in it."

"Ye...what?"

"Trevor wants to know if that's what goes into—"

"Yes, yes," she interrupted him faintly, "rye and bitters."

Thomas walked away, seeming to Caitlin like a movie character in a slow-motion frame. She narrowed her eyes against the smoke and looked in the direction he was headed.

Given her height and from where she stood with a clear line of sight over the heads of seated customers and between the row of men leaning on the bar, Caitlin had no difficulty seeing Trevor Morgan.

He was older—his tall body had filled out and he looked powerful in his dark polo-necked sweater, but it was Trevor nevertheless.

Caitlin took a deep breath, tasted smoke but didn't care. Awkwardly she ran a hand through her hair. It was as red as ever and as curly and unruly, but longer than when she'd last seen Trevor, way past her shoulders. Next she touched the corner of one eye as if she might smooth away the fine lines that hadn't been there nineteen years ago. She parted her lips and felt tears in her throat, not for what was—life took its course and people made choices they had to live with. No, the rush of sadness was for a memory of what used to be.

Thomas reached the bar and gestured to Trevor, who nodded and picked up a bottle. Another customer spoke to him and he laughed, the way she remembered him laughing, his head tipped back, eyes screwed up, teeth glinting. How old was he, thirty-seven? Yes, her eighteen-year-old friend was thirty-seven now and she thirty-six rather than seventeen.

The tears reached her eyes and she looked at the beamed ceiling. She was a silly emotional woman old enough not to be thrown at the sight of a childhood crush.

Only theirs hadn't been only a crush, had it? Those wonderful long days, carefree, full of plans for the future? What happened to the plans? Caitlin knew the answer. Life had happened, and distance and school…and eventually David. Her spine tightened. How she'd paid! Paid for a twenty-year-old girl's infatuation with a screenwriter ten years her senior in age and a hundred years her senior in experience. But it hadn't been all bad. They'd had eleven good years before the marriage cracked, and she did have Mary from the union. David would always have her thanks for Mary.

She took another deep breath, smiled at a man who bumped into her, returned her attention to Trevor...and met his eyes.

Through the smoke, she saw they were as gray as she remembered, almost silvery at a distance. He wasn't laughing now, not even smiling. The drinks he'd poured for Thomas were forgotten on the counter, and her uncle was involved in conversation with a man beside him. Trevor's face bore its own signs of time. His once-smooth brow was furrowed now, and deep grooves ran from beside his straight nose to the corners of his mouth. The mouth was the same—wide, turned upward. If she didn't know her own vision was blurred, she'd think there could be tears in his eyes, too.

In his still hands, Trevor held the money he'd been given for Thomas's drinks, but although he felt the textures of the notes and coins, all other senses and sounds receded. In the moving collage of ruddy-faced men and women, amid their sturdy, bulkily clad bodies, she was a tall graceful statue, unmoving, staring back at him as if only the two of them were in the room.

Awkwardly he raised a hand in a wave and tried to smile. She waved back, her blue eyes huge, her skin as translucent as it always was in his mind pictures of her.

At first, when her letters had come further and further apart, he'd felt desperate and helpless. Then, when she'd stopped writing altogether, he'd tried to make himself close her out. But whenever he'd walked on the cliffs or sat by the harbor watching sailboats and when he'd swum off one of the beaches, he'd felt her presence. Soon enough there had been the move to London and his marriage to Gwen—a happy marriage for the few years they'd been given—and then Caitlin had truly slipped into his past. Only when he'd given up his accounting job and returned alone to Tenby to take over from his father had he occasionally thought of her again.

"Are you dreaming, Trevor?"

Trevor started and focused on Thomas Rhys. Until tonight he'd forgotten that Thomas was Caitlin's uncle. She must be visiting him. "Ah, Thomas, you know I'm not a dreamer. Here's your change, man. Is that your niece you've got with you? Caitlin is her name, isn't it?" Phony. He knew the answers. But he must go through the formalities.

"Caitlin, yes." Thomas picked up the drinks then stopped in the act of turning away. "And if I hadn't forgotten! Of course, you two were friends when you were a couple of string beans, weren't you? You'll have to say hello. She'd like that. Our Caitlin needs some cheering up."

Sweat broke out on Trevor's palms as Thomas walked away. He was a fool to be afraid of meeting her again. Whatever juvenile things had passed between them were years behind. She'd probably forgotten altogether. But he was edgy. She needed cheering up? He sucked in his lower lip. And why would that be?

He watched Thomas approach Caitlin, hand over the drink and motion toward Trevor with his head. She dipped her face and the wonderful hair fell forward. Even more beautiful maybe? Longer, alive in the light from the fire. But she was thin, thinner than she should be. A soft black woolen dress, like nothing the women around here wore, fitted her snugly and accentuated her fragile shoulders, small breasts and tiny waist before flaring into a full skirt. He couldn't see her legs or feet but imagined she wore high heels. She was taller than most women in the bar and even many of the men, at least five foot ten. When they were kids he'd always been grateful for his six-foot-two frame because he'd felt strong and masculine beside her.

"Oh, Thomas, I don't think so," Caitlin said in answer to Thomas's suggestion that she say "hello to an old friend."

"We knew each other so long ago," Caitlin went on, "and I might make him uncomfortable." She didn't admit that she already felt uncomfortable and ridiculously sad and that she wanted to go back to the cottage and Mary.

"No such thing," Thomas insisted. "He's waiting to talk to you. Come on, Caitlin, girl."

A firm hand on her elbow, propelling her forward, made any further protest futile.

Then she was there, inches away, looking up into Trevor's face. And she couldn't speak at all, not even to say hi.

"Well, you two," Thomas said from somewhere behind Caitlin's shoulder. "I don't suppose you even know how much worry you caused my parents that summer, God rest their souls."

Trevor smiled. The dimples were there on each side of his mouth, and his left brow still raised slightly with his grin. "I remember. How about you, Caitlin?"

She found her voice. "Yes, I do. Hello, Trevor. How've you been?" She set her drink on the counter, using the action to anchor herself, and offered him her hand.

"I've been fine," he said and took not one but both of her hands in his. "Fine." Almost before she knew what he intended, he leaned over the counter and kissed her cheek. Beside her face he asked quietly, ''Do you feel as good as you look?''

She opened her mouth to breathe and smelled not smoke but Trevor, a clean smell, with a hint of the sea— or was it just that for her Trevor and the sea were synonymous? She steadied herself with a hand on his shoulder and felt the flexing of solid muscle beneath rough wool.

Then he drew back. ''Are you happy, *cari*?''

The last vestiges of air rushed from her lungs. *Cari.* The years were stripped away, and the gray in his thick hair, the frown and laughter lines on his brow and around his eyes and mouth. He was the boy beside her in the sunwarmed hollow in the cliffs.

''Caitlin?''

She shook her head and returned his smile, smiled more broadly and finally laughed. ''I'm just great, thanks. And you look great, too, Trevor. Good to see you again.''

''Likewise,'' he said, still holding her hand. ''We'll have to get together and talk about old times.''

She opened her mouth to agree at the same moment as he glanced down…and took away his hand. Her wedding ring shone on her finger, and the huge diamond solitaire she'd once been so proud to wear. Caitlin closed her eyes an instant. There was no point, might never ever be any other point in doing much talking with Trevor Morgan or any man who interested her. Even if she and David McBride had ceased to be husband and wife in any true sense five years ago, even if they had been legally separated for three years, she had yet to finalize the break.

''Well, I'd better be going,'' she said. Unthinking, she swallowed the manhattan and coughed as it burned down her throat. She lifted her chin. ''My daughter will be won-

dering where I am." Might as well make her position very
clear.

Trevor didn't answer, but his smile was gone. He sa-
luted her, bowing to look up at her under his dark arched
brows. A nerve twitched by one eye.

"Do you mind if we go, Uncle Thomas?" Caitlin
asked. "I promised Mary we'd only be a little while."

As she turned away she caught sight of something shining. Trevor also wore a wedding band.

"Paper shoes."

Trevor half heard the comment of a man at the bar. His
attention was on Caitlin's slender, retreating form.
Thomas, volubly unhappy at leaving, had downed the rest
of his beer and was shambling along in her wake.

The door opened, closed, and they were gone.

"Funny thing for a woman to do if you ask me," the
man to Trevor's right was saying. "Why would she want
to come to Tenby to do it? And in winter of all times?
My missus said the woman laughs at the wind. Ninety
miles an hour was, um, great, did she say? Thinks it helps
her concentrate. My missus is helping out a bit with cleaning up there at the old Davies's cottage where they're
staying and she was talking about it."

Trevor looked at Colin-crust as he was known, being
the local baker. The man's last name, if he'd ever known
it, eluded Trevor. "What did you say, Colin?"

"Her." Colin jerked his head in the direction of the
door. "The American woman. Thomas Rhys's niece."

"What about her?"

A ring of interested listeners, beer glasses held firmly
in workworn hands, drew closer around Colin.

"Like I told you," Colin said, his chest expanding as
he gained momentum, "she's some sort of fancy designer

from Los Angeles.'' He surveyed his audience. ''That's in California.''

There was a chorused grunt.

Trevor felt a small rush of irritation together with a proprietary sense to which he knew he had no right. ''She's Caitlin Rhys,'' he said and swiped a cloth over the counter. ''She spent a summer here years ago when she was...a kid.''

Colin puffed up even more. ''McBride's her name, now she's married. The missus says her husband's something in the pictures. Thomas wanted the woman and her daughter to stay with him at the old Rhys house, but she insisted on a place of her own. To work, she says.''

McBride. So that was her name now. Funny how in his mind she'd remained Caitlin Rhys of the red hair and bright laugh, eternally seventeen and certainly not married with a child. One of the barmen who worked for him asked a question and Trevor nodded distractedly.

Of course she would be married. She was beautiful, rich, charming. Women like that were always married. He'd learned to push aside the childish declarations of love they'd once made, and evidently so had she. But that wasn't news. He'd known as much within weeks of her return to America because weeks had been all it had taken for her to forget her promise to keep writing to him.

The reason for this irrational feeling of loss was that, just as Thomas had lightly suggested, he was a dreamer. He also spent too much time with nothing but his own thoughts for company. After Gwen's death he'd decided he didn't want to chance a replay of the kind of pain he'd suffered then. But now he'd had four years alone. It was time to take an interest in some of the women who let him know they noticed him. Yes. He squared his shoulders and plastered a smile on his face. No more spending all his free time on solitary reading punctuated by visits to his parents and Gwen's, and on coaching sessions with the local boys' rugby team. He was going to come to life as a man again.

"She does it for the pictures, I think," Colin was saying.

Trevor rested his elbows on the bar and supported his chin. "What exactly does the lady do for the movies?"

"Makes the paper shoes," Colin said, exasperation raising his voice. "I suppose someone else copies them in leather or something. How would I know? But that's what she does, and from her things—according to the missus, that is—she makes a lot of money. And the girl—her name's Mary—the missus says she's a nice little thing but she doesn't talk much. Doesn't eat anything, either, so—"

"So the missus says," Trevor finished for him, and the other men laughed. "They're staying in the Davies's cottage, did you say?" He shouldn't be asking, shouldn't care, but he couldn't help himself.

"That's right. And they don't go out...until tonight, that is. Everything's delivered—groceries, milk, meat. They've been doing the place up inside and all the supplies for that are delivered, too. Some man came down from *Cardiff* to help with the furniture and that stuff, mind you. Think of that. All the way from *Cardiff* just to tell you what kind of settee and chairs you should have."

Trevor smiled. Colin made Cardiff sound like a place on the moon rather than a city a few miles away. Finding out more about Caitlin tempted Trevor. He'd like to ask if her husband would be joining her, but the wiser path would be to forget she existed and turn the conversation to safer ground.

While he was thinking of a way to change the subject, Barry Thompson, the burly owner of a fishing fleet out of

Tenby, did the job for him. "How are our boys coming along, Trevor?"

"Ah, yes. How was the workout this afternoon?" Colin added.

"Our boys" were the Knights, a team of seventeen-year-old rugby players sponsored and coached by Trevor. This year there were high hopes of them finishing at the top of their league. Several boys were even favored to become members of the Welsh junior international team, and the whole town followed their progress with something near religious fanaticism. Local boys on a winning Welsh team against a squad fielded by England would put Tenby into orbit, as far as the natives were concerned.

Trevor picked up a stack of clean beer mats from beneath the counter and began to spread them. "The boys are improving," he said. The note of awe that entered every exchange about the team made him uneasy. "They may even turn out to be almost as good as we hope they are."

"Come on, Trevor boy—" Barry reached to slap Trevor's shoulder "—you're being humble. They'll pull it off. You see if they don't. With Michael Hearns and that Will Colly on our side how can we fail? Am I right, Jon?"

Trevor hadn't noticed the arrival of Jon Ellis, principal of Tenby's Progressional School. The man was tall, thin, dry—as if he'd turned to paper among the books and chalk that had filled his days until he'd become the school's principal two years earlier.

"Let's have it, Jon," Barry persisted. "You talk and we all believe. Those boys of ours are going to make us proud, aren't they?"

Jon Ellis looked up from the beer Trevor slid toward him. "Let's hope so," he said and took a slow swallow, rocking back onto his heels and training his eyes on his glass once more.

Trevor's stomach rolled. He'd been expecting trouble, and it looked as if it could be about to arrive.

"What's that supposed to mean?" another man asked, his stubbed chin jutting.

"Just what I say," Jon said without inflection. He met Trevor's eyes. "Young people have a way of getting carried away when they think they're important, don't they now?"

Trevor tensed his back, waiting.

"Heard any rumors have you, Trevor?" Jon continued. "Any complaints?"

This was it. "Some," Trevor said. Somehow he had to get the feet of some of the puffed-up idiots on the team back on the ground. They were almost becoming menaces.

"I've heard more than some," Jon said. "If I have to use a truant officer to get one or two of your stars in school, they won't be attending practices for a while."

A pool of silence formed amid the ruckus. The men drew closer as if to keep what was said among themselves.

Colin laughed and flapped a hand. "Take it easy, Jon. So one or two of the boys don't go to school now and again. Youngsters have always done those things."

Jon set down his beer with a crack and faced the other man. "Have they also thought they had a right to turn school dances into something no parents in their right minds would let their daughters attend?" He pulled his mouth into a straight line. "And does barging down a pavement arm in arm so everyone else has to walk in the street qualify as something kids have always done? Not in Tenby, Colin. Not in Tenby. They're getting above themselves, and if that doesn't change we're going to have to take a long look at what to do about it."

He'd known trouble was coming. He'd lectured the team about the rumors he'd heard and threatened them with being disbanded. But they'd ignored him. Trevor made a fist on the counter and as quickly shoved it into his pocket. He was angry, but showing it wouldn't help. He had to buy some time to convince his players that if they wanted to go on, they had to shape up.

"Drinks all around on the house," he shouted, attracting the attention of most patrons. At Jon he smiled benignly and winked. "Boys will be boys. Leave them to me. I'll have them sorted out in no time."

The words sounded good. They were hearty enough to make Jon Ellis's face crease into a smile of confidence.

Trevor wished he felt as confident. But he knew the petty crimes the school principal had chronicled were only a few of his miracle team's transgressions.

2

"How was school, darling?" Caitlin asked.

"I dunno."

Hunched low in her pink down coat, her long blond hair tucked inside an upturned collar, Mary came through the back door that opened directly into the kitchen where Caitlin worked at a big oak table. With the girl came the scent of fresh salt air and a rush of cold.

Caitlin pushed aside her sketch pad and wiped colored chalk from her hands with a damp towel. "What do you mean, sweetie, you don't know?"

"It was my first day, Mom." Mary shrugged an Esprit sport bag from her shoulder and dropped it to the floor. "All I did was say my name and where I come from about a hundred times. And put up with a lot of kids staring at me like I'm some sort of alien." She crossed her eyes and poked two fingers up behind her head. "I'm from the planet Los Angeles."

Caitlin covered a smile, remembering her own time in the same school. "It gets better, darling. They'll soon forget you're a foreigner, and you'll have fun."

"I don't care if they do," Mary said, taking off her coat.

"Of course you care," Caitlin said, but her heart sank. The early days of their time here had seemed to relax her tense daughter, but since yesterday Caitlin had again been seeing signs of the old uptight Mary. "Anyway, let's have a snack. Mrs. Johnson brought one of her husband's breads. Something called *Bara Brith*. It's got raisins and currants in it and candied peel. You eat it with butter and Mrs. J. says it's so good it's world famous."

"Not for me, thanks. Sounds gross."

The response was familiar. For months Caitlin had worried about Mary's lack of appetite. Without her coat, dressed in size two jeans and a huge red sweatshirt emblazoned with Coca Cola in white across the front, she looked frail.

"Oh, you've got to try this bread, Mary. I promised Mrs. J. we'd give her a report tomorrow, and I've been looking forward to a break with you."

The girl's eyes met hers, then slid away. She shrugged. "Okay." She sat at the table, her wrists protruding from her sleeves like knobby sticks.

Caitlin swallowed a sickening knot of anxiety and quickly moved around the kitchen, putting on the kettle, pouring milk for Mary, warming the bread in the hope that the wonderful smell would be tempting.

Then she sat across from her daughter, who was busy looking through the designs Caitlin was working on for a spring showing in Paris.

"These are super, Mom," she said. "I love all the bright colors. Different from last season, huh?"

"Winter's always a bit somber. But I sometimes prefer the mediums. I love working with skins. My lizard boots were a fantastic hit." She took a bite of bread and smiled at Mary. The girl picked a raisin out of her slice and chewed it carefully.

"What do you like best?" Mary asked. "The stuff you do for the clothing couturiers or theatrical designs?"

Caitlin selected a wooden shoe last and turned it this

way and that while she considered how to answer Mary.
The last was covered in fine silver mesh, something she
was experimenting with for an evening treatment. "I
guess it's hard to decide which I prefer. Maybe the couturiers. With them I'm more free. So much of the stage
and screen stuff is almost straight copying work." She set
down the last and swept wadded sheets of paper into a
plastic bag. "Tell me more about your day."

"There's nothing to tell, Mom. I did meet this cool girl
called Constance Trew. She's real popular because her
brother—his name's Owen—he's on some important
rugby team. She sat with me at lunch and walked as far
as the cliff trail with me after school."

"She sounds lovely." Caitlin blessed Constance Trew,
whoever she was. "Ask her home tomorrow. She could
have dinner with us."

"Aw, I'm sure, Mom. Just because she spoke to me for
a bit doesn't mean I can invite her home. She probably
wouldn't come anyway."

Back off, Caitlin warned herself. *Don't rush anything.*
"You're right, of course," she told Mary.

The past months, during which David's unscheduled
visits had become increasingly impossible, had turned
Mary into a nervous and ever more skinny shadow of the
happy child she used to be. Forcing David into a legal
separation three years ago had begun the process of their
daughter's deterioration, but then Mary had stabilized until her father started turning up more and more frequently
and always drunk.

Under the terms of their separation, David wasn't supposed to try to see Caitlin or Mary except by appointment.
He had followed legal instructions only as far as moving
into an apartment that was too close to Caitlin's house for
comfort. But Caitlin didn't have the heart to call the police

when he would arrive on her doorstep, invariably begging for "just a little understanding."

Being away from Los Angeles was as much, if not more, an attempt to help Mary as it was to give Caitlin space to make some decisions. But any change, for either of them, would take time.

Mary took several swallows of milk and stood up to carry her dishes to the sink. She hadn't eaten more than the single raisin. "Um, Mom—" she turned from the sink "—I don't suppose Dad called, did he?"

Caitlin picked up her scissors and a piece of construction paper, frantically searching for the right words to answer the question she'd known was coming.

"He didn't." Mary snatched the rope straps of her bag and headed for the door leading to the rest of the house.

"Wait a minute," Caitlin said. "I thought we made a pact. No more closing each other out."

"I need to look over the books I got. I'm behind everybody else."

These evasion tactics infuriated Caitlin. "The books can wait." She looked at her watch, the old rage at David blocking her throat like a ball of acid. "What time is it in L.A., Mary? If it's four here, that makes it what? Eight in the morning? When was the last time you remember your father up at eight in the morning?"

"So he doesn't get up till the afternoon anymore." Mary's dark eyes blazed, and an unnatural redness splotched her cheeks. "You know how often he works all night. He's got a different schedule than most people, that's all. Why won't you understand that? You've never understood Daddy."

With that Mary slammed from the room, rattling the door in its jamb.

Caitlin slumped in her chair and let her eyes rove over

the big kitchen she'd begun to like. But the bloom was off. The snowy lace curtains at the windows seemed drab; the wallpaper with its tiny blue daisies above the carved white wainscoting, hokey and out of character for a woman whose business was the design of high-fashion footwear.

Who was she kidding? There was no place to hide from reality. She might manage to steal a few hours of peace now and again while she was here, but David would never be far away because Mary loved him, as she was entitled to love her father. And through Mary, David would be kept in the forefront of everything Caitlin tried to do...unless she made the decision to go ahead and turn her separation into divorce. She felt vaguely sick. What would it take to divorce David without destroying Mary, who made no secret of her dream that they'd all be together as a family again one day?

With a sigh, Caitlin started cutting shapes from the construction paper. She would never stop being grateful for her art and for whatever magic had made her so good at it.

The decision of fourteen years ago, that she go back to school, was one of the best she'd made in her life. Mary had still been a baby and Caitlin was uncertain the timing was right, but David had endorsed the idea, insisting she'd waited long enough to start on the career she deserved to have. He used to be so proud of her achievements, before he changed and accused her of competing with him, before he stopped coming home at night and kind "friends" started telling her what they thought she ought to know— that David was frequently seen with other women—before he ceased wanting to sleep with Caitlin at all.

She pulled another wooden last toward her and started wrapping and gluing the paper shapes around it, checking her original sketch while deftly forming a high pump, with the inner sides cut low to show the curve of the instep. She had a unique way of working, and it had made her what she'd become, one of the top shoe designers in the world.

Her work usually shut out thoughts of David, but not today. This time in Wales was to have been her breathing space, her decision-making haven and, damn it, so it would be. She set the paper mock-up aside and picked up the fantastic mesh creation with its fan of pleats over the toe. Heel samples, most of Lucite, were stacked in a box. She selected, not Lucite, but a needle-thin aluminum spike which she held in place calculating balance and effect. Covered in silver satin and studded with tiny mirrored discs, her Cinder's Slippers were going to be a knockout.

What if she completely covered the heels with mirrors? At one time David had taken so much interest in everything she did.... How long ago had it been that their love had started to die?

Caitlin knew the figures. She'd tried to forget them, but they never went away. It had been four and a half years since David's last, abortive attempt to make love to her— if the fumblings of an impotent drunk could ever be referred to as love.

His career had been foundering for months by then, and they'd already started relying solely on Caitlin's resources. On that night she'd warned him that if he wanted to continue to live on her money, he was never to come near her again. And he hadn't. He came and went from a room on the other side of the house, her husband in name only. And for a while he treated her with truculent caution, knowing she shared a knowledge he wanted to shield from the world. But gradually the booze overcame his fear of exposure and the parties began, first small, intense gatherings kept to rooms where David could be sure Mary was never likely to appear, but gradually expanding to wild marathons that rocked the house.

Caitlin gave David another ultimatum: stop the parties or leave. Again he complied…for a while.

His sexual dysfunction was apparently permanent. She didn't need a degree in human sexual behavior to figure out that the parade of women was no more than a disguise he put on to hide his horror at feeling less than a man. In a way she was sorry for him, and she might have tried to urge him to seek professional help if there'd been any chance he would listen. There wasn't. To the outside world, David McBride intended to be viewed as a stud, a devil-may-care sorcerer to beautiful women. On the inside he was a failure in every sense of the word: as a writer whose work had slipped from promising to nonexistent and as a husband who had become no more than a leech who used his wife's money and connections to keep himself near the glitter of Hollywood that was his life's blood.

And finally Caitlin had been forced to take legal action to have him removed from the house permanently. Only her efforts hadn't produced a result that was permanent enough.

She was making her chance for a new start now, and she was making one for Mary. She'd cope. Maybe with Thomas's help she'd manage to come up with a few diversions for the girl. But David couldn't be allowed to slow Caitlin down. In a month she must go to the atelier she used in Paris. There she'd consult with the craftspeople who produced the prototypes of her shoes to be presented to couturiers. Then would come the rounds of the sleek fashion houses and the nervous hours of watching for reactions.

After that, as she had already promised herself, she

would return to Wales and evaluate how to deal with her personal life. If it weren't for Mary, she wouldn't hesitate to divorce David immediately. But Caitlin loved Mary too much to do anything without making sure she could cope.

The jangling sound of the phone in the hall stayed Caitlin's busy hands. The noise came in twin bursts, and she listened to several before she went to answer. She picked up the receiver and looked up the stairs, expecting to see Mary looking back. She wasn't.

"Hello," she said, rolling shoulders still sore from bending over the table. The sibilance of a long-distance call knotted her jaw. She was surprised David had waited so long to call for more money, or some intervention at whatever studio he'd decided to court.

"Baby?" Not David's, but her mother's voice.

Caitlin waited, garnering her strength for Eileen's latest barrage of complaints.

"Are you there, baby?" Eileen, an otherwise sophisticated woman, had never learned not to shriek on long-distance calls.

"I'm here, Mother. How are you?"

"I can't tell you, Caitlin. You don't want to know."

She didn't, but she'd listen anyway. "Something wrong, darling?" Caitlin pinched the bridge of her nose and felt movement beside her. Mary had crept down to sit on the stairs nearby.

"That idiot of a Parynsky gave someone else the part in *Silver Lady*," Eileen said. "Can you believe it? I'm perfect for that part, Caitlin. You know I am. I think I'm going to die of disappointment."

The voice had risen higher. Caitlin glanced at Mary, who must be able to hear the sound if not the words. Mary grimaced and shook her head. She was used to the histrionics of a grandmother who spent too much time alone, feeding not only on genuine grief at the loss of her husband, but also on a trace of rage at him for leaving her without his protective power. With Caitlin, Mary had suffered the silences, punctuated by wailing diatribes about the foolishness of directors who either didn't ask her to audition for the right parts or didn't choose her for them if they did ask.

"Caitlin," Eileen almost screamed. "Are you hearing what I'm telling you? That maniac Parynsky turned your mother down. Me, Eileen Allen Rhys. If your father had still been alive it wouldn't have happened."

"Listen, darling." Caitlin picked up the phone base from its little mahogany table and walked to the foot of the stairs to sit beside Mary. "Are you saying you had an audition?" If so, it would be the first in a very long time.

"We-ll. I called and said I could probably get there sometimes later in the week."

Caitlin clamped the handset between jaw and shoulder and closed her eyes. "Mother, did you break an audition appointment?"

"We-ll—"

"You did. You were supposed to show but you called with an excuse, and since they had to go on with the casting, they chose someone else. Isn't that the way it went?"

Eileen sniffed loudly.

"Parynsky didn't choose someone over you," Caitlin said softly. "You weren't there to compete in the first place."

"You don't understand," came Eileen's subdued response. "I thought he'd wait—"

"For how long? A week? A month? Mother, you wouldn't have gone in any case, because you aren't ready to act again. You want to be, but you aren't. We've gone over and over this. And I'm sure your therapist goes over it, too. Listen to her, Mother, and give yourself the time you need to get over losing Daddy, because that's what's still holding you up.''

The expected tears followed, the accusations leveled at Caitlin's insensitivity, then the making up and the promises that Eileen would work on becoming more independent. Finally, slightly mollified by Caitlin's sympathy and by hearing Mary's voice, Eileen hung up.

"Do you ever get over it when you lose someone for good, Mom?" Mary asked while Caitlin replaced the phone.

"You get used to it more than get over it," she told her. "I'll never forget my dad and neither will you, but we're both carrying on."

Mary lifted herself with a hand on each banister and swung back and forth. When she let go, she landed with a thump and said, "I don't think I could ever get over losing Daddy. I miss him when I don't see him."

"Sweetie," Caitlin began, but Mary shook her head and hurried back upstairs.

Mary was issuing a warning: don't try to shut my father out of my life. Caitlin's head ached.

An hour later, while she was cooking spaghetti for dinner, a loud rap came at the glass-paneled back door. She poured oil over the surface of water boiling in a pot on the stove and went to see who was visiting. Thomas, blowing into his hands and stamping his feet, came in.

"Thought I'd better come over and check up on you," he said. He came every day, usually right before a meal, with the excuse that it was up to him to make sure she and Mary were coping.

Caitlin smiled and held out her hand to take his overcoat and muffler. "It's been a good day," she told him, aware that she wasn't being entirely truthful. "I got a lot of work done. The groceries were delivered bright and early, Mrs. J. came, and Mary got through her first day in school without too much trouble—I think."

He looked at her sharply. "What do you mean, you think?"

"She's quiet, Thomas. She's never made friends easily and here it's likely to be more difficult." She laughed. "She said the kids treated her like an alien."

"Did they now?" Thomas raised the lid on the pan of sauce and sniffed appreciatively. "Well, I'll just have another word with Jon Ellis about that."

"No you won't," Caitlin said more vehemently than she'd intended. "Please don't do that. It could make things worse. Mary will be all right." She gave him a winning smile and added, "Have you had dinner?"

"Well..."

"Good. Then you'll join us for spaghetti. Sit at the table, and I'll get you a Scotch to warm you up."

Thomas did as she asked, visibly pleased. He'd been on his own too much, Caitlin thought. His obvious enjoyment of the hours he spent at the cottage showed how much he needed company.

After they'd eaten and Mary had returned to her room to listen to tapes and read the teen magazines she constantly devoured, Caitlin and Thomas went to sit by the fire in the tiny parlor.

Seated in matching chintz-covered chairs, they stared silently into the flames for a long time before Thomas spoke.

"This is none of my business," he began, reaching into his pocket for his pipe. "I told myself I'd stay out of it. But with your father gone there's no one else to look after you properly."

Caitlin noted that he spoke as if her mother didn't exist. She smiled a little sadly. Caitlin's mother loved her, but Red Rhys had always been the center of Eileen's existence, her daughter an afterthought, and Thomas knew as much.

He found a tin of tobacco and packed the bowl of his pipe, struck a match and drew in a series of hard puffs until the flakes glowed. He sat back. "You aren't really here for a quiet place to work, are you?"

Shock raised the tiny hairs on Caitlin's spine. "I don't know what you mean."

"Yes, you do. I may be a thorny old bachelor, but I'm not a fool. In some ways Red was an ostrich. Stuck his head in the sand and only brought it out to see what he wanted to see. I tried to talk to him about you and David McBride, but he kept saying you were all right. Even after the separation he made excuses, reckoned you both needed time apart to appreciate what you had together. Red was wrong, wasn't he? And that's the real reason you're here, isn't it? You're getting ready to divorce that... You are going to divorce him, aren't you?"

"I haven't—no. No, Thomas. At least, I'm not sure." Sometimes she was, but not when she saw how Mary clung to her father.

"Caitlin—" Thomas hooked both thumbs around his pipe and tapped the stem against his mouth "—I think you are sure. It's Mary that worries you, isn't it? You want to do the best for her, and so you should."

She nodded mutely. Pretending had become too much of an effort, and anyway Thomas made her feel safe.

"Does he run around with other women, the way some of those gossipy friends of yours over there say?"

"Who told you about that?"

"Your father mentioned it in a weak moment. Does David do that?"

How could she explain the farce David McBride really was? "Yes, I guess he does."

"Then what are you waiting for? Divorce the man and find someone who'll give you and Mary the kind of love you deserve."

"Mary loves David," Caitlin said. "Children deserve to have both parents if possible."

Thomas sucked hard on his pipe while he gazed at the fire. "Children are remarkably resourceful," he said. "I wonder if you aren't using Mary as an excuse for not making up your mind and taking final action. Are you afraid of being free?"

Caitlin bristled. "No. And that's not fair, Thomas. Mary does love him, very much. It hasn't been easy to hang on...."

"I'm sure it hasn't," Thomas agreed, his voice soft, his pale blue eyes fixed on Caitlin's.

She held her bottom lip in her teeth. Could he be right? Could she be putting off divorcing David because she hated the thought of all the fuss as much as she worried about Mary's reaction? And was there some sort of safety in her paper marriage?

"Mary's fifteen, you know," Thomas said. He warmed one big gnarled hand. "Before you know where you are, she'll be striking out into her own life. And where will you be then? Are you going to wait until you're too old to have anything worth sharing with someone else?"

The tone of his voice surprised Caitlin. Wistful? Thomas, she suddenly realized, was a lonely man. A rush of sympathy and annoyance at her self-absorption brought tears to Caitlin's eyes. "I'll remember what you've said," she told him. "Not that there's any hurry for me to do anything really."

"There's a hurry to get rid of that bloodsucker before he does any more harm to the two of you. And I think if Red knew how David plays on your poor mother's sympathies as well, he'd be with me in wanting you to get rid of the man."

That was a facet of her dilemma that Caitlin tried not to dwell on. Eileen, hungry for attention, was an easy target for David when he needed an extra loan. And Eileen was probably his only champion. She steadfastly pleaded his case to Caitlin. David was, Eileen often insisted, misunderstood and lonely, just as she was. In that pat litany Caitlin could almost hear David's voice.

"How do you think young Trevor Morgan looks?"

Caitlin started. Thomas had leaned forward to knock out his pipe into an ashtray made from a chunk of curly fossil.

"He looked…he looked good." Her hands couldn't be shaking. Was she so afraid of reacting to a man, any man, that she shook at the mention of a name?

"Mmm. I think he looks like you—lonely and trying to pretend he's not."

She played with the piping along the arm of her chair. "I wouldn't know about that. The last time we met we were children. Now I'm married and so is he. If he's not happy, I'm sorry." And she was. "But you may be imagining things there."

Thomas moved to the edge of his chair, frowning. "You don't know about Trevor, then?"

Caitlin shook her head. "The last I heard he was an accountant in London. Seeing him in the pub the other night was a shock."

"Ah, I see." Thomas stood up and returned to the

kitchen with Caitlin behind him. He pulled on his overcoat and wound the muffler around his neck.

She didn't want to but she asked, "What don't I know about Trevor Morgan?"

"Oh, it's history now. He married a girl from Tenby and they went to live in London. They were happy, I think. Nice little thing she was, Gwen. Quiet. Anyway, she got sick and had some kind of surgery in one of those big London hospitals. Don't know what it was that was wrong with her. Anyway, she died of what they called complications. It wasn't long after that Trevor's dad had a bit of an attack and couldn't manage the business." As if there were nothing more to be said, Thomas opened the door to leave.

"So?" Caitlin pressed.

"So, Trevor came home where he belongs to take over his father's place, of course. There are some who say he's never got over Gwen dying that way, so far from home in a place she didn't like. His mom and dad say he never will get over it, and so do Gwen's. But I don't know about that."

Caitlin held the doorknob while he went outside. In seconds the wind that whined through tortured trees along the cliff took Thomas's footsteps.

Come the weekend he'd take off for Cardiff and buy some new clothes. He hadn't paid much attention to his appearance for too long.

Trevor strolled along the pavement on one side of Tudor Square, glancing into store windows as he went. At the High Street end of the square there was a good men's shop. He could at least stop and have a look. Damn, he hated buying clothes. At least today was Wednesday, early-closing day, and it was already eleven, so he could put the subject out of his mind in an hour.

The bad part about early-closing day was that while the shops were open the town was crowded with shoving throngs determined to beat the clock.

For the second time in as many minutes, he left the sidewalk for the gutter to avoid being mown down. He was looking behind as he thudded into someone.

"Oh, I'm sorry."

The clear American voice could only belong to one woman. Trevor tensed. He, not Caitlin, had been the one to bring about the collision. Now he held her arms to steady her.

"My fault," he said, casting about for just the right next comment—something innocuous but pleasant before they went their separate ways. "We always were clumsy." The skin on his face went cold and felt two sizes too small. What an idiot.

But she laughed. "We were, weren't we? Some things never change." She looked at the passing crush. "Except I don't remember Tenby being quite this busy, even on early-closing day."

"It wasn't," he said, still holding her arms.

She looked at his hands and he released her. "How long have you been back in Tenby?" she asked.

He narrowed his eyes, remembering that she hadn't stopped writing until shortly after he'd left for school in London. Evidently she remembered, too. "I came home four years ago." No point in giving her the reasons or any other information about himself, for that matter. He wished there was. That thought should shake him, but it had come more than once in the past few days.

"Thomas told me about your wife. I'm very sorry, Trevor."

The air he breathed wouldn't fill his lungs. "Thank you." Sincerity darkened her beautiful eyes. A struggling autumn sun backlighted her tall slender frame, shone through the riot of windblown red curls. She had been a lovely girl; as a woman she was breathtaking.

"Well, I guess I'd better go find my supplies. We're in the old Davies's cottage you know, and there's still plenty to do."

"Ah." Trevor arranged his face as if he were hearing the news for the first time. "How long will you be staying?" He stopped himself from closing his eyes in self-derision. Asking questions was something he must not do. She was off-limits.

"All winter. Maybe into spring." She laughed, the young abandoned laugh he could have heard in his head without ever being with her. "Who knows. Mary and I may decide to stay for good—if we can make the cottage habitable. I've got to pick up more paintbrushes and a scraper. What do you call the shop where I get those?"

She didn't know when she'd be going home. And she talked of her daughter but not of the husband. And Thomas said she needed cheering up. With effort Trevor brought his attention back to what she'd asked. "Gimblet's is the place. All the way down toward St. Julian Street. And it's an ironmonger's." He smiled. She'd always loved the differences between American and Welsh terms.

"Ironmonger. That's it. I knew it was something funny."

"There's nothing funny about it to us." Was she lonely? Could she be here because her marriage wasn't working? Trevor gritted his teeth, hating himself for hoping for, or even considering, such things.

"Do you have children, Trevor?"

The question caught him off guard. So did a bicycle that came too near for comfort. He took Caitlin's elbow and guided her close to the shops. One of his customers from the White Knight passed by, touching his cap and taking just too long a look at Caitlin.

"No children," Trevor said simply. How did he seem to her? Old? Automatically his hand went to his stomach. At least he didn't have a pot, but neither was he the hard-muscled boy she'd known.

"Are you glad to be back in Tenby?" she asked. She tipped her head to the side, pulling up her collar.

"Yes. I've never regretted leaving London. How about you? I mean, do you like being back in Wales?"

"I love it here. But you know that." A faint, marvelous blush crept over her high cheekbones. She was feeling awkward, making conversation, nothing more.

He ran a hand through his hair, grateful that although turning gray it had remained thick. If he spent more time exercising for himself rather than simply helping the boys, he'd be in great shape in no time.

They both said, "Well," at the same time and grimaced.

Another moment and she'd be gone. Trevor cleared his throat and studied his shoes. Room for improvement there, too.

Caitlin looked at the top of his head. She liked the gray in his hair and the lines on his face. The lines showed he'd laughed and lived...and probably cried. She swallowed. He hadn't changed so much. He was still shy. Was she imagining things, or did he want to prolong this meeting as much as she did?

"I'd better get to the ironmonger's before they close." Her chuckle sounded forced, and when his eyes met hers again they held no humor.

"You'd better do that."

"Goodbye, then, Trevor."

"Goodbye." He raised a hand as if to touch her face, but buried it in a jacket pocket instead.

He moved back and she sidestepped around him. "See you," she said brightly. "Thomas thinks I need a local pub and since his is the White Knight he's elected it for me, too." Trevor was so still. Up close was he comparing her to the way she'd looked at seventeen and noticing how the years had changed her?

He had both hands in his pockets now. "I'll look forward to you coming in. Maybe I'll get better at your manhattans."

People passed between them, cutting them off. Caitlin turned and hurried away, barely registering the frequent bumps from shoulders and shopping baskets.

A few yards on she stopped and drew alongside the windows once more. A sense of loss, as if someone she'd loved very much had just died, took what sunshine there was out of the day and out of her heart. Yet again she told herself there was no point in grieving for what might have been. But she'd just stood and talked with Trevor, and although he was beyond her reach she'd felt what she had never expected to feel again, the ache of longing to love and be loved by a strong man.

She leaned against the glass, slowly rolled against it to stare unseeingly at passersby. Then she looked back the way she'd come.

Trevor stood where she'd left him, watching her.

He waved. Caitlin waved back, ducked her head and rushed toward St. Julian Street.

3

"Mom asked you to talk to me. That's why she told me to bring the book by after school, isn't it?"

Thomas grunted. Mary was smart, quick, but then she would be—just like her mother. "Caitlin stayed here when she was a year or two older than you." A schoolteacher he might have been, but he hadn't had any experience counseling unhappy teenaged girls.

Mary didn't answer. She sank lower in one of the old overstuffed chairs that had sat lumpily in the parlor from when he was a small boy, as long as he could remember in fact. Cabbage roses cavorting over the fabric had once been bright pink. Now they were no more than comfortably familiar splotches of blushed brown. He liked those chairs.

"My parents, your great-grandparents, never stopped talking about that summer Caitlin came. She woke up this house, I can tell you." The banter felt stilted but he'd promised Caitlin some help with Mary and he'd have to do the best he could.

"What did she like to do then?" Mary wriggled a little straighter, a flicker of interest finally and blessedly on her face. "Did she draw stuff all the time like she does now, and make things? I mean, like the shoes—only other things?"

He fumbled for his pipe, buying time. A slight opening

was in sight but it could close instantly if he didn't say the right things. "She drew some. And painted. Watercolors if I remember properly. But mostly she was outside, swimming, sailing, hiking." The memory of Caitlin as a skinny seventeen-year-old with a blistered nose made him smile. "That summer was probably the best she ever..." The tongue, the silly loose tongue. "She enjoyed herself here, Mary. And you will, too, if you want to."

"Hmm." She turned the collar of her shirt up, dragged the ends of her sleeves over her hands and pulled her feet onto the chair.

Thomas noted her sharp knees through faded jeans. Caitlin was right, the girl was much too thin. "Your mom did sort of suggest we have a chat." As his old mother had told him, honesty was the best course in the end.

"I knew it." Her chin, planted on a fist, clamped her mouth shut. He might have to reevaluate the honesty angle.

He stuck the empty pipe between his teeth and chewed the stem. "Sometimes it's hard to explain ourselves to the people we love the most. That's why your mom thought it might be easier for you to talk with me."

"I love you, Uncle Thomas."

The odd stinging in his eyes caught him off guard. He grunted again and fiddled with his tin of tobacco on the mahogany table close to his own chair. "Are you settling into school now?"

"Yes."

Did an old man tell a little girl he loved her, too, or would she think he was funny, emotional? Anyway, he couldn't do it. "Making friends, are you?"

"Some. Constance is coming by for me at five-thirty. She's got dance lessons first, then we'll walk home together."

"Constance?" Thomas frowned, sorting through the many names of his old students and trying to connect one of them with an offspring named Constance.

"Trew," Caitlin supplied. "She lives up Slippery Back. Usually we go as far as our cottage together, then she cuts across the fields to get home. This is out of her way, but we get along. We like to talk, so I thought I'd take her to meet Mom today. Constance doesn't have a compact disc player so I said she could come and listen to mine."

Trew, Trew? Slippery Back? "Ah, Jimmy Trew's girl. I hope she's better at her arithmetic than her father was. Although he does well with his roofing business from what I hear, so maybe he learned more about his numbers than I thought."

"She's got a brother, too. His name's Owen."

"Is that right?" Thomas glanced at the girl. She played with a loose thread on her jeans. He smiled. Maybe there was hope here. That was a touch of dreamy interest he saw, wasn't it? Ah, the young and their crushes. They could hurt, but they could also be invaluable to a youngster with a fragile ego.

"Mary." He didn't have much time. "Your mother's not happy, you know."

She colored and turned her face away.

"She and your dad have been separated a long time and—"

"They'll get back together." Her head snapped around, the glitter in her brown eyes, took him by surprise. "We'll be a family again," Mary continued. "There's a few things they don't understand about each other, that's all."

A classic case of ostrichitis, Thomas thought, despairing. "And what are those things, Mary?"

She shrugged. "I don't know. That Daddy's different from most people, I guess."

"And your mother, what about her? Is there something about her that your father doesn't understand?"

"Everybody's mom and dad gets a divorce." A catch in her voice panicked Thomas. He couldn't bear it if she cried. "We're not like other families. We used to have fun. Mom always said we were different because we all loved each other. Why did it have to change?"

He cursed himself for agreeing to get into this conversation. "Mary," he began without being sure what he was going to say. "Mary, could it be that you're not being fair on Caitlin? Divorce isn't unusual when two people aren't happy together anymore."

Her fists, thumping the chair arms, startled him. "I know all that, Uncle Thomas. I'm not a child anymore. But why does everyone have to get a divorce? I don't want it to happen to us. I wouldn't get to see my dad, I know I wouldn't. And they *could* be happy together if...if..."

"If you could wish them back in love with each other?"

A small sound warned him that his fears were coming true—Mary was starting to cry softly. "Don't," he said. "I'm sorry if I'm a hard old man. That comes of not really having children of my own, apart from the ones in school. But I do care about you and your mother. I want to do what your grandfather would have done if he were still alive."

"You...don't...know." Her shoulders heaved and the long blond hair hid her face.

"I think I do. He'd have said that you should go on loving both of your parents and supporting them, but not giving either of them more pressure."

"You think I'm a spoiled brat. A nuisance."

He had really botched it. "No, I don't, young lady. Just a very mixed-up girl with the same values as her mother. Don't you think your mother would have given up on her marriage years ago if she didn't believe in trying to work things out?"

"I don't know."

And she didn't, Thomas decided ruefully. He got up and stroked the back of her head awkwardly. "It's all right now. Don't you worry. Everything will work out."

He was trying to make a fifteen-year-old who'd been sheltered by her mother and, to a point, by her father accept that the promises they'd made her, of security and unity, could no longer be kept. He knew from everything Caitlin had told him that she'd set out to give Mary a glitz-free environment even though they lived amid the fastest-moving society in the world. Grudgingly he admitted to himself that David McBride had wanted that too before he went off on whatever crazy tangent had beckoned him.

"Listen, Mary, can we make a deal?"

She lifted her face. "What deal?" Her dark lashes stuck out in wet spikes.

"That you'll come and talk to me about things that bother you? I may be a bit rusty at talking, but I like it and…well, I don't mind a bit of company now and again. I know you have to pass your cottage to get here, but you could come after school some days and cheer up a lonely old man."

"If you really want me to." She looked dubious, and Thomas reckoned she was more unsure about how good a confidant he'd make than whether or not he wanted her company. And her doubts were founded on that score although he'd do his best to make her trust him.

There was the food thing. He'd forgotten the food. "I've got a fresh seedcake in the kitchen," he said in a rush. "Bought it specially when I knew you were coming."

"Seedcake?" Her features screwed into a disgusted mask.

He had to laugh. "Yes, seedcake. Caraway seed. You must have had it before."

"No, I don't like cake. I mean…I'm not hungry."

Now she thought she'd been rude and was flustered. Thomas scrutinized her thin frame again. Caitlin was justified in being concerned about how much the child was eating.

"There are some biscuits, if you'd rather. Or nice brown bread and butter. That used to be your mother's favorite."

"I don't think so. Constance will be here any minute." And a rap at the door came on cue. "There. That must be Constance now." She leaped up and ran into the hall.

Thomas scrubbed at his jaw. He hadn't done so badly, had he? The girl liked him. He felt a small, unaccustomed warmth. Yes, his brother's granddaughter did like him—and he was glad about that.

Voices approached the parlor. Voice, singular. A masculine voice speaking low.

Mary came back into the room and now her face was scarlet. "Um, this is Owen Trew."

Thomas assumed a deeply serious expression. "How do you do, Owen?"

"How do you do, sir?"

The boy—young man—shifted from foot to foot behind Mary. A big, well-built specimen, Thomas noted recognizing Jimmy Trew in his tall, dark-haired son.

"Constance didn't finish her, er, chores," Mary said. "So she had to go straight home. Owen came to tell me."

"I see," Thomas said, and wondered if he didn't see much better than black-eyed Owen would ever imagine. "Aren't you on Trevor Morgan's famous team, boyo?"

Owen stood even taller, making Mary seem more diminutive. "Yes, sir. We've got a game tonight. We'll be playing the Footmen from Pembroke."

"Hot team?" Thomas prayed his lingo wasn't too out of date.

"Fair," Owen told him. "But they don't have Mr. Morgan." Something close to adoration came into the boy's eyes, and Thomas experienced a sliver of apprehension. He wasn't sure how he felt about this rugby fever that had invaded the town...or the single-minded homage the team paid Trevor.

"Why is the other side called the Footmen?" Mary asked. Her skin had regained its clear ivory color.

"After a pub," Owen said, his whole attention on her. "Oh."

Silence pressed in for several moments before Thomas rallied. Someone had to take charge around here. "I don't suppose you want to hang around for tea, Owen. You'd better be on your way to practice or whatever. Make sure Mary gets home safely." He bowed his head to hide a smirk. "Remember me to your father. Ask him how his fractions are these days."

"Fractions, sir?"

"He'll know what you mean. Now run along with you." he waved them into the hall and saw them out the front door.

Back in his favorite chair, he finally got around to packing his pipe and lighting it. Circles within circles. Generation after generation. How many years was it since

Caitlin walked the cliff edge with Trevor Morgan? Not so many to an old man. Twenty, maybe. Maybe less. And now Mary, Caitlin's daughter, was walking the same trail with another good Welsh boy.

Thomas took several contented puffs. They said you couldn't turn the clock back, but sometimes things did come all the way around in those circles he'd thought about. Not that he was exactly sure what he had in mind...was he?

She was a little thing. That was what he'd first noticed about her. Little and pretty and quiet—and fair. The other boys on the team had teased him after they'd seen him talking to her in the Common Room. Cradle snatcher, they'd called him. And why would he be interested in a girl built like a skateboard without wheels anyway? He'd ignored them, except to laugh a little. If they wanted to see her like that, so much the better. She might be small, but there was nothing unfeminine about her shape and he was crazy about the way he felt beside her.

"Are you nervous about the game?"

He jumped at the sound of her voice, then felt foolish. "A bit. I always am, but that's supposed to be good."

"Why?"

He couldn't see her face. The wind swirled her hair forward and she was watching the ground as she walked.

"They say it means you're on your toes and ready to go."

"Is that what it means for you?"

Her voice was terrific, soft but clear and with that accent Constance said she'd kill to have. He didn't blame her. "Yeah," he said after thinking a moment. Then he puffed up his cheeks and let the air whistle out. "No, that's a lie. I'm just plain scared and I think everyone else is, too." She made him feel like telling her anything she wanted to know.

"It was kind of you to come and let me know about Constance."

He swallowed. If Connie ever let the truth out he'd throttle her. "No problem," he said, hunching his shoulders. It had cost him a week of washing-up duty to get that rotten sister of his to let him take her place this afternoon. "I like walking up here. The sea's wild on the rocks down there." Now he sounded like a soppy poet.

"So do I," Mary responded and immediately felt the stupid blush coming again. He was really something, the best-looking boy in school, and he was nice—more than nice. And he was talking to her as if he liked her. All the boys in school back home called her "sticks" or "bird bones" or "Scotch tape," but Owen treated her the way she'd seen boys treat girls they liked.

"Hold up a minute," Owen said suddenly.

Mary did as he asked, pushing the hair out of her eyes.

He leaned over her and lifted a bramble spray out of her path. "These things are vicious," he said, letting the vine go when she'd passed. "Particularly if you can't see."

His laugh brought her to another stop.

"Through all that hair." He brushed it back and held each side of her face. "There. Now I can take a good look at your face, Mary McBride. Mmm. Not so bad. You could probably show it now and again without frightening too many people to death."

She studied him, unsure what to say, but sure of what she felt. His big hands were warm on her skin and the warmth spread all over her. But he was only being kind to his sister's friend, treating her as he would Constance.

He held her an instant longer then dropped his hands. "Have you ever been to a rugger game?"

"No." Her heart thumped in a funny way. "They don't play it in school in the States."

"Would you like to see it?"

Her heart thudded now. It hurt in her throat. "Yes, I would."

"Then I'll take you tonight. I'll drop you off at your place and come back at six-fifteen. You'll have to sit through warm-ups but you'll enjoy that. We're pretty awesome."

Now it was her turn to laugh. "You're also pretty humble."

"Hey, kid—" he cocked his head to one side "—who's gonna root for a bunch of guys who don't know how good they are?"

"You sound American when you talk like that. Welsh with American words, I should say."

"I hope that's a compliment. Here's your castle, Rapunzel. Tell your mom you're leaving at six-fifteen."

He was incorrigible. "She may not—" But Owen was already racing at a suicidal pace down the path. "Mom may not want me to go," Mary said for her own benefit as she opened the gate to the cottage's small dormant garden.

Owen leaped and dodged, resisting the temptation to look back. She'd started to protest, but he could tell she wanted to come, and since he didn't have a phone at home, she couldn't call to put him off. Not that she would.

Tonight the other fellows would see he'd brought "that toothpick" to the game. Even though she'd be sitting with Connie, the gang would work out that she was really there for him. Then they'd take a closer look at "skateboard."

He let out a whoop, grabbed a tree to swing around a

bend and slipped on mud to land on his rear. The chill air stung his throat. They'd take a real close look.

"Eat your hearts out, guys," Owen yelled.

"Yes, operator, I'll accept the charges."

She'd expected the call, been surprised David had taken so long about making it, so why wasn't she prepared?

"Sweetheart? Is that you?"

She closed her eyes and sank onto the small chair she'd bought to set beside the phone table. "It's me, David." When he called her sweetheart she hated him, truly hated him. He used the word to play on the old, good memories of what they'd once had together.

"Sweetheart, you know what I'm going to say, don't you?"

Yes, she knew, more or less. "David, will you do me a big favor?"

"Of course, sweetheart, name it."

"*Don't* call me sweetheart. It makes me sick."

Silence.

"What do you want?"

"For you to come back home to me and bring Mary."

Here it came, the whining, the lies about his reasons for giving a damn where she was. "I'm not doing that, David."

"You've got to." His voice dropped until she had to press the phone closer to her ear. "I can't make it without you, Caitlin. Do you understand?"

"You and I don't have a home together, David. You have yours and I have mine. And most of the time you're perfectly happy with that."

"I wasn't the one who wanted the separation."

She was so weary. "You were the one who made it impossible for us to live together."

"You never understood me."

"You sound like a record. And I did understand you once. It wasn't my fault you started chasing your lost youth or whatever you were doing."

What sounded suspiciously like a sob came along the line. He was probably drunk or on his way to being drunk.

"David, let's not continue this now. You aren't yourself and I'm tired. Good—"

"No! No, Caitlin, don't hang up. Listen, I need money. Not a lot. Just enough to get by the next week or so. A few grand would do it."

He felt no shame in begging and he never begged for peanuts.

"Forget it. It doesn't cost me thousands to live for a week or so and if you'd get your act together, you could manage your own life. The answer's no."

"You don't understand—"

"I *do* understand. Find someone else to finance your parties."

"When did you get so hard, Caitlin?"

When you set out to make me feel like nothing, she wanted to say. "Goodbye, David."

"Caitlin! Let me talk to Mary, please."

"She's not here." And she thanked God she'd capitulated and allowed their daughter to go with that boy who looked too much like a man for comfort.

"Where is she?" David's voice turned tough. "It's got to be nine at night where you are. What do you mean she's not there?"

"She's out with some friends, David. She's having a good time and you should be grateful. The poor kid's had few enough of those lately, thanks to you." Caitlin rested her head against the wall. She didn't want to say half the things that were coming out of her mouth but she always lost control with David.

"I don't like her being out at night. She needs a father around to look after her."

Caitlin laughed mirthlessly. "You seem to be able to forget that whenever it suits you. I'm hanging up now."

"Caitlin! I need that money."

"Go to the bank."

"You know I don't have money in the bank."

"You used to."

"Why do you want to hurt me? I think I should come to Wales, sweetheart. If we could have some time alone and away from the old memories we'd sort everything out."

A tide of nausea doubled Caitlin over.

"Did you hear what I said? I'm coming to Wales to talk some sense into you. You can't separate me from my child and refuse to help me out when I need a hand. I'll make the arrangements."

Caitlin breathed slowly through her mouth. "David," she said carefully, "I'll cable instructions to my bank tomorrow. Five thousand is all you get. Don't contact me again."

4

"What the…get away from there!" Trevor yelled at a small figure framed between the goalposts.

She either didn't hear or didn't understand. The little idiot would get clobbered if she stayed where she was. Starting to run he shouted "Boys—" over his shoulder "—back to the other end. Push-ups till I say otherwise." He'd called a practice scrum and the team had already divided and bound together in their two facing lines, heads down and driving at each other, waiting for the ball to be hooked between them.

By the time he got close to the girl he was panting steamy clouds into the cold afternoon air. "You know better than to stand there."

Already pale, she blanched alarmingly. And she still didn't budge. Good Lord, he'd frightened her half to death.

"Look," he said, lowering his voice. "I didn't mean to shout, but I don't want you to get hurt."

"Sorry," she whispered, and backed away. A pretty blond girl with huge brown eyes and… There was something familiar about her.

"Just a minute," he said, and she stopped. "What's your name?"

"I didn't mean to do anything wrong." Her eyes had become bigger than ever. "I didn't know I shouldn't stand here." Her shoulder bag was clutched to her chest. The accent had already told him that his hunch about her was probably correct.

"You're not in trouble." He smiled. Obviously she thought he would report her to someone at school. "I just wondered what your name is."

"Mary McBride."

He opened his mouth but couldn't think what to say next. The sensation in his chest, his legs was new. An ache. This was Caitlin's daughter....

"May I go now, please?"

Dimly he heard the growls and shouts of the boys going through their routines. "Caitlin Rhys is your mother," he said, and felt foolish. "Caitlin McBride, that is. I knew her when her name was Rhys."

The girl frowned. "Rhys is my middle name, too. Mom never said anything about knowing someone here—except for Uncle Thomas." She was pretty, with definite traces of Caitlin in her, except for the coloring. He wondered if her father was blond and dark-eyed. And the next feeling to hit was something he detested—jealousy. How could he be jealous of a man he'd never met? Unfortunately Trevor knew the answer. He wasn't completely over what had started between him and Caitlin all those years ago.

Mary McBride was watching his face and waiting. Of course, she must wonder why they were having this conversation. "I'm Trevor Morgan," he said, and felt inane.

"Oh." A smile transformed her somber face and made her so like Caitlin that he caught his breath. "Owen talks about you."

It was Trevor's turn to frown. "Owen? Ah, Owen Trew. You know him?"

She blushed furiously. "He's my friend's brother. He

brought me to the game last night. I'd never seen rugger played before.''

Trevor was swept back in time to when a red-haired girl had come to watch him play on this field. He looked again at Mary. History repeating itself maybe? A twinge of bittersweet nostalgia gripped him.

''And did you enjoy watching?''

''I...I didn't really understand it. But Owen's going to explain everything to me.'' The blush swept back.

''I'll bet he...I'm sure he'll be glad to do that. Owen's a very special boy. Good player, too. You know, your mother came with me to watch games here.''

Her expression said that she couldn't imagine her mother and an old fogy like him going anywhere. ''My mother came to see games?''

''She certainly did. And she was quiet, like you, but she still shouted for me....'' He swallowed and felt his own face pale. He mustn't say anything to embarrass Caitlin. ''She shouted for the whole team.''

''Mom shouted? She never does that.'' She giggled, hunching her shoulders.

Trevor laughed, too. ''I know how you feel. When I was a kid I couldn't believe my folks had done the things I did.''

She only smiled.

This could have been his child, his and Caitlin's. The thought was like a blow. He made himself smile. ''You remind me of your mother. She was a lovely reserved girl. But she knew how to laugh.'' Shouts from the other end of the field grew wilder. ''I'd better get back. You're what I would expect in a daughter of Caitlin's. She's lucky and so are you.''

Another flush started. Poor kid. He was thoroughly confusing her. "Goodbye, Mary. If you want to watch, sit on the bleachers, okay?"

"I have to go home now." Already she was backing away again. Her sudden brilliant smile surprised him. Then she ran toward the school buildings, her hair flying, the breeze ballooning her bright pink jacket.

Shivering a little, Trevor zipped his sweat jacket all the way to the neck while he watched her go. "Do you have children?" Caitlin had asked. After she'd left him in the street, after that odd suspended moment when they'd looked back at each other, he had thought about the question or, more importantly, about Caitlin's having a child. He'd given up on the shopping expedition and returned to the pub, still thinking, still making himself search for whatever it was that bothered him. And, at last, he'd faced the truth: he'd once expected to become Caitlin's lover, her first and only lover. He had no right, but the vision of her in the arms of another man had enraged him.

He had no right.

"Mr. Morgan!"

"Coming." He jogged downfield.

Where was McBride? Why did Caitlin need cheering up, as Thomas had suggested? Could there be any harm in finding out?

Staying on schedule was essential. Caitlin sorted through leather and fabric samples on the kitchen table. Concentration had been hard since David's call of yesterday. She'd arranged the bank transfer and tried to put him out of her mind, but his threat to come to Wales haunted her. Would she dare to breach the terms of their separation so seriously? With David, she never knew anything for sure.

A swatch of soft jade-green kid caught her eye, and she

fingered it, flipping through sketches to find a dressy pump with spectator-toe treatment. This design should go over well. She'd decided to make its curvaceous Louis heel her trademark for daytime shoes this year. Soon her drawings must be in Paris, and a matter of weeks after that she'd go there herself to discuss and oversee any final changes. She enjoyed every moment once she was involved, but today she couldn't imagine either being ready or having enough energy to cope.

"Mrs. McBride?"

Ethel Johnson, whispering behind her, startled Caitlin. "Yes, Mrs. J?"

"I've done the bedrooms and the bathroom." The woman made a habit of tiptoeing around Caitlin's kitchen workroom and speaking in whispers. "And I telephoned Andrew Briggs about the garden. He'll come up and take a look, he says." Her ruddy face grew more mottled as she spoke. She pulled a floral apron over her head, dislodging wisps of iron-gray hair from a knot at her nape.

"Thank you, Mrs. J." Caitlin found herself whispering, too, and said more firmly. "I'll see you tomorrow."

"That you will." She put on a shapeless gray coat and settled a red woolen beret firmly on her head. With a string shopping bag in hand she opened the back door and collided with Mary.

"Sorry, Mrs. J.," Mary said breathlessly and slipped past the housekeeper. "I want to talk to you, Mom." Her coat and bag had already hit the floor.

"Mary, could you please close the door?"

A sneaker, applied to Caitlin's fresh paint, sent the door rattling shut on its hinges.

"Mom, I want you to tell me all about rugby."

"What?" *Rugby?* Then Caitlin remembered it had been a rugby game that the boy had taken Mary to last night.

She'd come home in such high spirits that Caitlin had worried Mary would get a migraine—the expected finale to excitement for her—but there was no headache and the good mood had still been present this morning. The boy had been polite, big, good-looking, but he'd seemed so much older than...

"Mom!" Mary's voice rose. "You know the rules, and I want you to teach me."

"*I* know the rules?"

"Yes. Mr. Morgan told me you do—or he said you went to a lot of games—so you must know more than me."

Caitlin dropped the green leather on the table. "What are you talking about?" Her hands turned cold and she rubbed them together.

"I met that Trevor Morgan...Mr. Morgan, the one who owns the big pub in the town and coaches the rugby team Owen's on. He's a great coach, Owen says. I saw him last night and he shouts a lot but the boys all think he's great. Owen says he's the best ever, a—a guru, Owen says. And I'd like to surprise Owen by knowing all about it next time he takes me."

The words tumbled out—more words than Caitlin had heard Mary speak in months. That pleased her, but only took up part of her mind. Mary had talked to Trevor, and Trevor had mentioned that summer when they'd been friends.

"Where did you meet Mr. Morgan?" she asked slowly.

"At the playing field. Will you tell me the rules, Mom?"

"I don't know much, but I'll try. What were you doing at the field? You're late home."

She shouldn't have said that. Mary's smile vanished and she perched tensely on the edge of a chair.

"I'm sorry I'm late. I only went to see the practice for a few minutes. Constance stayed after school to help in the home ec room so I waited for her."

And Mary went to watch Owen whatever his name was, just as Caitlin had gone to watch Trevor so many times. But Mary was only fifteen, too young to be running around after some boy. Caitlin's aching fingers let her know they were clenched. She spread them on her jean-clad thighs.

"Mom, it's all right, isn't it? For me to be a bit late, I mean?"

Let go, Caitlin warned herself. Don't do what your mother and father did to you...discouraged any friendship that didn't promise some advantage. She smiled. "Sure it's all right. How come you talked to Trevor Morgan?" Her heart moved uncomfortably.

Mary looked at the floor. "I was where I shouldn't be and he told me to move."

Caitlin frowned. "Was he angry with you?" She'd never seen Trevor angry.

"At first. But he said it was only because he was afraid I'd get hurt. Mom, he said you were his friend when you visited here before and that you—" Mary stopped, wiggled to sit on her hands and looked awkward.

"I what?" Caitlin prompted.

"Only that you were friends, I guess. I could tell he really likes you." She turned pink.

Caitlin crossed her arms tightly. He really liked her? He certainly had when they were teenagers. But did he still like her now? Why should he? They were strangers again. Strangers who had a definite effect on each other. She was dreaming again—a sure sign of how unsettled and lonely she'd become.

"Mom?" Mary, obviously puzzled by Caitlin's silence, touched her knee. "Mom, is something wrong?"

"No, nothing, sweetheart." She must concentrate on Mary. "I'm glad you're settling in so well here."

"It's kind of fun," Mary admitted. "There's only Constance and Owen who talk to me much but that's okay. The rest of the kids still seem kind of suspicious, like they aren't sure I'm not one of those aliens I told you about."

Caitlin chuckled. "They'll come around. And two friends are a good start."

"Yep. I really like Owen." A dreamy preoccupation smoothed her features before she caught Caitlin's eye and said quickly, "I like Constance a real lot. And I liked your friend, Mr. Morgan, too."

Part of Caitlin wanted to hear why Mary liked Trevor, to hear anything at all about the man he'd become, but another part shied away from thinking about him. "He's nice," she said and the words sounded ridiculous, as if she was describing the mailman.

"Do you know what he said?"

Caitlin shook her head and Mary giggled, that young, unself-conscious giggle Caitlin had always loved.

"He said—" and she puckered her brow "—he said I reminded him of you because— No, that wasn't it."

"What did he say?" Caitlin realized she'd moved forward in her chair and eased back again.

"He said I reminded him of you. Then he said you were a...a lovely, reserved girl but you knew how to laugh. There." She grinned. "That's it. *And*— Are you ready for this?"

"Ready," Caitlin said, feeling weak, feeling as if her blood had drained away.

"He said you used to *shout* at rugby games," Mary

announced triumphantly. "My quiet mother used to shout, just like all the other kids."

Caitlin laughed because she was supposed to. Mary's glee was sweet and infectious, but, damn it, what she'd just said had brought Caitlin close to tears. The memories were so sharp. She smelled the oranges they used to suck through a hole in the peel, heard the kids yelling, heard her own voice raised and remembered feeling bashful each time she realized she *had* shouted. And then there had been Trevor—big, wonderful to look at, with his gray eyes glittering, his face flushed, his straight hair sticking out, slick with sweat—and always it seemed he'd be wearing a liberal layer of gleaming mud.

"Mom?"

She blinked, clearing her fuzzy vision. "Yes, hon?"

"You okay?"

"Of course I am." And she was. "I'm fine. Anything else you want to tell me?"

Mary gripped her hands between her knees. "Only that Mr. Morgan said we're lucky to have each other. We are, aren't we?" She bobbed up and hugged Caitlin, kissed her cheek.

"We sure are." Caitlin returned the hug, held on tightly and closed her eyes against tears. Trevor didn't have anyone, did he? At least she was luckier than him. The thought should have brought more satisfaction, but she'd rather that he were happy, too.

"You're breaking my neck, Mom," Mary mumbled into Caitlin's shoulder.

"Yeah." She let go and stood up. "Enough of this mush, huh? I forgot to tell you your dad called while you were out last night." Mary needed to feel contact with her father, regardless of how much Caitlin wished she could forget David.

"He did? Oh, I missed talking to him. What did he say?" Mary jiggled while she spoke.

"Not a lot. He was just checking in. I'm sure he'll call again soon." She controlled a tightening in her jaw muscles. He undoubtedly would whether she wanted it or not. "But he said he loves you, honey—and that he misses you."

Mary stopped moving. "I love him, too," she said, then looked squarely at Caitlin. "You do still love daddy, don't you, Mom? A little bit anyway?"

This was one question Mary had never asked directly before, and Caitlin hadn't considered what she'd say. She touched Mary's cheek but couldn't muster a smile. "You'll have to leave things between your father and me to us. Don't forget how much you mean—to both of us. You always will."

"But—"

"No buts, Mary. Enough said. Now, let's think about dinner."

"I don't want dinner."

Irritation blunted Caitlin's concern. "Mary, don't use that old weapon on me."

"I don't know what you mean."

"Yes, you do. You know I worry about how little you eat, and whenever things don't go your way, you take advantage of that."

"I do not." Mary swept up her coat and bag.

"*Don't* walk out of here angry." Caitlin's stomach cramped sickeningly. "People die from not eating, and I don't only mean people who can't get the food they need."

"Aw, Mom, knock it off."

"Mary!"

Slouching, Mary stood with her weight on one foot,

glaring at Caitlin. "You think I'm a little kid who doesn't know anything. 'People die from not eating.' I know that and I'm not sick or anything. I just don't have a big appetite and I'm not hungry now. Can I have something later, please?"

She'd been warned not to make too big an issue out of this problem. "Sure, sure. Forgive me for shooting off like that. I've got my own concerns, Mary. That's not news to you. Try to understand that it doesn't help when you keep pushing me about your father. We have big problems, and they aren't going to go away."

"But they could if you—"

"Mary." Caitlin heard the menace in her own voice, but she'd had enough for one day—for a lifetime if it came to that.

"Fine, Mom. I get the picture. Butt out. Okay if I go to my room now?"

It was a question that didn't need an answer. Caitlin sat at the table again and heard the door close behind Mary.

She should go through the couturiers' sketches for the spring collections again. A big part, perhaps the biggest part, of her task was to balance her designs with the projected clothing styles for each upcoming season.

Impatiently she flipped pages. Skirt lengths were all over the place. At any other time she'd enjoy the challenge that brought. Tonight it was an annoyance.

The best thing that could happen to Mary would be for her to get thoroughly involved with a peer group here. In future there must be as little censorship of activities as possible—if only Caitlin could be sure they posed no threat to Mary.

Stopping work because she was upset was a luxury she couldn't afford. A sketch of a short evening gown made of layered puffs of scarlet moiré caught her eye. This year she was definitely caught up with novelty shoes. Something in matching moiré with rhinestone straps, perhaps. Very high heels again. And pray for a model with insurable legs.

She opened her pad and drew with quick, deft strokes. From above her head came the bass thud of Mary's stereo equipment.

God, let Mary be happy, she prayed. Let me find a way to give her what she needs without sealing myself off from what I need for the rest of my life.

Caitlin set the pencil down carefully. What did she need? What was she really thinking about, trying to sort out?

Forever. For always.

She shivered. The wind rattled the windows. If she closed her eyes and concentrated she could hear the way the wind sounded in the graceful marram grass along the cliff. She could feel the sun warming the air, smell salt and feel sand scrunch beneath her bare legs...and she could feel Trevor's mouth on hers. They'd promised that one day they'd be together forever.

They'd had something special, she and Trevor, even though they were different. Caitlin opened her eyes and picked up the pencil. If she'd known Trevor would be here now and that he'd be ''available,'' as they said, would she have risked coming? She'd never forgotten him. Even when she and David were happy together she'd occasionally wondered how Trevor was. Not with the longing she'd had in the first year or two after her summer in Tenby, but with a gentle wish for his happiness. Yes, coming here again could have been a dreadful mistake.

What if they had managed to fulfill the promises they'd made each other? Would the differences between them have gradually formed a schism? Would they have eventually grown disenchanted? Were happy liaisons between men and women a myth?

She'd probably never know, but while she was here she'd do well to make sure she stayed out of Trevor Morgan's way.

Four hours later she put her materials away for the night. At seven Mary had appeared and asked if she could take a sandwich up to her room. Determined to keep the peace, Caitlin agreed, then forced herself back to work. Now her brain felt like used gum and it was time to stop.

She took a glass of white wine upstairs and set it on the table beside the antique brass bed she'd bought in Cardiff. A shower in the only partially renovated bathroom down the hall, then she'd settle in with her book and the wine and hope the combination would help her sleep.

The phone rang, jarring her so hard that she sat down on the bed before picking up the receiver. Her nerves were shot.

It would be David again, she knew it. Maybe there'd been a mix-up with the money transfer. Hardly able to breathe, she put the handset to her ear and listened.

"Hello?" The accent was Welsh, not American. And there was no long-distance static. Probably a wrong number, thank God.

"Hello?" he repeated.

She hadn't answered. "Er, yes, hello."

"Is that you, Caitlin?"

She became absolutely still. The phone was formless in her hand. "Yes."

"This is Trevor, Caitlin, Trevor Morgan. You remember?"

Did she remember? Why would he ask that? "Of

course I remember." And he asked because he was as nervous as she was.

Now he was silent. She could hear him breathing.

"Trevor, Mary told me about this afternoon. I'm sorry if she got in the way, but she didn't mean to. It won't happen again, I promise."

"No, no," he said hurriedly, "I'm not calling about that. She's lovely, Caitlin, lovely. She reminded me of you."

"So she told me."

"She told you?" He gave a short laugh. "Poor kid probably thought I was nuts."

"No, she thought you were nice." Her lungs felt tight, as if she were hyperventilating. *Get hold of yourself.*

"Caitlin, could I take you out to dinner?"

Keeping a grip on the phone took two hands. She'd misheard him. Trevor knew she was married because she'd told him. He wouldn't ask her out.

"Caitlin, did you hear what I said?"

Nothing would come, not a word.

For several seconds Trevor was silent, too, then his voice came, low, as soft as she remembered, and loaded with embarrassment. "I've made a mistake. Forgive me, please. I should never have called."

"Trevor—"

"Will you forget this, Caitlin? What was I thinking about, intruding on you like that? Loneliness does—" He paused and his swallow was audible. "This is awful. Just forget the whole thing. Good—"

"Trevor, please be quiet." Caitlin sucked in her bottom lip, amazed at what she'd said. "I mean, please don't hang up. You were going to say something about loneliness. I know all about that, friend. I could write a book on it." She couldn't, oh, she couldn't be saying this. Yet she was and she wanted to tell him more. He'd always listened and understood...and cared.

"What's wrong, *cari*?"

The gentleness, the old soul-wrapping gentleness was there. His voice was deeper, a man's voice rather than that of a boy verging on manhood, but she could feel what she'd felt in him from the beginning...a spirit that matched her own almost frighteningly.

"Talk to me, Caitlin," Trevor urged softly.

She shouldn't be doing this but she couldn't stop. "When would you like to have dinner, Trevor?"

5

Plantegenet.

Caitlin read the sign beside the door of the restaurant. The place was old, ancient, its lights shining out wavery and yellow from bottle-thick glass set in crooked lead framing.

"I don't remember this," Caitlin told Trevor. She still couldn't believe she was out with him, alone, that he stood inches behind her, that she could touch him if she wanted to.

"It wasn't a restaurant when you were here before. Just a house the owners made a fortune from, selling it to these people."

She could believe that. In a prime central location, the building, a high step up from a narrow alley, bulged mysteriously, as if the centuries had weighted and distorted its gray stone walls.

"Will this be all right, Caitlin? Or would you rather go somewhere else?"

She faced him, met his eyes for the first time since he'd picked her up. "It looks wonderful." *He* looked wonderful.

He didn't move. Neither did Caitlin. At seven-thirty, the time they'd agreed upon, Trevor had arrived at the front door of the cottage, and she'd been waiting, hoping to leave without more questions from Mary. But Mary had followed her to the door and given Trevor one of her widest, most beguiling smiles. Evidently Trevor had made a hit, even though his first meeting with Mary had been less than ideal. Caitlin knew she should be grateful that explaining the dinner date away as "getting together with an old friend to talk about old times" had raised no suspicion. Not that it should. That was exactly what she was doing.

"Shall we go in, then?"

"Yes, yes."

Trevor took her arm, slid his hand carefully under her elbow to guide her up the steep step. And Caitlin blessed the darkness that hid the involuntary tightening in her face at his touch. But neither the dark nor the wreathing mist would disguise the tension he must feel in her body.

While Trevor opened the door and ushered her into a warm interior, she made much of taking off her gloves, unbuttoning her coat, sliding off a green and gray silk scarf. By the time she gave up her coat to him, she'd recovered enough composure to murmur appreciative comments about their surroundings.

"It is nice, isn't it?" Trevor agreed when she exclaimed over a Jacobean settle.

She went to warm her hands by a fire in what must once have been a separate sitting room. Now the room, used as a lounge for waiting customers, was open to the dining area. The walls, some exposed stone, some rough plastered, supported a ceiling banded with dark and dipping beams. Caitlin was enchanted. "How old is this place?"

When Trevor didn't answer, she turned and found him still standing where she'd left him, on the threshold with her coat in his hands. Seeing him there—watching her, unsmiling—froze her in place.

"I'll just hang these up," he said, and even at a distance she heard the forced steadiness in his tone.

She sat on a Victorian ladies' chair of heavy but faded blue damask and waited until Trevor had spoken to a young man in jeans and sweatshirt who appeared to be the maître d'. *Incongruous* would be her mother's term for the place. Eileen had never liked anything about "that funny little country your father came from."

When Trevor talked he used his hands. He'd done that as a teenager…and he'd shown the same animation and attention with whatever he was doing then as he did now. Tonight he wore a suit. She'd never seen him in a suit before, Caitlin realized. But she wouldn't have. He looked…different, sophisticated? The years had been good to him. His broad shoulders were broader than ever and his body mature, powerful, but with no sign of extra flesh. The suit was dark and well cut, his shirt white. She wasn't sure she'd noted the color of his tie, but it was also dark, and the natural olive quality of his skin gave him a tanned appearance against his collar. He was handsome, very handsome. She bowed her head and smiled. What would he think if he knew she was analyzing his appearance and liking everything she saw? What would he think if he knew she felt many of the old sensations she'd felt when they were seventeen and eighteen, when the very sight of him had made her shaky all over? The difference was that then the attraction had been uncomplicated. Sexuality, although present, wasn't fully developed. But they weren't seventeen and eighteen anymore, and every nuance of the effect Trevor had on her was easily identified.

They were only here to talk about old times.

Trevor came to stand over her. "If we want to, we can

eat in the bar. It's an interesting room. Used to be the kitchen when this was still a house."

Caitlin hadn't noticed a bar. "This is your bailiwick, Trevor. You decide."

For a moment he looked uncertain. Then he offered her his hand, and when she held it he said, "The bar. Just to show you I can be masterful and make decisions."

Caitlin had no doubt he could be masterful. She could feel strength emanating from him, and it excited her. Just as quickly she reminded herself that she probably shouldn't be here, that she was courting complications in an already complicated life. There was no doubt that she and Trevor could very easily pick up where they'd left off, and this time they'd be unlikely to spend much time swimming and sailing and walking the cliffs.

"Sit there," Trevor said when he'd led her through a velvet curtain into a flagstoned area with a bar on a book-lined platform at one side. "Right there, in the corner. It'll be comfortable."

Caitlin did as she was told and didn't fail to notice that he'd have to sit beside her on the upholstered bench recessed into a rough wall. A small stained-glass window in the alcove glowed bloodred and gold.

"This is the oddest place, Trevor," she told him when he'd slid in, so close their knees touched. "I asked you how old it is, but you didn't hear me."

He puffed out his cheeks. "I'm not sure. The alley we came in from is called Quay Hill, and farther down Quay Hill there's a place called the Tudor Merchant's House. I know that dates back to the 1500s. But this town is old, a mishmash from Norman to now." He chuckled. "You always were a bundle of questions. I like you in that color, by the way. Gray suits you. I like you in dresses, too." His gaze flickered down over the soft wool sheath.

She took an instant to compose herself. "Thanks. I like you in a suit. I suppose you wore them all the time in London, but I only remember you in jeans and shorts."

He shrugged. "And I only used to remember you in jeans and shorts. But since I saw you in the pub that first night I…" He paused, running a forefinger up the bridge of his straight nose. "I'm giving myself away again. You did bowl me over a bit. You looked as if you'd come to the wrong party."

Caitlin laughed shortly. "Is that a compliment?" And she winced. He'd think she was fishing.

A girl chose that moment to ask if they wanted a drink before dinner. Trevor ordered a martini for himself and, without asking Caitlin, a manhattan.

"You have become masterful, haven't you?" she said, leaning toward him.

"Only on the outside," he responded quietly. Tentatively, as if he expected her to draw back, he touched first her cheek, then her hair. His fingers lingered on her hair before he drew back and folded his arms. "I've wanted to do that since I picked you up tonight. I never forgot the way your hair felt."

In that moment nothing existed for Caitlin but Trevor.

"Does that offend you?" The uncertainty was back. "Caitlin, did I do the wrong thing asking you out this evening?"

"I don't know," she said, too quickly to decide if honesty was wise.

"Does that mean you only came to save my feelings?"

Who was fishing now? "I came because…I came because I'm as lonely as hell, Trevor, and once you were the only person in the world who understood me. You never judged and you…you loved me in that great innocent way you had. It didn't matter what I did, you were there and we could talk. Trevor, do you remember how we used to talk? I need that now." When she stopped speaking she closed her eyes and pressed her fingers to her temples. This was mad, totally unlike her. He'd get the wrong idea, think she was making a pass at him or something. She cringed.

"Hey, hey." Trevor slid an arm around her shoulders and pulled her close. "Sh. It's okay. I wouldn't have needed a degree in psychology to figure out you've got something heavy on your mind. I'm your friend, remember? You can talk to me. We made a promise or two a long time ago. Do you remember, we said we'd..." His face was close to hers, and she saw his eyes grow darker. "We promised to be friends forever. We didn't really know what we were talking about then, but I guess this was the kind of time we had in mind."

The drinks arrived. Caitlin sipped her manhattan. Trevor ignored his glass. He kept his arm around her, and his eyes on her face. She mustn't give in to what he made her feel. But she wanted to tell him everything about her life from the day they'd parted until now, and so very much, she wanted to have him hold her.

"I'm fine," she told him, inching away.

Trevor immediately removed his arm and picked up his drink. When she glanced sideways at him his face was impassive.

"You're one of the last people in the world I'd want to hurt, Trevor," she said and every word took effort. Coming *had* been a mistake, a self-indulgent foolishness. "I've never forgotten you. But I shouldn't be taking advantage of an old friendship just because I'm not too sure of myself these days."

He twirled the olive on its toothpick. "You can only

take advantage of someone if you force them to do something they don't want to do."

"I'm okay, really." The old lie came increasingly easily. "When you called I was feeling a bit sorry for myself, that's all. But that was yesterday and today I'm my usual feisty self."

"Sure you are." He continued to play with the toothpick. "That's why you just gave that speech about the way I always understood you, right?" His gray eyes took her in quickly, and she turned hot. He lifted the glass to rest against his lower lip, "I loved that speech by the way. And everything you said goes double for me." The swallow he took almost finished the martini.

"Trevor, I shouldn't have said those things."

"Of course not. But you did, and so did I—with your help. Whether you like it or not, *cari*, it's probably a fact that sometime or other in a lifetime we meet the great love. There are people who get lucky and end up with that love. The rest of us—" he covered her hand on top of the table, squeezed quickly and picked up his glass again "—we poor devils get a glimpse and then never forgive ourselves for letting it get away."

Her shy young friend had turned into a very articulate man. She tried to laugh. "We're getting pretty heavy here, buddy. Don't tell me you've spent nineteen years pining for the days when we swam and sailed—and threw sand at each other." She sounded sarcastic but if she didn't lighten this up, she'd be in worse shape than she already was.

Trevor leaned back and rested his head against the wall. The window cast a pink-gold shadow over his angular face, turned his eyes to gleaming pewter. "I haven't spent all the time thinking about it. Gwen and I had a good marriage.'' He glanced at her. ''Do you remember Gwen? She was in my year at school. Gwen Williams.''

Caitlin liked him for the open sadness she felt in him at the mention of his dead wife. ''I don't think so.'' She thought a minute and nodded. ''Yes, I do. Of course I do. Her parents owned a grocery store.''

''That's right. Bronwyn and Snowy Williams. Great people. It was terrible for them when Gwen died. They've been good to me, but I know they think it was London that killed her—which is rubbish of course. She died of peritonitis. There was an appendectomy, but it was too late. I always wonder if the Williams blame me in a way.''

''Of course, they don't.'' Before she could think, she grasped one of his hands in both of hers. Rather than letting go, she rubbed it, smoothed his long, square-tipped fingers. ''I do remember Gwen, though. She was little with short curly hair. Dark brown eyes. An athlete, right? A runner?''

Trevor nodded, smiling slightly.

''Aha, Trevor Morgan, the truth comes out.'' The lightness she tried for began to work. A laugh bubbled in her throat. ''That truth is that you toyed with me. And all the time you were on the lookout for a little woman. I never was your type and that's why you stopped writing to me.'' As soon as the words were out, even as she lifted her chin in mock hauteur, she regretted the comment.

''What do you mean?'' Before she could withdraw, he twined their fingers together. ''*I* stopped writing?''

''Never mind. That was a long time ago. We were too young.''

''No, I do mind.'' He was hurting her hand. ''You said I stopped writing.''

''You did,'' she said in a small voice. ''I wrote for weeks after the last time I heard from you. Then I gave

up. It felt so awful.'' When she looked at him she knew
he'd see tears in her eyes, and she felt ridiculous. "Kids
can be silly, can't they?''

"Some kids. We weren't. Caitlin, you were the one
who stopped writing. I got three letters and a card from
you after I got to London. Then nothing. I was frantic but
I didn't know what to do.''

"That's not possible—''

"You're saying I'm lying?''

"No, of course not, but—''

"Caitlin, I registered one letter and you signed for it. I
even got the money together to make a call, but you
wouldn't talk to me.''

She stared at him, slowly comprehending what had
never occurred to her before tonight. "I never signed for
a letter, Trevor. I never got it. And I…oh, Trevor, I never
refused to talk to you on the phone. Who answered?''

He shook his head, a muscle moving convulsively in
his jaw. "I don't know, a woman. But you did sign. I got
the receipt back.''

"That wasn't my signature. I swear it.''

"Are you saying someone deliberately stopped me
from contacting you?''

Caitlin drew in a shaky breath. "Yes. You don't understand my folks. They had…they had 'expectations' for
me, as they called them.''

"So you think they intercepted my letters and wouldn't
let me talk to you?''

She nodded miserably, feeling sick with regret and a
sense of loss. "I wouldn't have thought it of them, but
that must have been it.''

"But you never wrote anything about not hearing from
me.''

"Not in the letters you got. But I didn't ask you why

you weren't sending anything to me until after I stopped getting your letters.''

He raised expressive brows. "So? What point are you making?"

This was better left alone. "Let's forget it, Trevor. It all happened a lifetime ago and it doesn't matter anymore."

"Doesn't it? Aren't we talking about something that might have changed the course of two lives?" Frustration grated in his voice. "Explain the rest of it to me."

"If you insist. But isn't it obvious what happened?"

"Not to me. But then, we always knew I was the backward one from the backwater town. Maybe I'm too slow to catch on."

"Don't do that," she snapped, and felt no regret. That she'd lived in the fast lane had always brought out the worst in Trevor, and she hated his barbs as much now as when he'd first used them. "Obviously my parents decided to take a hand in my fate. They must have intercepted my letters, too."

"How could they do that? Can you tamper with the mail where you come from?"

Heat washed up her neck. "No, you can't. Unless the mail is set out for someone else to take."

He stared and the start of a sneer turned Caitlin's stomach. "As in a servant?"

Pride was the only barrier to tears. "That's the way it was, Trevor," she told him, with the merest crack in her voice. "I'm sorry it still bothers you that we come from different backgrounds. Not that you appear to be suffering."

"Oh, hell." Trevor screwed up his eyes. "Forgive me. I'm always saying things like that to you. Always did have to say them. The reason hasn't changed. And it was never your fault. When I first heard about where you came from and about your family I was in awe, afraid to come near you. But I couldn't help coming near you anyway." His laugh was self-conscious. "I shouldn't say this, but damn your family, Caitlin."

"It's a bit late for that," she said, but she damned them too. "And we'd have grown out of each other anyway."

"Would we?" He looked at her briefly before raising his glass to take a draining swallow. "Are you sure?"

"Aren't you? We've been together, how long? An hour now? And already we're picking at each other."

Trevor put down his glass, turned it slowly by the stem. "We're bound to be a bit edgy. It's been a long time."

"No," Caitlin said. "No, you're missing the point. We're saying the same things to each other as we did before. Oh, they're different because we're different, older, but it's the same stuff really. You were never that comfortable with me."

"That's not true—"

"Yes, it is. Face the truth, Trevor. You were... threatened somehow by where I came from, the kind of people I came from. And you sound as if you still are."

"I'm not threatened," he said, making a fist on the table. "Why should I be threatened?"

"Because we've lived very differently from each other. That doesn't bother me, Trevor. Never did. But it was an issue with you when we were kids, and I think if we'd...if we'd come together the way we planned, we'd eventually have started tearing at each other."

"I don't believe that."

She looked away from his rigid face, his persistent fiddling with the empty glass. "Let's drop this. We didn't get together, so what's the point of hashing over what might have happened if we had?''

"None, I suppose. But I still say that we had a right to make our own decisions. And I also say that, good or bad, our lives might be very different today if your parents hadn't got in the way.''

The sickening sensation came back, the feeling of having been cheated. "Possibly. But we'll never know now, will we?'' But one day she would say something to her mother. Caitlin had little doubt it had been her mother rather than her father who had tampered with her correspondence. And the past was past, but there would be some satisfaction in seeing Eileen Rhys, actress, try to squirm her way out of the small-minded thing she'd done to her daughter.

Caitlin learned that Plantagenet served Greek food, but not why Greek food was served in a restaurant named after an early English royal family. She and Trevor ate spicy Greek pizza, which Trevor selected from a menu chalked on a huge board propped on the mantel above a fireplace. Pizza, he said, would make her feel at home. Caitlin hardly tasted a bite. They spoke little as they ate and left without dessert or coffee.

"Hell, it's cold,'' Trevor muttered outside the restaurant. "Is that coat warm enough? You go back inside and I'll get the car.''

The streets in town were narrow and he'd parked his Jag by the lifeboat station at the harbor, a few minutes walk south of the restaurant. The dark green Jag had surprised Caitlin until she recalled that he had been successful in London and was now running a thriving business in Tenby.

"No, you won't get the car,'' she said, belting her

camel hair coat. "I'm perfectly warm and I need to walk after all that food."

Instead of looking at him, she peered down Quay Hill. Opposite was a tiny shop called Caldy Island, which she remembered sold perfumes made by monks living on an island that lay three miles from Tenby harbor. Beyond the shop, worn steps curved downward and out of sight around a bend.

"Caitlin?" Trevor spoke as quietly as usual but with an intensity that sharpened every nerve in her. "I'd like to walk with you. Will you tell me a little of what's going on in your life if we do? I don't want to barge in where I'm not wanted, but you know about me...or some of it anyway, and I'd like to know about you."

In the light from a lantern bolted high on the building behind him, she caught a glint in his eyes. "Okay, but there isn't much to tell." Not much that she was prepared to share. Her life would sound sordid compared to his.

Taking his proffered hand, she walked beside him down the steps, past the old Tudor Merchant's House he pointed out and on to a street he named as Crackwell. Here they turned east and Caitlin could hear the sea below them to her right. They must be above North Walk, which skirted the beach and eventually led to the cliffs where she lived, with Thomas's house a mile or so beyond.

"What time is it?" she asked. "I'd forgotten how quiet this town could be at night."

"Not late. Ten-thirty. We Welsh are a quiet bunch." He chuckled. "That is, when we're not singing or arguing. Stoic, they call us, remember?"

"Hmm." Mist swirled about each light they passed, and she moved a little closer to Trevor. The smell of tar mixed with salt rose from the harbor. "I used to think you were mysterious because you were quiet. Then I found out you were just plain ornery.''

He stopped abruptly, and she grasped his arm. "What's the matter, Trevor? Does the truth hurt?"

"You always had a wicked tongue. I *am* mysterious. A more even-tempered man you'll never meet. Ask my mother."

She smothered a laugh as they moved on. "I only met your mother once, but it was obvious you had her snowed."

"You'll have to meet her again. I've still got her snowed."

"We're going away from the car, aren't we?" Caitlin looked over her shoulder. They'd have to go the other way to get to the car park.

"You said you wanted to walk. I thought we'd go to Brother John's garden. Do you remember it? The little garden built by one of the old stewards from Caldy Island?"

"Yes." And she also remembered that it was secluded. How could she want so much to be alone with Trevor yet be so afraid at the same time?

Their shoes clipped on slick cobbles, echoed off walls and unlighted windows.

"Here we are." Trevor opened a wrought-iron gate.

Caitlin recalled how the sunken garden overhung the cliffside, how in daylight there could be a sensation of seeing the ocean from a plane. She hung back.

"Come on, I'll protect you from any hobgoblins lurking about." He laughed and pulled her into an ivy-shrouded bower. "There's a bench in here somewhere. We can sit and listen to the water. But watch your step."

"I can't see a thing." But she could feel, feel him as

if they were locked in each other's arms. "Maybe walking in the dark wasn't such a good idea."

"Why?" With a hand at her waist he urged her gently in front of him. "You never used to be afraid of the dark. Here we are." He guided her to sit on a slatted bench.

Caitlin didn't lean back. She never used to be afraid of the dark? She wasn't now. The point he was evidently missing was that there were a few things she never used to be but that definitely applied now, such as being married. Separated or not, she was still David's wife, and they had a child she never intended to hurt. Involvement with Trevor, or any man, could do more to undermine Mary than Caitlin was willing to risk.

Trevor sensed Caitlin was withdrawing further and further from him. He leaned forward, resting his forearms on his knees and stared at the dim outline of the walls around the garden. If he didn't handle her right, there might never be another time alone like this. Gut instinct, together with the comments she'd already made, told him her marriage wasn't picture perfect. He might yet have a chance with her.

"Where's your husband?" He gritted his teeth in the darkness. If there was an award for tact, he'd never be in the running.

He heard her indrawn breath. "In Los Angeles."

"Will he be joining you here?"

"No."

Marriage was forever. He believed that. He shouldn't be glad that Caitlin's might not be. "You said you didn't know how long you'd be in Tenby. Won't your husband miss you if you stay away very long?"

She stood up and moved in front of him. Trevor stayed where he was, watching the way her hair lifted and whipped forward around her hunched shoulders. He should drop the subject.

"David misses me."

He looked away, not liking himself for being disappointed. "And you miss him," he said flatly.

"No. But I don't want to talk about it, Trevor. I think I should go home. Thomas was going over to keep Mary company, but I shouldn't leave them too long."

Back off, Trevor, my lad. But pure hope fueled his undisciplined tongue. "Thomas will take good care of Mary. I want you with me for a while." He got up and held her shoulders. "What is it with you and...David?"

"Not now." But she leaned against him before stepping away. "It's complicated and I've got a long way to go on my own before I know where to begin explaining what's on my mind to someone else."

Someone else? He didn't want to be just someone else, not to Caitlin. And he wasn't giving up so easily on at least getting a hint of what was wrong for her.

He'd try a change in tactics. "Mary's a sweet little thing. Evidently Owen Trew thinks so, too."

Caitlin turned and her face was a study in light and shadow. "She only met him a few days ago. They're just children."

"So were we."

Her bowed head sent her hair cascading forward. "That was different. We were older."

"A couple of years. And children mature earlier now."

"She isn't ready for a boyfriend."

"Caitlin." He lifted her chin with a finger and thumb. "A while ago we were angry that your parents interfered with our friendship. Are you going to do the same thing to Mary?"

"Of course not. I'm a typical mother, that's all, not

ready for her little girl to grow up. Anyway, we're making something out of nothing.''

He wouldn't pursue that. He'd already seen the way Owen looked at Mary, and *nothing* wouldn't be the word he'd use to describe what he saw in the boy's face.

"It's too cold out here. Let's go back to the White Knight for a drink. Then I promise I'll give up and take you home." Surely there was some way to make her relax with him.

"I don't think so. Thanks anyway, Trevor."

"Curfew? I thought you were a big girl now." A barrier had stood solidly between them all night, and it was getting steadily thicker and higher. "I don't want you to go yet."

She made a move to pass him, and he caught her arm. "This was wrong," she said. "If you wanted to prove that what we started once could start again, you've done it. We could get involved with each other very easily. Only we won't allow that to happen, and you already know why."

He didn't…and he didn't accept. "Can't we be friends?" She couldn't know how his heart had leaped into his throat at her admission that she felt something special with him.

"I doubt it."

"Please come back to my place and talk some more." He released her and held up his hands. "I'll behave, I promise. I always did. You were the aggressive one."

The hoped-for laugh didn't come. "I know that," Caitlin said. "And I've got a hunch I haven't changed around you, Trevor. Damn, I can't believe what I'm saying. Why is it I don't feel I have to protect my pride with you?"

"Because you don't." Taking her in his arms would feel so good. It would also end any chance he had of going forward with her. "Ma'am—" he bowed his head "—would you please come with me, and trust, just trust?"

Her sigh fanned his cheek, and he closed his eyes.

"Lead on," she said. "But I can't stay long."

On the way down Crackwell Street to the car he kept his hands in his pockets. He would prove he meant what he'd said. His behavior would be above reproach. No pressure from this boy.

Caitlin slipped her arm through his and he smiled. Years didn't count for much. She felt as natural at his side as she ever had.

The drive to the pub took less than ten minutes. Trevor blessed his timing when he pulled the Jag into the forecourt and saw all the lights were turned low for the night. Nip Lymer, the Londoner who managed the White Knight whenever Trevor wanted or needed to be away, had closed up and would already have left for home.

Trevor got out of the car and went around to open the passenger door. "Okay, friend. My flat upstairs, or the bar? The choice is yours. Wherever you'd feel more comfortable is fine with me."

"I like the bar."

By the time he locked the car door she was walking toward the front entrance.

Fine. Have it your way. You're at least as afraid of your own reactions as of mine. He grinned as he followed her.

Nip had banked down the fire in the bar but embers still glowed through the ash. "Good," he said to Caitlin, rubbing his hands. "The fire didn't go out. I'll get it going properly."

"Don't bother for me."

He smiled at her, took her coat and shrugged off his

own. "If you say so. But I'll bother for me." With the precision he'd learned from his father, he stirred the coals, speared them with slivers of kindling and piled fresh fuel on top. "There. That'll be roaring in no time. Give me your coat and tell me what you'll have. I'm an expert on manhattans now. I've been practicing."

She laughed.

Mr. Smooth had done it again. "Okay, okay, so I still give myself away every time I open my mouth. You're right, I did read up about them and mix a couple because I hoped to make them for you again."

"You always were too darned honest, Trevor." She wasn't laughing anymore. "That was one of the things that made it so easy to...being fond of you didn't take a whole lot of effort."

He mustn't allow awkward silences, even if she did keep saying those little things that hit him like tough-sweet blows. "So, a manhattan?"

"No. But I will make sure you have a chance to show me how good you've gotten at them some time."

"Promise?"

"Promise. I don't think I need anything now though, Trevor."

His hands were dirty from the fire. He looked at them with something approaching gratitude. Any diversion was better than none at all. "Let me wash my hands. But think of something I can get you, please."

"I'll try."

While he ran water into the sink behind the bar, Caitlin's high heels tapped on the wooden floors.

"Your bird's asleep," she said, raising her voice. "Why doesn't he fall off his perch?"

"Don't ask me. He's been there as long as I can remember, and he sleeps that way every night and never falls off.''

''Trevor.''

''Yes.''

''I wish we could go back.''

The water sounded thunderous. He turned it off slowly and dried his hands. ''No one can do that.''

''I know. Dumb thing to say.''

''Not so dumb. I wish the same thing.''

''Forget I said it.''

''I don't want to. Say it again—'' he walked around and approached her carefully ''—and again and again.''

Her hands rested on her hips and she stared down into the fire. Was she angry?

''Caitlin, why aren't you happy?''

''I shouldn't have told you I wasn't. I don't have any right to prey on you just because I know you so well.'' She sounded…bitter? ''Isn't that crazy? Nineteen years ago we were close for a few months, and I feel I know you better than I've ever known another human being.''

''Including your husband?'' Another false step, but he couldn't help himself.

''Including my husband,'' she said distantly. ''We had some good years, Trevor. David was a good man when we were married. But he caved in. He became Hollywood, the worst of Hollywood, the phony part.''

If he'd learned anything over the years it had been the importance of caution. Now he needed to use what understanding he had of how and when to employ it. ''You've had a bad time, haven't you?''

She lifted her hair from her shoulders, and he followed the beautiful, slender lines of her body. Perhaps too slender, but lithe and desirable enough to awaken responses he couldn't give in to now.

"It wasn't all bad," she said at last. "And I have Mary—and my work. I've got everything I need."

"Everything?"

"Yes." She responded too quickly, too vehemently.

He'd back off a little. "You design shoes, I'm told. I never knew anyone who did that."

"We aren't a common breed." She shook her head. "That sounds pigheaded. I only meant that it's a narrow field and a hard one to succeed in. I've been lucky."

"I bet you're wonderful at it. Will you show me what you do?"

She hesitated. "You'd be bored sick."

"Do I have to beg?" If she didn't gather by now that nothing about her would ever bore him, she never would.

"I'll show you, I'll show you. Soon, okay?"

"Okay. I'm going to hold you to it. Can't I give you something?"

Wood scraped on wood as she pulled a chair close to the fire. "You can give me a little time, a little peace." She sat down and rested her chin on her fists. "Sit with me, Trevor, and help me pretend we never lost track of each other."

He placed a chair to face hers and sat. "Why are you still married?"

"I don't want to talk about that. I just am and will probably go on being married unless I can sort out one big problem."

"Let me help you with the problem."

She shook her head.

"I don't understand why you're holding back," he said.

Caitlin was here again, close, yet as far away as she'd ever been since she left him before. That much he understood very well.

"Remember our place on the cliffs?" she asked. The

attitude of her body, her determined voice, warned him not to push her about David McBride, damn the man.

"You know I remember."

"What comes back the clearest, Trevor?"

He was only human and he'd gone over those times again and again, embellishing each little encounter. "This." Leaning toward her, he gathered both her hands into one of his. Then he arranged them so they rested on his wrists. "Next step is yours."

She tried to withdraw, but he clasped her fingers. "No, no. You asked me what comes back and you don't get off that easily. What did you do to a poor innocent boy that day?"

"Trevor, I can't."

"Oh, but I think you can."

For what seemed a very long time she stared into his eyes before bringing her mouth close and brushing her lips against his in a feathery touch.

"I was a forward minx. Leading a pure—"

She never finished. His hands spanned her waist with ease and soft fabric swished against his pants as he lifted her onto his knees.

He met her eyes for an instant. They shone. Apprehension? Invitation? He didn't care. She uttered no protest, and beneath his mouth, hers opened.

She turned in his arms, wound her fingers in his hair, made small, keening noises in her throat. Their tongues touched, reached, and her grip on him became wild. His arousal was instant.

"*Cari,*" he murmured, kissing her jaw, her cheekbones, her closed eyes, ranging his hands over her back to wrap her more tightly against him. "Let me love you. We need each other."

Her stillness penetrated his ardor slowly. She became passive, rested her face against his neck.

His heart beat an erratic tattoo, and need pulsed in his every cell. In the middle of his brain a small cold place formed. He'd blown it, gone too fast. All the lectures to himself had been useless. *He'd blown it.*

"Caitlin?" He tried to lift her away, to see her face, but she clung tighter. "Oh, Caitlin, I'm sorry. Forgive a stupid man for not thinking far enough."

She said nothing and he felt moisture on his skin. He'd made her cry. Idiot that he was, he'd promised understanding and space, and she'd taken the trust he offered. Then he'd ruined everything.

"Caitlin—"

"Shut up," she said, so softly he wasn't sure he'd heard correctly. "Shut up and kiss me again. The same way. Then don't you say another word before you take me home."

6

Trevor drove along the narrow lanes from Caitlin's cottage toward the Croft. Minutes would take him back into town and home.

He didn't want to go home.

Speeding around a corner, he braked too hard and went into a skid along a hedgerow. The Jag screeched a hundred yards, scraping the paint work on brambles, before it slewed and stopped.

Silence closed him in with the hard beat of his heart. What the hell was he going to do? What was happening to his well-ordered life? He cradled the steering wheel and rested his brow on flexed knuckles.

No, Caitlin had told him at her door, no, they mustn't be together again, not the way they had been tonight. And she'd reiterated the reasons: she wasn't free, and even if she were, they'd become too different from each other, had always been too different from each other. Still, he didn't buy a word of it.

He switched off the ignition, got out of the car and looked back the way he'd come. If he cut across the fields in the direction of Thomas Rhys's house, the house where Caitlin had stayed in her teens, there'd be no trouble finding the place where he'd spent so many hours with her. He'd returned often enough since.

A suit and slippery-soled dress shoes made poor hiking

clothes. He went anyway, absently aware of mud underfoot, of stickery things fingering his clothes, of the scent of mist-rimed gorse.

A mile or so east of the Davies's cottage he veered toward the sea, hearing and smelling rather than seeing how close it was. Loose rubble clacking away, spinning palely, stopped him from taking one step too close to the cliff edge.

Peering at the ground, he inched onward until he found the wind-winnowed bowl he sought and then leaped down. The sand was too wet for him to sit.

This was not rational behavior, he told himself. This was the act of a man in danger of losing his objectivity, something he'd taken more years than most to cultivate.

To his right, a light shone beyond the harbor, on the tip of Castle Hill. A few more lights glimmered in the town. And nearer, a glow showed in what must be the back of Caitlin's cottage.

He must think things through carefully, plan what to do next. And he would do something about Caitlin, no matter how she tried to head him off.

They couldn't be together the way they'd been tonight? What exactly did that mean? That they must not be alone with one another? Fine. He'd find ways to be with her and with someone else at the same time. Mary should be the perfect choice of chaperon. The girl seemed to like him and that could turn out to his advantage.

The deep breath he took turned his lungs cold, made his throat sting. He could think clearly here because he felt Caitlin's presence.

When he'd kissed her earlier his mind had darted back to this place. He pursed his lips. Their kisses tonight had been very different from those of the past, and that was as they should be, as he wanted them to be. But the passion he'd felt simmering an hour or so ago had begun right here when a girl touched her inexperienced mouth to his. The heat in his body now was a sexual thing but still there was that other thing, that link with her. When they'd originally lost touch and the link had seemed broken, he'd been almost immobilized. Now he felt it again, as strong as ever.

First love was a practice run, they said, a fragile frivolous experiment never meant to last. But fragile creations sometimes grew stronger and stronger, and judging from what he felt now, that's the way it would have been had he and Caitlin kept the promises made on this ground. Was it too late? Was Trevor Morgan, local jock hero, a lonely dreaming fool to hope otherwise?

He couldn't honestly deny that they were opposites in many ways. Caitlin, so gentle and quiet, must have found his preoccupation with rough sports a puzzle. He could see now how she'd pretended interest to please him. And he understood little or nothing of the way she'd lived and continued to live.

Differences could be overcome, were overcome all the time. Opposites attract, went the old saying, and he and Caitlin weren't total opposites anyway. If they'd been able to grow together...

He must put the truth about their failed correspondence out of his mind. Anger was destructive and he needed to keep his head. Dwelling on what the Rhyses had done to Caitlin and to him could only cause impotent fury.

Caitlin's husband missed her, but she didn't miss him. David used to be a good man but not anymore. And she no longer wanted him. Trevor would bet his life on Caitlin's desire to move on from her marriage. So what was holding her back?

"I'll find out, *cari*," he announced aloud to a moonless sky. "And then we'll see if there is any going back."

Tomorrow he'd start his offensive.

"What's wrong, Trevor?" Caitlin entered the bar and let the heavy door swing shut behind her. In the dim interior that smelled of aged beer and used cigarette smoke she was momentarily blind, but she saw his silhouette in a mirror. "Mrs. J. said you called and said you needed to see me. Desperate she said it was. Are you all—"

Although it was midafternoon and the pub was technically closed, she and Trevor weren't alone. A tall man stood in the shadows to one side of the fireplace, the parrot perched on his shoulder. Caitlin didn't need to be told this was Sam Morgan, Trevor's father. She'd remember him even if the likeness wasn't unmistakable.

"Hello, Caitlin." Trevor's voice was flat. He came from behind the bar. "This is my father, Sam Morgan."

"I know," she said, growing uncomfortable. "Nice to see you again, Mr. Morgan."

"Likewise," the man said, sounding anything but pleased. "I heard you were back in Tenby."

"For a while. I'm not sure how long. But I expect Trevor's told you all that."

"Trevor hasn't told me anything. If someone else hadn't mentioned it, I wouldn't know you were here." He moved forward until she saw that he'd grown thinner with the years and that his thick hair had turned iron gray. The features were an older pattern for Trevor's, strikingly defined, with high cheekbones and a perfectly straight nose. Even the mouth was a copy—wide, the upper lip narrow, the lower full. But the eyes were different. The eyes were pale and, at this moment, hostile.

Caitlin backed up, unsure what to say. What had she

done to cause this man's obvious dislike of her? "You're busy, Trevor. Why don't you give me a call later and tell me whatever it was you had to say?"

Trevor squared his shoulders inside a bulky old fisherman's sweater of oiled navy-blue wool. "Don't go, please. Dad dropped by unexpectedly."

Sam Morgan muttered something, then pretended to be talking to the bird.

"Mrs. Johnson overdid the message a bit." Trevor laughed. "I did say I wanted to talk to you as soon as possible but not that it was an emergency. Thank you for last night, by the way. I had a wonderful time."

Ignoring the antagonistic vibes from the older man was impossible. "So did I," Caitlin responded in a low voice. Wonderful wasn't an apt description for how she'd felt after Trevor left her. She'd never been more disturbed or tossed through a night with such a sense of longing as she had once he'd driven away.

"You two are seeing each other?"

The question startled Caitlin. She looked at Trevor and he smiled tightly, shook his head, signaling, she assumed, that he would take care of his father.

"Dad, Caitlin and I are old friends. You know that. Yes, we're seeing each other."

She opened her mouth to protest but couldn't think how. This was a small town. News, particularly gossip, traveled fast, and she didn't want ideas put into Mary's head.

Sam Morgan untangled the parrot's claws from the shoulder of his jacket and placed the bird on its perch. "Aren't you married, Mrs., er—"

She felt shaky. "McBride. Yes, sir, I am married. And I have a daughter, Mary. Maybe your informants have told you about her, too?"

"Hmm."

He didn't need to say more, his meaning was implicit. She was a married woman and had no right to lead his son astray. A rare flash of anger brought blood to her face. "Trevor, if there's nothing I can do for you, I'd better get back to work."

"No! No, *cari*."

Morgan senior shifted, and Caitlin's jaw tightened until it ached.

"That's why I called," Trevor continued after only a missed beat. "You promised to show me the way you work and I wondered if this would be a good day."

And for that he'd left a message that brought Mrs. J. breathlessly to the door when Caitlin got home from the post office? "Well, I suppose—"

"Good. It was great of you to drop in, Dad. Tell Mom I'll be over for lunch on Sunday."

"I'll do that." He followed Trevor who grabbed a worn pea jacket from a chair and pulled it on. "Gwen's folks will be there, too, son."

Trevor looked blankly at his father. "Aren't they always?"

They reached the door, and Trevor locked it behind them.

"We'd invite you for lunch, too, Mrs. McBride," Sam Morgan said, "but I'm sure you understand that it wouldn't look good."

"I—"

"Don't be so old-fashioned, Dad." Trevor's laugh wasn't convincing.

Caitlin felt the closest thing she remembered to rage, mixed with a sense of injustice. "Thank you, Mr. Morgan. I'm not free on Sunday anyway." She walked away.

Trevor caught up with her and fell into step before Caitlin reached the sidewalk. "I'm sorry," he said and sounded it. "He has a way of dropping by when I least expect it. I think he misses the pub."

"I'm sure." She was too upset to deal with any of this. "And he also disapproves of me. I think he's afraid I'll corrupt his little boy."

"Hey." He swung her around so fast she grabbed his coat for support. "My dad was rude. He's a funny, old-world man and sometimes he says things he shouldn't. He doesn't bother me, so why does he bother you? And why the put-down? Does it make you feel better to make me feel worse?"

Caitlin squirmed but she made herself meet his eyes. "I'm sorry. That was lousy of me. I felt embarrassed and kind of...grubby. Trevor, I couldn't handle it, that's all. And we *aren't* seeing each other, so why did you tell him we are?"

"Because we are." He let her go and looked serenely over her shoulder as if something in the distance pleased him.

"We are not. I told you we couldn't—"

"Be alone together. Yes, I know. So we won't be. Mary should be home by the time we get to your place, right?"

She narrowed her eyes at him. "You manipulative—"

"Ah, ah, Caitlin. Don't say something you'll regret. Get in the car." She hadn't noticed they were beside the Jag.

"I walked down," she told him.

"Well, you don't have to walk back, do you? Please get in." He opened the door and she silently did as he asked. Why couldn't she just let herself enjoy the way she felt with him? The reason was instantly there, and she crossed her arms tightly.

"Boy, the best-laid plans. I really did just want to ask

if I could come over and watch you for a while,'' Trevor said after he slid behind the wheel and started the engine.

"We can't be anything to each other, Trevor."

"Because you're married to a man you don't like?'' He steered into traffic.

"I didn't say that." She must be transparent to him, just as she always had been.

"You didn't have to say it. If you care about someone, you miss them." He glanced at her. "Take it from me."

"I don't have to. I already know that. It doesn't change a thing. My life is set and there isn't room for more complications."

"But when you got a message from me, you came rushing to my place because you thought I needed you. I'd say you're not having an easy time shutting me out."

She swiveled toward him, her breathing short. "That's not fair. I don't care what you say. You gave Mrs. J. the impression something was wrong. And I did what any friend would do."

"That's right. You came running, and from the look on your face you were worried sick." A flush accented his high cheekbones.

"If you want me to feel a fool you can congratulate yourself." She sank lower and stared out the window. Rain had started falling again. It hit the glass and washed upward in jerky sheets. She shoved her hands inside her sleeves.

Trevor drove on in silence until he turned the car from the Croft onto the lane leading to her cottage. "I'm sorry, okay?"

She didn't answer.

"Caitlin Rhys McBride, this man hates himself for saying some of the things he just said. Lately he hasn't had a lot of practice dealing with women he cares about. Will you forgive him?''

Her heart tightened. If she had to guess, she'd say Gwen Williams Morgan was the last woman before herself that Trevor had dealt with. And if she asked him, he'd probably admit as much.

"Caitlin, *please*?''

"I'm the one who needs forgiveness,'' she told him. "Now forget it.''

Trevor shrugged. Experience had taught him not to press her too far too fast. Not that he usually remembered in time.

When they arrived at the cottage, Caitlin led him directly to a big well-lighted kitchen. She pulled out a ladder-backed chair from a giant and cluttered table. "Sit. I'll put the kettle on. Mary should be here any minute and Thomas will probably come with her. She goes up to see him after school most days and he usually comes back—just to see she's safe, he says. Actually, I think it's Mrs. J.'s cakes that draw him.''

"Thomas must like having you here.'' But it was too bad the man was likely to show up now, Trevor decided. "I never saw how this place looked before, but you've done a lot, haven't you?'' He admired the airy effect she'd accomplished—all pale blue and white with the old wooden floors refinished to a high Swedish shine. "It's nice.''

"Thanks. I would have expected you to prefer dark places like your pub.''

"You haven't seen where I actually live yet.'' He watched for her reaction.

Her gaze flickered to his and immediately darted away.

She was as aware of the force field between them as he was.

He pulled a box across the table toward him. "What's all this stuff?"

Caitlin had filled the kettle. Now she set it on the stove and turned on a burner. "That 'stuff' is what I work with. You're holding a box of sample heels."

"Pretty fancy, aren't they?" A silver spike piercing a crystal globe caught his eye and he held it up. "Would a woman actually *wear* something like this?"

She chuckled and came to lean on his shoulder. "I'm focusing a lot of my attention on evening designs this year. And yes, a woman would actually wear that. Look at this one. It's an idea I'm fooling around with, and I only picked up the prototype yesterday."

While she spoke she unconsciously rested a hand on the side of his neck and her breasts pressed softly against his back while she shifted piles of sketches.

Trevor closed his eyes and realized he was holding his breath. He'd swear she wore nothing under her black cashmere sweater. Her skin, the skin that was usually hidden from sun and wind, would be so white against that black sweater.

"Here it is."

She straightened, moved a chair close to his and sat down.

Trevor blinked rapidly, glad she was too involved in the thing she was holding to notice she'd aroused him.

"See." A heel shaped like an empty gold cage, very narrow at the tip, caught the light. "Strong but almost weightless and very flashy. Can't you see this with a completely plain gold-kid upper and a gold-sequined halter dress like this—" She shuffled papers and produced a drawing of a skimpy number that reached mid-thigh. "Or something in shocking pink. The naked look, like this—" Another picture showed a model wearing a skirt of ruffled layers and something that appeared to have a chiffon bodice sheer enough to show the the woman's nipples.

Trevor swallowed. "Great," he murmured, completely out of his depth. Confronted by a woman in the pink creation he'd be unlikely to check out her shoes. He cleared his throat. "You said you got the prototype yesterday—the heel. Where do they come from?"

"Paris." Caitlin leaned back in her chair and put her hands in the pockets of her black pants. He noticed her own shoes were simple, flat, also black, and that her feet were long and elegantly shaped. Everything about her fascinated him.

"Who sends them? Do they come up with heels and you figure out what shoes will go with them?"

She laughed explosively, jerking forward and folding her hands around his arm. "Trevor! That's priceless." With visible effort, she sobered her expression. "I'm sorry. How would you know? I draw everything here, or wherever I happen to be working. Then I send my drawings to my atelier, my workroom, in Paris where they make up samples and send them back for me to approve or decide on changes. At this stage I'm still playing around a bit, so I often come up with ideas for a heel or a new material and I ask for a mock-up. I see everything in model form before I make up my mind if the concept works."

Enthusiasm and confidence shone in her eyes and he felt oddly proud. "So you thought up a heel like a cage and your workmen made it? I didn't have any idea how any of this worked. What happens when—"

"Mom, are you home?"

Mary, catapulting through the kitchen door, effectively shattered the intimacy of the moment.

"Here, sweetie," Caitlin said.

Trevor noted that instead of smiling she cast an uncertain look in his direction.

Mary concentrated on him, too, but only for an instant. A quick frown suggested that she sensed something intangible, unfamiliar. He and Caitlin must make too domestic a picture. He'd have to tread carefully if he was to keep Mary on his side, something he could only do if she didn't see him as a rival to the father she undoubtedly still loved.

The moment passed. Mary waved at him and looked outside. "Uncle Thomas is here, too."

"Uncle Thomas isn't going to be here much longer if this young lady keeps running me around the way she does." Thomas puffed into the kitchen, his ears cold despite burning lungs. "She forgets I'm an old man who needs to take his time."

"Baloney," Mary said, pulling him forward. "This is Mr. Morgan, Uncle Thomas. He's the coach I was telling you about."

Thomas hadn't noticed Trevor sitting there: his face was slightly flushed and Caitlin's more so. "Good day to you, Trevor. Mary kept talking about a Mr. Morgan, and somehow I didn't put you together with the name."

"Hello, Thomas," Trevor said, and Thomas heard a wary note. The idiot of a boy must think Caitlin's aged and undoubtedly straight-laced single uncle might not approve of her being alone with a man. That was something Thomas intended to work on.

"Tea?" Caitlin hopped up like a marionette on shortened strings. "The kettle's on...."

The kettle was whistling steadily, had been when he and Mary walked through the door. A little preoccupation around here, maybe? Thomas quelled a satisfied smile.

"Can't stay for tea," he said briskly, his mouth watering for a cup and for a piece of that Ethel Johnson's cake "Got to get back and...there's something I want to show Mary, but I thought I'd better check in with you first."

"What?" Mary asked immediately, her eyes glowing with curiosity. "You never said anything."

"That's because I wanted it to be a surprise. Okay with you if I kidnap your daughter for an hour or so, Caitlin?" His mind raced, searching for what he could produce to interest Mary.

"Well, I suppose so. What about dinner? Come back here for dinner." There was a layer of apprehension there. Discomfort at what he might really think about her being with Trevor? Or mistrust of herself and Trevor if they were left alone? He couldn't stop a smirk, but he coughed into his fist, feigning deep thought.

"Will you come for dinner?"

"I could, I suppose. It's been a long time since I had a chance to really talk to Trevor. Smoke a pipe, do you, Trevor?"

"Er, no, sir." Trevor looked at Caitlin and continued quickly, "But I'll be glad to keep you company while you smoke yours, Thomas. *After* I help with the dishes, of course." And he turned a winning smile on Caitlin, who blushed a deeper but charming shade of pink.

Good boy, Thomas thought. This might not be as difficult as he'd expected. But then, Trevor Morgan had been a single-minded devil even as an eleven-year-old.

"That's settled then," Thomas said. "Come on, Mary. How's seven-thirty, Caitlin?" Two hours shouldn't be long enough for too much trouble to develop. But then again, it might even be long enough for... What did he know? He was an old man and a bachelor.

Caitlin agreed to "seven-thirty" in a weak voice.

Mary, watching silently until now, startled him. She

hugged her mother and, after an uncertain pause, quickly hugged Trevor, too. In another instant she was leading the way outside.

He stopped, remembering a snippet about Trevor. "Do you know you were the best math student I ever had?" He looked significantly at Caitlin whose eyes seemed to have grown a size or two and who was having difficulty keeping her lips together. "Always remember, Caitlin. Only logical men make good mathematicians and logical men can be relied on."

He swept out, wrapping his muffler more tightly around his neck and silently congratulating himself. Perhaps Mary would be interested in the model soldiers he'd made over the years. No, not for a girl. There had to be old photographs in the attic. That was it, he'd show her photographs, let her sit in the dusty attic among the junk Caitlin called memorabilia. Girls liked that stuff. So did interfering old men.

The click of the door latch closing sounded like a gunshot to Caitlin. Thomas was throwing her at Trevor. Her own uncle was playing matchmaker when he knew she was still a married woman and had made no definite plans to change that status.

Trevor's laughter was the next sound to jar her. "Foxy devil," he sputtered. "I do believe your uncle wants us to be alone."

"You're imagining things. He only came for the reason he said he did. And *you* invited yourself to dinner."

He managed a hint of mock contrition. "Only because I didn't want to embarrass him."

"Sure, Trevor, sure."

"If you don't want me to stay I can leave. Tell Thomas I got called back to the pub. If I don't contact Nip Lymer to take over, I'll have to go anyway."

"Call him," she said without thinking. Damn, she wanted him to stay and she wanted him to go and she didn't know what she wanted at all anymore.

"I will," Trevor almost whispered. "Thank you, *cari*."

"You're welcome. Ready for more instruction on the craft of shoe making and design? I can make shoes, you know. Not that I very often do anymore. But I still recreate my designs three-dimensionally from paper or whatever works and do some hand-sewing, embroidery, beading and so on for special orders."

"Not now," he said, and she gave in to the delight of basking in his warm sensuous appraisal. "I'll want to know every detail later, but no more today. What I'd really like to do is out but—"

"Trevor—"

"Sh, let me finish. I'm only a man, and nineteen years is long enough to wait to be with the woman you dreamed of as your first lover."

The warmth in her own body turned to intense, aching heat that throbbed in her womb. "Don't talk like that, please."

"No, no, I won't. I mustn't." But he stood up and pulled her to her feet. "Not till you let me know it's time."

She opened her mouth to say there would never be a time for them. But she didn't want to, didn't want to believe it was true. "Don't pursue it, Trevor. I'm not free."

"You're still married." He brushed back her hair, tangling it in his fingers and kissed the corner of her mouth. Caitlin closed her eyes and stood very still. "You've got a husband who wants you, although you don't want him." He pressed his lips fully to hers, but she turned her head and rested her face on his shoulder.

"Caitlin," he whispered. "Don't you believe in fate, just a little bit?"

Her arms, flung around his neck, gripping tightly, caught him off balance and he backed into the table, spanning her waist. "Hold me, Trevor. Don't talk."

"What is it?" Why did she persist in holding back when she clearly didn't want to? "Caitlin, I'm not going away and I'm not letting up until you tell me what's wrong with you. Does this man you're married to frighten you? Is he some kind of threat?"

He stroked her back, brought his hands to rest on her slender hips. She was crying soundlessly.

"Caitlin." Firmly, he pushed her far enough away to see her face. "*Tell* me. You're here to get away from this husband of yours, right?"

She nodded.

"You don't love him anymore?"

"No."

"When did you stop loving him?"

"Years ago."

Relief, hope, were misplaced as yet. "But he still loves you?"

"No."

He frowned. Mascara splotched her cheeks, and he rubbed at it with his thumbs. "But you told me he wants you home."

"We don't live together. We've been legally separated for three years. I said he misses me."

"I don't understand any of this." But he wanted to, God how he wanted to.

"David went wrong somewhere, Trevor." She blinked, breathing through her mouth. He hated causing this distress but there could be no stopping. "He was a good man, a brilliant man. He's a writer, scripts...only he doesn't get work anymore.''

She tried to rest her face on his chest again but he stopped her. "Go on," he said. If she didn't work this through, there was no hope for her, for him with her.

"He got in with a bad crowd. Parties and booze. Oh, Trevor, he drank himself to nothingness. Now he misses me, but only because he needs me.''

"Because he's lonely, you mean?" That he could understand.

"No, because he doesn't have any money most of the time and because I still have connections in the film industry. He...uses me.''

Trevor stared at her. "Why do you let him?" He turned away, ramming a hand into his hair. "Where's the problem, Caitlin? Divorce the bastard. And if he tries to give you any trouble refer him to me. I'll—''

"He's Mary's father.''

Her voice cut through his fury. Cool, detached, she made the statement like the closing lines of a speech. No more to be said.

Trevor walked a slow circle, stopping in front of her. "Yes, I assumed David was Mary's father. What does that have to do with the fact that you should divorce the man, should have divorced him years ago?''

"She adores him, and he...David loves Mary very much in his own way.''

"And what way is that? When it suits him and he doesn't have a party to go to?''

"You're reacting, not thinking. You don't know David. He's had his problems.''

"Haven't we all?''

"Of course." Stress tightened the skin on her face. Her cheekbones shone. "But it's all irrelevant. I can't, no, I won't do anything to make Mary more insecure than she already is. These last three years have been very hard on her. She's gone from being a physically frail little girl who was emotionally secure to a borderline anorexic with a muddled mind.'' She paused, teeth driven into her bottom lip, a desperate light in her eyes. ''Mary's all right, or she will be. She's starting to get better now she's in a calm atmosphere, and I'm going to work things out so she doesn't take any steps backward.''

Trevor's stomach did jumping jacks. He lifted his chin to swallow. ''What do you mean by that? Work things out?''

She shook her head. ''I know why you're asking. Don't think I wouldn't like to start over with you. I'm not blind or numb, I can feel what there could be between us. But my life's such a mess and I don't know how long it'll take to straighten out.''

Without thinking, he gathered her fiercely into his arms. ''I don't give a damn how long it takes. But you are going to get rid of David, aren't you?''

Her fingers, sliding beneath his sweater to spread wide on the skin of his back, jammed air into his windpipe. ''That's why I came here,'' she said, her lips on his throat. ''I want to be free, Trevor. I *need* to be free. But if I do it at all, it has to be slowly so that Mary gets used to the idea and doesn't think she's going to be cut off from her father. She's afraid of that, so she convinces herself the separation is temporary and we'll all be together again one day.''

He felt her struggle, and he felt his own suffocating triumph tangled with dread. If, if, if. There couldn't be any if about this. ''I'll help you with Mary,'' he said, meaning every word. ''She likes me. And she'll get used to the idea of you and her father being divorced. It happens."

Caitlin ran her nails up and down his spine and her body leaped at his stiffening. "Mary isn't ready to accept that her father and I can't put our family back together. And also I won't have her hurt by an attachment to another father figure."

"You mean me?" Trevor leaned away, framing her face with his big hands. "How would I hurt her?"

"By becoming part of her life. You're right, she does like you. But if she comes to like you too much, to rely on you, it'll only be another blow when you aren't around anymore."

He flinched as if she'd struck him. "I intend to be around, Caitlin. Are you telling me you don't want that?"

She'd hurt him, but one of them had to be realistic. "What I do or don't want isn't the issue, not all of it. When you've been disappointed once you can't pretend it might not happen again."

"I'll never willingly disappoint you. Neither of us can be sure how things will work out. But give us a chance, my love. At least do that much and we'll see."

He held her closer, pressed his hips to hers in a reflexive movement. She concentrated on the neck of his sweater. His erection was natural; it was also a warning she couldn't ignore. A dull, exquisite throbbing in her breasts and thighs made clear thought a feat.

"Trevor, what you'd like at this minute is to go to bed."

He blushed and the effect startled Caitlin. She smiled, touching his cheeks. "I've become very blunt. Sorry."

"Blunt and honest. Isn't that what you'd like, too?"

It was her turn for embarrassment. "You know it is. And that's why we're going to have this conversation just once. I'm trying to decide when and how to divorce David. If I pull it off, and by that I mean when and if I've set the divorce wheels in motion, then I'll be free. I'll be free to do what I like with my life—'' she met his eyes, glanced at his beautiful mouth ''—and my body. But understand that I can't make love with you until I'm sure I am ready to initiate the divorce. It wouldn't be fair on you, and I'd be betraying myself. If I'm ready for a lover, I'm ready to make the final break with David.''

"You are blunt." Trevor leaned to kiss her forehead. "And so wise. But I'm patient and we're going to be together, you know that, don't you, *cari*?''

7

"Next thing we know, Trevor, boy, you'll be having one of those jukebox things in here."

Trevor grinned at Colin-crust whose elbows rested in the same spots, one each side of a lager pump, where they rested every night until closing time.

"Now, Colin, don't tell me you're not a man who enjoys a bit of music."

Colin grumbled into his glass. A speck of froth clung to the tip of his purple nose. Trevor had finally given in to the younger clement that had been steadily growing in number among his regulars and installed a stereo system. Colin wasn't the only customer disgruntled at the change, but they'd get over it and Trevor knew well that they enjoyed a reason for argument.

Caitlin would be dropping by later. He smiled to himself. Thomas would bring her, and after the pub closed, she'd sit with Trevor by the fire here or in his flat upstairs, and they'd talk and dance their tantalizing dance of "look but don't touch" until he took her home. The pattern had been the same for two weeks since that first dinner at her cottage. She came to him, or he went to her or took her out hiking or shopping or sea-gazing, often with Mary along.

Mary troubled him. On the surface she gave all the right signals. She seemed determined to be happy that he spent time with them. But the small doubt persisted. Did she really want him around her mother, or was she, in her too-mature mind, computing what she saw and felt and watching for confirmation that he could be in line to take her father's place?

So far Caitlin hadn't mentioned the subject, which probably meant he was worrying about nothing. But Mary couldn't be allowed to ruin Caitlin's chances for a full life, even if it wasn't destined to be with him. Trevor was almost certain, though, that he and Caitlin would have a future. He was breaking down her defenses. Little by little she relaxed with him. Before long, maybe tonight, she'd decide she knew what she was going to do. She'd declare herself, and David McBride would be relegated completely to her past.

Let it be tonight. Let her tell him she'd decided to stay with him tonight. He checked his watch. Another two hours before ten-thirty and closing time.

"Hear you've been busy lately, Trevor." Fishing hadn't been good and Barry Thompson spent more time drinking Crabbers Nip, the strong bottled ale he favored, than he did on his boat.

Trevor continued drying a glass. There was a surliness in Barry's tone.

"Not talking, eh?" Barry nudged Colin. "Seen our Trevor's lady friend, have you, Crust? That redhead from America?"

"I've seen her," Colin said offhandedly, avoiding Trevor's eyes.

"Known her a long time, have you, Trevor? Old friends, like?"

"Caitlin and I met when we were teenagers." He didn't like the direction of this interrogation. "Thomas Rhys is her uncle—her father's brother. She stayed in Tenby with her grandparents for a few weeks when she was seventeen."

Barry laughed, a bawdy chuckle that showed yellow teeth. "I don't think he's telling us everything, do you, Crust?"

Colin sniffed and wiped the back of a hand over his mouth. "I reckon that's none of your business. Caitlin McBride is a nice woman, so I'm told."

Trevor was both surprised and grateful at the defense from Colin, who was usually the first to sink his teeth into any snippet of gossip. Then he remembered that Colin's wife worked for Caitlin. The Johnsons were proud people and they wouldn't want any talk about Ethel's employer.

Andrew Briggs, a wiry, bowlegged man of few words came to stand shoulder to shoulder with Colin. Trevor groaned to himself. Andrew had started working on Caitlin's garden and he'd seen him there several times. He and Caitlin had nothing to be ashamed of, and, for himself, Trevor didn't give a damn what anyone thought anyway, but for Caitlin, he detested the prospect of suggestive talk.

"Evening to you, Andrew." Barry swayed forward and fixed Briggs with a bleary glare. "Just the man we need to draw out our closed-mouthed hero, here."

"Evening, Trevor," Andrew said, ignoring Barry. "Pint of the best please. And a gin chaser."

"Gin chaser?" Barry bellowed. "That new job of yours with Trevor's lady must pay well."

Andrew stared straight ahead, and Trevor had an uncomfortable sensation that Andrew and Colin felt they needed to cover up for him, even if only to protect themselves.

Saturday nights were always busy and Nip Lymer was on duty together with two other barmen. "Nip." Trevor stopped the little man as he passed. "Take over for me here. Spot needs fresh water." Anything to break up the discussion Barry was determined to continue.

"I'll do it," Nip said, and darted away to get the bird's dish before Trevor could respond.

Another man joined the klatch at the bar. "Big game tomorrow then, Trevor?" Len Colly was the father of Will Colly, one of the Knights' most talented players.

"Big," Trevor agreed. "But the boys are up to it." At any other time Trevor would have gritted his teeth to cope with the blustering older Colly who wore his son's rugby accomplishments as if they were his own. Tonight Trevor blessed Len's presence. "This Cardiff team should give us a run for our money."

"Nah." Colly waved a tankard, slopping beer. "No chance for them. Not when they come up against my Will."

Trevor made himself smile. "Will's one of the best. The whole bunch of our boys work well together." The truth was that on the field Will was magic, off the field the boy was an arrogant bully.

"That thing with the windows blew over, then?" Colin asked, turning his attention on Len. "Lunchtime, Jon Ellis was telling me he didn't know—"

"Over with," Len cut in, his small dark eyes darting to Trevor and away again. "Finished."

"What windows?" Trevor drew a pint into Colin's pewter tankard. "What did Jon say to you?"

Colin waited until Trevor set the tankard down and turned the handle in his direction. "Not a lot. You know our Jon. Not a big talker."

"Need any help tomorrow?" Will asked, hitching up his belt beneath a pendulous belly. "I'd be glad to help with that field lining."

No one around here wanted to talk about windows. "Back up, Will. Has there been some problem I ought to know about? Don't try keeping me in the dark, because it won't work."

Len glowered at Colin. "There's those as should stick to their puff pastry. Gossiping around town like an old woman can make trouble for other folks."

"Watch out who you call an old lady," Colin said, bringing his face close to Len's. "I wasn't gossiping. I thought Trevor here would know about the school windows being broken and how someone said they saw three boys from the team running away about that time."

"Nobody saw anything." Will pounded a fist on the counter. "Jealousy, that's what it is. Slander. I'd prosecute if anyone said my boy had anything to do with it."

Trevor tossed his cloth on the bar. "Who said they saw the boys?" This wasn't the first rumor of trouble he'd heard, and he wouldn't be responsible for helping a group of promising teenagers turn into hoodlums.

"The janitor," Colin said.

"Could have been any of the kids." Len pulled back his lips from his teeth. "If anything goes wrong, it's always the team. People reckon the boys have swelled heads and need to be taught a few lessons."

"Maybe they do," Trevor muttered. Whether or not there was proof that some of his players were involved in this incident, it was time to have a heart-to-heart with his arrogant little "stars."

Len gulped beer, choked and coughed until his jowls wobbled and turned puce. "What if their heads are a bit swelled," he sputtered. "They've brought more excitement to this town than we've seen in years. And they're the best. Who says they don't have a right to let off steam?"

"Damn it, Len." Trevor leaned across the bar. "Sportsmen are supposed to be just that, sportsmen. These lads are in the limelight, and they should want to set an example of how to be good at something and still be a bit humble. If they can't cope with a little success, they shouldn't be playing at all. They aren't an all-Wales squad, are they? And if this nonsense goes on, they may never get a chance to go anywhere in rugger."

"Meaning?" Len bristled.

"Meaning that if I hear many more stories like this one, there won't be a team." That development would hurt him as much as anyone but he'd learn to live with it.

"Like hell—"

"Seems to me—" Barry Thompson interrupted in a loud voice "—that Trevor should be taking a look at his part in all this."

A silent pool formed amid the furor in the rest of the room.

Trevor spread his arms, gripping the edge of the bar. "Want to expand on that, Barry?" He didn't like the man, but there were plenty who were snowed by the blustering manner.

"Seems to me—" Barry swayed, his eyelids drooping "—that you're the coach. The Mr. Know-it-all around here. You should have known if your little golden boys were in trouble."

"Ease up, Barry," Andrew Briggs said, riveting a hard stare on Barry. "Trevor coaches the boys. He isn't their keeper. And you're plastered out of your mind, man."

"Too busy with Mrs. Paper-shoes," Barry went on as if he hadn't heard Andrew. "She's always here after closing, y'know. And I'll bet our Trevor's at her place a fair amount. You'd know that, Andrew. You must look up from your spade from time to time."

Andrew looked helplessly at Trevor. "A man ought to be able to have his own life," he said. "And another man ought to know how to mind his own business."

The way his hands formed reflexively into fists helped clear the fury in Trevor's mind. The temptation to punch Barry's offending mouth was the result of too much pressure, too much doubt about which way Caitlin would decide to jump. He couldn't allow himself to become a different man because he was personally frustrated.

Barry hadn't finished. "All I meant was that if Trevor wasn't so preoccupied, he'd know someone had accused members of his team of breaking windows. I'm the last man to begrudge another a bit of...fun."

"You son of a bitch." Trevor grabbed the man's sweater and just as quickly Colin and Andrew straight-armed him, holding him off. "Don't you ever talk about Caitlin Rhys as if she were a cheap floozie. What the hell do you mean by a bit of fun?"

"Not a thing." The grin of alcoholic anesthesia made a fool's mask out of Barry's face. "But it's McBride now, isn't it? Is she widowed, then?"

"That's none of your damn—"

"Trevor," Andrew warned. "Let it be."

"No, not a widow, I suppose," Barry persisted. Caution wasn't even a memory for him. "Maybe she's divorced."

Trevor couldn't take anymore. "She will be. Not that it's any of your damned business." He calmed down almost at once, shrugging away from Andrew and Colin's restraining hands. "You're over the limit, Barry. Get home and sober up."

"I'm finishing my beer."

"You're going home. With or without help." Trevor started for the flap leading to the other side of the counter.

"Hey, Trevor, you should see this."

Nip Lymer had been clearing glasses from tables and now he returned slowly, glancing back at the leaded windows.

Trevor was only interested in getting Barry Thompson out of the pub before he caused more trouble.

"One of those limousine things. You know, the big long cars, black with windows you can't see in. Parked in the lot it is. He's put it sideways over four spaces." Nip set down the ten glasses he'd speared, one on each finger, and thumb. He winked at the group of interested faces. "Maybe it's visiting royalty."

When the door opened, the man who came in wore a navy-blue chauffeur's uniform, complete with gold-braided cap. He removed the cap and held it stiffly under his arm.

"Maybe their highnesses prefer to be served in their car," Andrew whispered amid a wave of chuckles. "Hey, Colin, could you pop around to your place and rustle up a few of those…petits things?"

"Give 'em a meat pasty," Len Colly said. "Bring 'em down to earth."

The driver threaded his way to the counter and spoke to Trevor. "They told me at the petrol station that you'd be able to help me," he said. "I need a place to stay for the night. They said most hotels are closed by this time of the year."

"No problem." Trevor took a notebook and wrote down an address. "The Esplanade's open and it's good. Nice rooms, residents' bar, good food and it's close to everything. You can call from here, if you like."

"Thanks," the man said, putting his cap down. "I'll take a Watney's first."

The crew at the bar were silent again.

"Brought a fellow down from London," the driver said expansively, rocking back onto his heels. "Nice little town you've got here."

His effort brought a chorus of agreement.

"Taking the man back to London tomorrow, are you?" Nip asked and Trevor grinned. Nip's curiosity would kill him yet.

"No, he doesn't know when he's going back for sure, he says. I just decided I might as well have a sleep before I get going."

"Must be pretty expensive. Riding all that way in your type of, er, car," Andrew said.

The man nodded. "Doesn't happen very often. This long a trip, I mean. But this fellow's someone big from America. Come down to meet up with his wife, he said. Second honeymoon."

Trevor's mouth dried out. All feeling left his hands.

"Big?" Nip moved closer, an avid light in his eyes.

"Movies, he said," the driver elaborated. "Writes them he says. And his wife's important, too. She designs shoes."

8

"I will, Thomas, I will." Caitlin tucked an afghan around his legs and put more coals on the fire.

"You could call him from here." Thomas's voice was a throaty croak.

"Stop worrying and stop talking," Caitlin ordered. "When I get back to the cottage will be soon enough."

"Why not take my car and drive into town?"

"No." She laughed. "Thanks anyway, but that beast of yours terrifies me. I should probably look into buying a car myself, only I'd as soon walk most of the time."

Thomas started taking off the afghan. "All I've got is a cold. I can drop you off."

Caitlin stilled his hand and retucked. "You'll do no such thing, you old matchmaker, you. Why are you pushing me at Trevor so hard?"

He sniffed, then blew his nose explosively. "I'm not. I just want you to have a friend of your own age here."

"Ah. That explains it of course. Quit worrying about me. Trevor is my friend. And when I get home I'll let him know why I'm not coming. We don't have to see each other every night. He'll probably welcome a quiet evening on his own."

"He will not." Thomas frowned thunderously. "You young people can't see past the ends of your noses half the time."

"Enough, Thomas. You're to take it easy. I've got to

get back to Mary." Caitlin would miss seeing Trevor, but then, she wouldn't be surprised if he came to her. The ever more familiar warmth began and she busied herself pouring Thomas a whiskey. "Have this before you go to bed. I'll be over in the morning."

As she left he was grumbling about being "fussed over," but she smiled. Thomas was a happy man these days and it showed. She and Mary had become his family, the focus of his lonely life. How would he feel when they left Wales?

The evening was mild. An almost warm breeze fanned her face, carrying with it all the subtle wild scents of the cliffs and the ocean. Leaving this place was something she couldn't deal with herself, not yet.

Walking to the cottage took half an hour. Caitlin was still glad she'd opted for her own place rather than taking Thomas up on his offer to share his house with her and Mary. He might love them, but he was set in his ways and she liked her independence.

The kitchen light was off. She glanced upward. There was no glow from Mary's bedroom lamp. Caitlin hastened her pace, not stopping to close the back garden gate behind her. Mary was a night owl and usually had to be told to go to sleep.

The kitchen door wasn't locked. Her heart leaped sickeningly as she went inside, a hand held in front of her, groping along the wall for the light switch.

She never reached it.

"Surprise!"

The brilliant glare of the overhead fixture flooded the room, dazzling Caitlin. She squinted. "Mary, that's not funny. You scared me."

Mary, her face unnaturally flushed, stood by the sink. "Mom—"

"Hello, darling."

Every living force in Caitlin seemed to pause. She couldn't catch her breath. Turning her head slowly she saw what she'd prayed she would never see, not here. David, his hands sunk deep in the pockets of beige pleated pants, shrugged away from a wall and came toward her. His pink-and-beige striped jacket, the cuffs turned back, was hooked behind his arms.

Nausea swept through her.

"Aren't you going to say anything, darling? Like welcome, husband dear?" He turned his thin, handsomely dark face to Mary and smiled. "Mary's thrilled to have me, aren't you, sweetie?"

"Oh, Daddy." She crossed the space between them quickly and threaded her arm through his. "Mom, we knew you'd love this. You always liked surprises."

Faintness blurred her vision and she closed her eyes for an instant. "You knew your father was coming, Mary?"

The girl giggled. "Yes. I phoned Daddy from a call box, like he told me to. He said I could do it once a week and reverse the charges and we came up with this. He doesn't have to work for a while so he's going to stay with us." Despite the laughter there was apprehension in Mary's eyes. "You are pleased, aren't you, Mom?"

Caitlin pressed her lips together to stop them from trembling. Then she said, "Of course I am, Mary. If you are, I am."

"You were right, Daddy," Mary said, her voice skating higher. "All we need is some time together as a family again. Mom, I've made some hors d'oeuvres and Daddy brought champagne. He says I can have some, too."

Oh, David, how can you do this? How low can you sink—to use our little girl? "That sounds fine."

She gave Mary a moment to get busy taking dishes from the refrigerator before looking fully at David. He wore his best innocent-but-misunderstood expression. His almost black eyes pleaded for sympathy. The pale pink shirt he wore, open at the neck, showed off his "California" tan, which in his case came from a tanning booth. But no tanning booth could hide the slackening jaw, the deep lines of discontent, the destruction living too well for too long had wreaked on his still-compelling face.

"It's good to see you, love." He turned the corners of his mouth up. There was no sign of gray in his curly black hair. "I knew this was the right thing to do—" he nodded significantly at Mary's back "—for all of us."

"Sit down, David." She detested him, really detested him. "Did you come straight down from Heathrow?"

"You bet I did. Couldn't wait to get here. Hired a limo and told the driver to hit it. We didn't even stop for coffee."

"The driver must have appreciated that." How could she be in a room with him and not let her feelings show?

David arched a brow. "He was well paid for his time."

Well paid with her money. "I'm sure he was."

"Sit down, everyone," Mary said. Her movements were jerky, and Caitlin's muscles tightened unbearably. "Daddy, you'll have to open the champagne." She'd put a plate of canapés, obviously professionally made, and another of finger sandwiches on the table, flanked by blue and white checked napkins. Three champagne glasses stood beside a bottle of Rothschild. Caitlin didn't need to check the label up close to know she was looking at the price of a week's groceries for most people.

"Mary says you do your work in the kitchen these days. That's charming. Quite a change from your studio back home." That David found her simple cottage more amusing than charming didn't need to be said. "You sit down first." He swept out a chair with a gallant flourish.

Caitlin sank to the seat, grateful to relieve her rubbery

legs. Mary had packed away the sketches and shoe lasts that had been left on the table for a late work session.

David opened the champagne and Caitlin saw the first sign of a crack in his facade. His hands shook. She watched the thin stream of pale liquid fall into the first glass.

The doorbell rang.

Caitlin didn't move, couldn't move. Her heart sounded in her ears like a drum.

"I'll get it," Mary said after looking from Caitlin to her father's questioning face.

"Bit late for callers," David said, frowning at his watch. "Ten. It's lonely out here. I'd better go with Mary."

"No." Caitlin got up, supporting her weight on the table with splayed fingers. "There's nothing to worry about. This isn't Los Angeles." And she knew who their caller would be. She heard Trevor saying, "Hello, Mary. Where's your mother?" from the hall.

He strode past the girl, every nerve in his body on alert. "Caitlin? Caitlin, where are you?"

As usual, the light was on in the kitchen. If he paused, thought at all, he'd change his mind about doing this, and he didn't want to change his mind. He had to make sure Caitlin was all right.

"Hello, Trevor. Come in." Caitlin sat at the table. A thin, dark-haired man in clothes Trevor recognized as being the expensive, designer variety, hovered beside her, a bottle of champagne in one hand.

"This is my father."

Trevor glanced back at Mary. Her face was flushed, her eyes feverishly brilliant. "I see." He bit down on the inside of his mouth and held out a hand. "How do you do? David McBride, isn't it?"

The man hesitated, set down the bottle and shook

hands. The grip was a single squeeze quickly released. "Yeah, that's right." And he took Trevor in from the toes of his worn loafers to the rolled neck of his baggy sweater. He made no attempt to ask Trevor's name.

"This is Trevor Morgan," Caitlin said in a voice that sounded like a stranger's. "He's an old friend."

Her eyes held a message he wanted desperately to understand. All he could be sure of was that she was intensely distressed. "Are you all—"

"Trevor, David decided to come and surprise Mary and me." She gave a high, unnatural laugh. "David's always been big on surprises."

She was signaling that she didn't want her husband to know there was anything between her and Trevor. Not that there was so much between them.

He fixed a smile firmly in place. "Nice to meet you, David. Mary's told me a lot about you." No way would he suggest that David McBride was a topic he discussed with Caitlin.

McBride raised expressive brows. "I don't think you mentioned how you know my family."

His family. Hate, the real basic kind, must feel like this.

"Trevor and I knew each other when we were children," Caitlin said, and he heard her swallow.

The bastard had her terrified for some reason. "Not exactly children," he said. "We met when Caitlin spent a summer with her grandparents. We were teenagers."

"Really?" McBride cocked his arrogant head. "Oh, I remember. Eileen mentioned some boy you had a crush on." He smiled benignly at Caitlin whose face blazed. "Eileen said she and Red had some bad moments until…" He closed his mouth in a secret, smug smile. "But all that was a long time ago."

"Eileen?" Trevor looked at Caitlin.

"My mother." Understanding passed between them.

Caitlin's mother must have told this man how she and Red Rhys had intercepted their daughter's correspondence to make sure she didn't get involved with some Welsh bumpkin. Trevor wondered if Mrs. Rhys was still as pleased with her choice of a son-in-law.

"By the way, darling," McBride said, bending over Caitlin while he gave her a glass of champagne. "Eileen sends her love, but she's going to call tonight anyway. She said she doesn't want to miss all the fun. It took every bit of persuasiveness I've got to stop her from coming with me."

The sensation came to Trevor that he'd moved outside a tableau to watch as a spectator. He had to leave. For himself and for Caitlin. There were undercurrents here he didn't understand, might never understand, but Caitlin didn't want him here either.

"I'd offer you a drink, but…" McBride let the sentence trail off.

"Thanks, I don't want one." For Caitlin, he must make this easy. "I just stopped by to make sure Caitlin and Mary were okay."

"Really. Do you make a habit of that?" McBride's fingers circled the back of Caitlin's neck and Trevor's jaw locked.

"Trevor's been very good to us."

"Yes," Mary said without any trace of awkwardness. "He's taken us out a lot and he helped when one of the pipes broke and Uncle Thomas couldn't fix it."

McBride squared his shoulders. "Surely they have plumbers, even here?"

The man wasn't worth his anger. "I happened to be around. Look, sorry to butt in like this. Good to meet you, McBride. Enjoy your visit."

"I think this may turn out to be more than a visit," the man said with a warm smile at Caitlin. "My family and

I have a lot of catching up to do, and I think this is going to be a good place to do it. By the way—'' he flashed a grin in Trevor's general direction ''—thanks for being a friend to Caitlin and Mary. I worried about them without me around.''

Trevor backed toward the hall and for the first time Caitlin showed something other than sluggish apprehension. She got up. ''I'll see you out, Trevor.''

''No need, darling,'' McBride cut in. ''I'll do it. Although if Mr. Morgan knows his own way…''

''*I'll* see Trevor out,'' Caitlin insisted and followed him to the front door and outside into a night turned subtly colder. She closed the door and crossed her arms.

''What the hell's going on here?'' Trevor whispered. ''Did he just show up unannounced?''

She nodded.

''Why don't you tell him to get lost?''

''You know why. You can *see* why, Trevor.''

''God…no, I can't. You're going to have to explain.''

She rocked forward and stared down at her feet. ''You'll have to back off. At least until I try to work through this. Maybe for good.''

He couldn't believe he'd heard her correctly. ''What are you saying to me? This creep you don't want in your life shows up and you're going to accept him back with open arms? And good old Trevor can take a hike? What is that?''

''It's all I can say right now. If you can't work out that I've got one priority in my life and only one right now, so be it.''

He looked at the sky and let out a long sigh. ''Mary. Of course, the kid's in seventh heaven because she thinks Mommy and Daddy are going to get back together and you don't have the guts to tell her the truth.'' She flinched when he caught her by the shoulders. ''She's got to grow up sooner or later. She'll have her own life eventually. By then it may be too late for you to find one of your own. What then?''

Her eyes glittered. "I guess I'll just have to take my chances," she said softly. "Right now I'm not making any final decisions."

"So that means the question of divorce is out of the picture?''

Her breath touched his face. "I didn't say that. What I did say was that my daughter's happiness comes first, and you'll have to accept that. Maybe it would be best if we forgot we'd ever met again. They say you can't go back, and it's looking to me like whoever 'they' are have that one right."

He released her. "I see. And he's staying here with you?''

She tried to turn away but he stopped her.

"Answer me. Where is your 'husband' going to sleep while he's here?''

A choking sound came from Caitlin's throat. "You can think what you like. There's plenty you don't know about me, Trevor, and you probably never will know because you can't get past your own physical needs."

She raised her hand and for a second he expected her to slap him. Instead she lowered her arms and reached back to open the door. "Good night, Trevor. Thanks for everything."

He stood, cold hands thrust deep in his pants pockets, for a long time after she closed him out.

Mary came first. He wasn't even in the running. Caitlin would take the man she'd insisted she couldn't stand the sight of back into her home—into her bed—because hiding behind her daughter's needs was easier than facing her own.

The Jag was a few yards down the lane. He'd parked

it there to avoid the mud puddle near the front gate. He walked slowly, skirted the soggy ground and climbed into his car.

What were Caitlin's needs? He switched on the ignition, shifted into reverse and backed toward a wide spot between the hedgerows. Had he been taken for a fool? He and Caitlin came from different worlds, different enough to be planets apart. Was it so unlikely that she'd needed an amusing diversion? She lived in the land of make-believe. She could easily have played out the type of soap opera script her slick husband probably wrote. What proof did Trevor have that she hadn't made up every word about McBride being a man she couldn't stand?

He drove away. There were no answers, not that he could get at, and he wasn't hanging around waiting for Caitlin McBride to decide she needed the company of a patsy again.

Trevor drove faster. His head pulsed. The muscles in his belly and thighs stiffened until he pounded a fist against the dashboard. If the two of them were in that cottage together, they were, as far as the world was concerned, there as man and wife.

Damn it all. The woman had lied to him, sucked him in. But she wouldn't again.

"He doesn't look fit, does he, Livie?" Bronwyn Williams heaped more potatoes on Trevor's plate while she spoke to his mother.

"Pale," his mother agreed. "But we all know what you've been going through, Trevor. No need to talk about it. We're glad it's over, that's all."

Trevor, a forkful of parsnips on the way to his mouth, paused to look at his mother's serious blue eyes. Normally he'd ask what she meant, but he knew and couldn't face a discussion about Caitlin.

"We are glad," Bronwyn agreed. Trevor never looked at her without remembering Gwen. In time his dead wife would have been her mother's double, still pretty with dark curly hair but the girlish slimness turned softly rounded.

Snowy Williams ate in stolid silence, his leonine head—crowned with the shock of white hair that had spawned his nickname—bent low over his plate. In contrast, Trevor's father picked and pushed at his food.

These Sunday lunches were becoming a weekly trial, with Trevor the defendant of the day.

"Good thing," Trevor's father announced suddenly. "Woman like that wouldn't do you any good in the end. Foreigners don't fit in with us."

Trevor set down his fork and crossed his arms. "What do you mean by a 'woman like that,' Dad?"

"Oh, nothing. I was rambling, that's all. Thinking out loud." There had been no mention of Caitlin or the appearance of her husband over a week ago, until today.

"Not good enough," Trevor persisted. "What kind of woman is Caitlin supposed to be? That is who you're talking about?"

"Yes." Snowy finished his meal. "And you don't need us to explain what we mean. She took you for a fool, boyo. Strung you along, then dropped you when her husband showed up. Not that I'm sorry. Now you can get on with what should be occupying your mind."

He must not lose his temper, not with these people who really loved him. "What should be occupying my mind, Snowy?" He'd called his father-in-law by his first name from the time of the engagement to Gwen.

"The pub and the boys," his father said before Snowy could reply. "You've got a business to run and a success on your hands with that team—if the little blighters don't get into so much trouble that they end up in reform school.''

"Hey, slow down." Trevor choked on the last bite of food he'd taken and reached for his water glass. "I'm getting sick of this. First, the pub is doing just fine, thanks, Dad. Second, I'm coaching those kids, not adopting them. Besides, from what I've heard in the last few days, they aren't doing anything out of line at the moment. And, in case you've forgotten, we're undefeated this season, so we must be doing something right—"

"Stop it," his mother interrupted. "Stop it right now, all of you. Everything's going to be as it should be. Those are wonderful boys, and Trevor's a wonderful coach. There's nothing to worry about." She smiled at him. "Except perhaps finding you a nice Welsh girl to settle down with again."

The effect could not have been more electric if she'd hit him. He felt his mouth open. "Mom—"

"No, no." She waved for silence. "Bronwyn and I have been talking about it." Grunts came from the other two men, but she didn't appear to hear. "Gwen would have wanted you to marry again. You've been on your own long enough and that's why we've all had this worry about that American woman. You're...what's the word, Bronwyn?"

"Susceptible," Bronwyn supplied. "Too ready to be taken in by a pretty face with nothing on her mind but fun. There's many a fine young woman in this town who'd love to look after you, Trevor. Look around a bit. Open your eyes, boy."

He couldn't believe it. They were planning his life for him, telling him how to proceed, what he could and couldn't do. He'd become the only child of not just one set of doting parents, but two.

"I've got to go." Almost knocking over his chair, he left the table and strode toward the dining-room door.

"You haven't finished," Bronwyn said, sounding outraged that he'd leave food on his plate in her house. "You always finish."

He faced them. "It's too bad you never do finish. When it comes to organizing my life, that is. First, you don't know Caitlin Rhys—Caitlin McBride. She's a good woman who loves her daughter too much to cut her off from her father. That's why she didn't send the man packing the minute he came."

"He's still there," Snowy commented, not looking at Trevor. "And she's not right for you anyway. An American and a rich one. All she'd do to you in the end would be to decide she was bored with your life. Then you'd either have to let her go or follow her wherever she wanted to be. And you aren't made for life away from here. We've already seen that."

Caution made him pause for a breath. The Williams had lost almost everything when they'd lost Gwen. He would not deliberately hurt them.

"I was fine in London as long as I had Gwen. She never liked it, I admit, but we were happy. I was a lucky man. But you're wrong about Caitlin. You don't know her. She's special and you should give her a chance."

He walked out without another word. He'd voiced what he believed, that Caitlin was caught in a trap formed of her own integrity. Given time, she'd find a way to solve the dilemma she faced and they'd both be happy. They would be.

As he neared the corner of Upper Frog Street he lengthened his stride and decided to carry on to the harbor. The tide would be out. Watching the boats and the gulls, the drying sand whip along, always raised his spirits. Then he'd go back home and concentrate on work. Things were going to work out. He wished he could help Caitlin, but interference would only complicate what she must be trying so hard to do—to get rid of David as quickly and painlessly as possible.

"Trevor!"

Mary's voice brought him to a halt at the corner. The girl ran toward him from a narrow side street.

"Hello, there, young Mary. You look radiant today." And she did.

"We're going out for lunch," she informed him. "To celebrate. A place called Plantagenet. Do you know it?"

"Yes," Trevor said. "I know it."

"Of course you do." She giggled. "You and Mom went there. No wonder she thought of it. Mom, here's Trevor."

The light in the side street was poor, and he squinted past Mary. With one hand Caitlin held David McBride's elbow while she pointed toward the High Street. She hadn't heard Mary's call.

"What are you celebrating?" Trevor asked.

"Being together again," Mary said. "I've got to go. See you, Trevor."

"See you, Mary."

He heard David McBride laugh.

9

Glass clinked on glass. Caitlin covered her face. Drinking, whining, drinking, begging, drinking, threatening. On and on it went, a replay of the old scene she'd vowed never to live with again.

"You never appreciated me," David muttered behind her.

She lifted her head and stared at the sketch in front of her. These drawings had to be finished and sent to Paris within a few days, but she couldn't concentrate.

"D'you hear me, Caitlin?" David scraped out a chair and slumped down beside her. He held two glasses of Scotch and pushed one toward her. "You never damn well understood me."

"Keep your voice down," she whispered, ignoring the drink. "Mary will hear you."

David put a wavering finger to his mouth. "Sh. Yeah, yeah. Okay, so listen to me, will ya?"

She picked up a slim purple chalk and drew swiftly, outlining a shoe cut away to the insole on both sides and with a heel shaped like a backwards comma.

"Stop that." He lurched toward her, brought down his hand on hers, breaking the chalk and marring the sketch. "You've got your damn successes, your place in the sun. You always had your place in the sun. Now it's my turn, baby, and you're gonna make sure I get it."

"Look what you've done." Caitlin tried to brush away ground chalk. "I don't have time for this or for you. You're not supposed to be here. I could have you arrested for breaking the restraining order."

"The hell you can. Not here, baby."

"Don't call me baby. I'm not one of your bimbos." The sketch would have to be done again.

The contents of David's glass, splattering across her papers, dappling the swatches of leather and fabric piled to one side, froze Caitlin in place. She took an instant to grasp what he'd done before she leaped up, grabbed a towel and mopped frantically at her samples.

"You crazy man. You lunatic. David, you've got to get out of here. Go! Or so help me I'll make sure you never see Mary again."

"You wouldn't do that."

"Try me."

He leaned back, his eyes unfocused, and began drinking from the glass he'd brought for her. "Mary loves me and she's unstable." He slurred the words together. "I don't think you want our little girl upset again. She's happy now. And that's because I'm back in her life."

Caitlin paused, the cloth dangling from her hand. "David, do you care about Mary?" That had always been his one saving grace in her eyes, his supposed love for his daughter. "Or is she really just a pawn you use to keep me on a string?"

He set the glass down and got shakily to his feet. Mottled color rose in his face. "You don't have the right to suggest that." He wiped his mouth. "My girl is my girl. You can't change that. Make up any stories you want, you won't get anyone to believe I don't idolize Mary."

"You've got a hell of a way of showing it."

"Whose fault is that? You drove me away...kicked me out of my own house so I couldn't be with her."

Caitlin took a measured breath. "It's my house. And when you did live there you were too busy with your 'social' life to give any time to Mary."

He shook his head. "I don't wanna go into that. That's history you use when you want to put me down. There's something we gotta talk about, now, while Mary's asleep."

"What?" She was tired. The charades, the phony posing for Mary's sake, were wearing her down.

"Hey, lunch was great today, wasn't it?" David swayed toward her, rested a heavy arm on her shoulder. "That place you took us to was quaint."

"Get to the point, David." Lunch had been hell. David had suggested the outing in front of Mary, trapping Caitlin. And Plantagenet had been the only place she could think of. But every corner of the restaurant reminded her of Trevor and their meal there...and of the way they'd parted the night David arrived. On the way to Plantagenet, Mary, who'd been hanging back in front of a store window, caught up and said she'd spoken to Trevor. Caitlin looked, but there'd been no sign of him. Mary had told him where they were going. What had he thought? That her times with him meant so little that she felt nothing about taking someone else to places they'd been? By now he'd probably decided she was a hassle he didn't need.

"I've got it, baby—Caitlin. I've got what it takes, I tell you."

She'd only half heard him. "What?"

"I'm going places. Finally, I'm gonna show 'em all that David McBride's a man they shouldn't have passed over. Caitlin, your husband is a genius and I've got people who're ready to back me up on that."

He was pathetic. "What people would those be?"

"Eileen, for one." Waving the glass, he paced back and forth. "Your mother has always known I've got what it takes to be a great writer. And there are others."

Caitlin tried not to think of her mother. Eileen had called several times since David's arrival, begging for reconciliation, pleading David's case as the misunderstood artist. David had always been able to con Eileen.

"These others," Caitlin said, "are they backers? Are they putting money into whatever project you're working on?" David working? That would be a change.

"Not backers, baby. I don't want to share this with anyone. These are the people I'm gonna need to do things for me."

"People who will make a bundle out of your ego, do you mean?"

"Knock it off." His voice reached a raging pitch. "I've got the script of all times, baby. Your husband is going to be up there getting his little Oscar next year. And all I need is the money."

"You aren't my husband." Her hands were frozen. They squeaked as she rubbed them together.

"Not in the biblical sense, but—"

"Not in any sense. We're legally separated and as far as I'm concerned you're proving it's time to change that to something permanent."

He stood still and pointed at her. "You won't divorce me. Mary wants us together and you won't let her stop hoping for that."

A clear place formed in Caitlin's brain. "David, you don't want us. Oh, you want to see Mary from time to time, but you wouldn't want responsibility for her, not the real responsibility that goes with parenting."

"For God's sake, forget about Mary for once. I want

money. I need money. A lot of it." His eyes cleared and he moved closer. "This script. It's the one I tell you, Caitlin, the big one and I want it all. I'm gonna have it all."

She could smell liquor on his breath and turned her head away. "I just gave you money."

"Peanuts." His laugh was derisive. "It's got to be big bucks. This time it's gonna be all mine. The script, the casting, the production end—everything. Mine. No outsiders are gonna tell me what to do with this. There'll be no big mouth telling me what to do or putting the brakes on the purse strings, because I'm gonna hold 'em. Understand?"

"No, David. I don't understand." She did understand that he was talking like an egotistical maniac and that he was steadily getting drunker.

"Then listen, my pet, and listen carefully. You are my answer. You've got the money I need, or you can get it. You're the one with the solid-gold connections, and finally you're gonna use them for me. It's payoff time, baby. You're going to finance *Pounce*."

"*Pounce?*" The booze was talking, giving him courage he'd never have on his own.

"My movie. *My* movie."

"No." Caitlin shook her head slowly. "Not another penny, David. I told you that the last time."

When he clutched her shoulders she couldn't stop a cry of shock. "Shut up," he warned her, nodding upward. "You'll pay and you'll like it. And if you don't like it, you'll keep quiet. You owe me. You've taken everything that mattered to me."

Her legs trembled, her whole body. "Go to bed," she said.

"Caitlin—"

"Go to bed, David." She shrugged away. "Sleep it off. You're not making sense. And make sure you're off that couch before Mary gets up in the morning."

"We're going to finish this," he said, a grim note of menace in his voice. "Now."

Caitlin stared at him for an instant before walking around him and going to the door. "We're going to finish it, David. But not while you're drunk. We'll talk tomorrow."

"You owe me." The menace was gone. His eyes glistened.

"Don't say that again," Caitlin told him. "I don't owe you a damned thing. No one does."

As she went into the hall she heard him mutter, "You owe me and you're gonna pay."

Trevor drove slowly down Jones Street and pulled the Jag to a stop outside the police station. "I don't think I should do this," he said to Len Colly, who sat beside him.

"They're only boys. And they're a bit hotheaded." Ray Best, father of another member of the Knights team spoke from the narrow back seat. "Don't tell me you never got into a bit of trouble when you were young, Trevor."

"Yes, Trevor. These are—"

"Your sons." Trevor finished for Len who smelled of stale beer and sweat. "And if either of you had an ounce of sense, you'd want them to learn a lesson. If they don't get it through their thick heads now that you can't terrorize people just because you think you're a big shot, when will they?"

"This will set them straight enough," Len said, his voice weak and gravelly. "They'll have had enough of a shock spending half the night at the police station."

"What am I supposed to do?"

"We told you," Ray said. "Persuade the cops there won't be any more trouble. You're respected in the town. Vouch for the boys."

Trevor slid down in his seat and rested his head back. After the pub closed he'd gone walking for hours, trying to shut out the memory of Caitlin and McBride together, the sound of the man's laugh. When he got back at almost one in the morning, Ray and Len were waiting for him.

"Let's go over this again. Will and Robin were caught smashing windows, right?"

"Well—"

"No, Len. Give it to me straight. In that empty shop front toward Castle Hill? The one that belongs to the Andersons?"

"That's right," Len muttered. "They weren't the only kids involved, though."

"They were the ones who got caught," Trevor said wearily. "How many others were there?"

"They wouldn't say," Ray said. "The police tried to get it out of them but they clammed up—little idiots."

Trevor sighed. "If there's one reason I'll go in and help Robin and Will, it's because at least they're loyal to their friends." Maybe it was time to take a long look at whether or not his charmed rugger team should continue to play…as much to set the parents' priorities straight as the boys'.

"So you'll do it?" Len leaned toward him and Trevor felt sick.

"Yes. I'll do it. But I won't do it again. Stay here."

An hour later he returned to the car with Robin Best and Will Colly in tow. He opened the passenger door of his car. "Okay," he said. "Take them home."

Len and Ray scrambled from the car. Ray said, "What

happened?'' and caught Trevor's sleeve. Ray was a tall man, thin and stooped.

Trevor squeezed his eyes shut. He felt as if grit lined his lids. "Officer Peebles didn't want to back off," he said.

Robin shifted at his side. "Stupid old gaffer. You set him straight, though, Mr. Morgan."

"You little idiot." Trevor swung the stocky boy around so hard he stumbled into the wall. "I saved your tail in there because I think there's something in you worth saving. When you talk like that I'm tempted to march you right back inside."

"He didn't mean anything," Ray mumbled.

"No? I think he did. I think if we don't set these little thugs straight, we're going to be without a team."

Will Colly sniffed. "Cool it, Rob. We're sorry, Mr. Morgan." He slumped against the wall, resting his head. His face was pale and sweaty, but Trevor felt no pity.

"You're sorry? Good, and you'd better stay sorry. I put my name on the line for you in there. I vouched for you and said I'd keep you on the straight and narrow. Also, I agreed to pay the bills for the damage, but you two will be paying me back—"

"We'll pay," Ray said quickly. "How much, Trevor?"

Trevor rounded on him. "You *won't* pay. They will." He hooked a thumb at the boys. "The issue here is responsibility."

"But where will they—"

"By working for me, Ray," Trevor said. "They'll work off every penny. You'll both be at the pub on Saturday morning. Every Saturday morning."

"But there's practice," Robin Best protested. He wasn't one of Trevor's favorites on the team.

"Not until eleven. That gives you four hours to wash

glasses, scrub floors, clean lavatories, clean up the beer garden. There'll be plenty to do.''

"What am I supposed to say to people?" Robin muttered.

"You mean you actually have pride? You're afraid you'll be shown up as a little kid who has to be punished?" Trevor felt control slipping away. "Len, Ray, give me a few minutes with these two charmers. We've got to get a point or two straight—now."

Silently the two men moved a few yards away and Trevor turned on the boys. "This may be pointless, but I've got to try, for all our sakes."

Will sat on his haunches and rested his brow on a fist. "We've got the message, Mr. Morgan. I'm sorry for what I did, honest I am." The kid was tired and scared.

"You're sorry, Will? How about Robin here? Does he—"

"Why the big deal?" Robin cut in. "Okay, so we weren't smart. We got caught. But we didn't kill anybody or nothing."

Suspending the boy from the team was probably the thing to do. "You caused stress to people who don't need it," Trevor said, taking his time with each word. "Do you know what I'm saying?"

Robin cocked his head, frowning. "What d'you mean? Our dads?"

"He means our dads and a bunch of other people," Will said, surprising Trevor. "We were stupid."

"What I really meant was that you broke windows in an empty shop—"

"Exactly. Empty." Robin spread his hands.

Trevor looked at the dark sky. "Empty, full. What difference does it make, except no one was physically hurt? The Andersons closed the shop because it wasn't making money. They don't have much and they need to sell the place. Now they also need to replace windows. Fortunately you'll be footing the bill. But why should you cause them any more grief?"

A muffled noise from Will made Trevor bend over the boy. "What is it? Are you sick?"

"Nah." Will bounced to his feet. "Tired, that's all. We'll work off the bill, won't we Robin? And we are sorry about the Andersons."

"Good." Trevor didn't wait to speak to Len and Ray before getting into his car. As he closed the door he heard Robin whine, "*Seven* on a Saturday morning? That's when I watch the telly."

Two weeks. He'd give the team two weeks to show him they could behave like humans. If they didn't come through, he was out and that meant they were out, too.

Caitlin tiptoed downstairs. She'd spent more of the night awake than asleep. David must leave before he did more damage than he already had. At this point she'd been his only victim. If she could get him out gracefully, there was hope that Mary need not be hurt.

She pushed open the door to the small parlor that had been David's bedroom since he arrived.

"Well, well. If it isn't my champion come to wish me good-morning."

David's voice, thick and still slurred, brought goosebumps out all over her body. He lay supine on top of the quilt covering the couch. Red silk pajamas, the top wrongly buttoned, were wrinkled around him, and his beard, always heavy, showed darkly against his fading tan.

"Get up," she ordered. "You're leaving today."

"Like hell, lady."

She made fists. "*Get* up, David. Shave, dress, put a smile on your face and tell Mary you've been called back to the States unexpectedly."

He raised onto his elbows, smiling crookedly. "Neat, my love. Forget it unless you're ready to give me what I want. And I told you last night what that is."

"I'm not—" she lowered her voice "—I'm not giving you money. If I did, you'd go through it in a few weeks or months and be back for more. You've got to go it alone, David. For God's sake, you're forty-six. Isn't it time you grew up?"

"I married you, you bitch. I let you be a part of everything I had."

"Thank you." She blinked, close to tears. "Thanks a whole bunch for all you've done for me." Anger and pity made a destructive combination.

"You owe me." He stood up, ran his fingers through his hair and sat down again with a thud. "You owe me."

"*Don't* say that again. I owe you nothing. You gave me one thing that's worth a damn. Thank you for our beautiful daughter, David."

He scrubbed at his face. "We had some good years."

"Yes—"

"We could have more."

"No, no we couldn't. Who are you kidding? You don't want to be anywhere near me. You made that plain years ago."

His arm shot out and he pulled her down beside him. "I knew you'd come to that. And it's your fault if…if… You did it to me. You and your damned ambition smashed me. I had to be your shadow. What man can stay a man in the shadow of a woman?"

Caitlin clamped her teeth together. She twisted her wrist free of his hand. "A man who's really a man doesn't feel threatened by a wife who's a success. Your impotency had nothing to do with me. You lost whatever you lost all on your own."

"Don't," he said, a break in his voice. "Don't say it."

"You already said it. You said I made you less than a man, and you're talking about the fact that you can't have sex."

"And that's the real reason you want to get rid of me." He turned on her suddenly, pushing her down, pinning her shoulders against the arm of the couch.

"Let me go." She struggled, but he pressed his weight on top of her. Pain darted through her neck where the wood trim on the couch caught her spine. "Let me go, David."

"Not until I've said what I should have said the night I got here. You emasculated me with your damned career. 'Look at Caitlin. Isn't she wonderful? Caitlin this, Caitlin that.'"

She mustn't panic. Her throat was so tight she could hardly breathe. "Because I was a success you became a failure? That makes a whole lot of sense." There wasn't any sense in him. Wildness flared in his eyes.

"You've got something going with that Welsh guy, haven't you?" He shook her and she winced. "And you want me out of the way so you can carry on your affair in peace."

"That's not true."

"No, maybe it's not." He sneered, leaning harder and harder on her. "You're not woman enough for that, are you? If you were any kind of a woman, you'd have been able to make sure I didn't have any problems with sex. It was you, you cold bitch, who did this to me. I've been through hell because of you."

The strength came from deep inside, from her brain,

her rage, and she kicked, twisted, knocked him to the floor.

"You bastard. You gave me so much, didn't you? What you did was to take and cheat and lie and ruin what could have been beautiful. You're impotent because you're an alcoholic. Didn't anyone ever tell you that, David? Alcoholism and impotency go together. And it was you who stopped sleeping with me, not the reverse. You did that because you were ashamed. And you reacted to the shame by parading women in front of me, pretending you could do with them what you couldn't do with me. But that was all a lie, wasn't it?"

His sobbing shocked her. She recoiled, slid to sit on the edge of the couch. "Stop it. Stop it, for God's sake, before Mary hears." The noise got louder. "Forget all this, David. Give it up and go home."

"I need money."

"Work for it like the rest of us. I wouldn't be helping you by giving it to you."

"Caitlin, please." He reached for her hand but she pulled it away. Her head ached and her back, and she felt utterly, overwhelmingly ill.

"I'm divorcing you, David. No more waiting. If you don't fight me, the grounds will be painless—incompatibility, no airing of dirty linen. Mary will have to cope the best way she can, we all will."

Mary backed away from the parlor door. Her arms and legs shook and her skin broke out in icy sweat.

She moved slowly at first, passing through the kitchen without seeing it. Her mind was blank as she took her coat from a peg by the door.

Then she was outside and running, running. Mom was divorcing Dad. "Mary will have to cope." The cold air made funny sounds in her throat. And Dad had cried, but he'd been saying bad things to her mother. They weren't the people she'd thought they were, but she loved them. Daddy wouldn't be able to see her after the divorce, because Mom would make him stay away.

She ran until pain in her side stopped her. "I'm never going back." She gasped, sending milky vapor clouds into the dawn sky. "I'm never going back."

10

"Hold on. Just hold your horses." Who would come hammering on an old man's door before six in the morning? He coughed and sniffed. Damn this cold.

He'd barely slid the bolt off the front door when Mary barreled into the hall, gasping.

"What is it? Mary, what's happened?" Something must be wrong with Caitlin. The child's face was ashen and he could see her thin body shaking.

"They're getting a divorce," she said, and tears sprang into her eyes. "Uncle Thomas, Mom's going to divorce Dad and it's all going to be horrible."

"Ah." He wrapped his threadbare woolen robe more tightly around him. "Come into the kitchen, Mary. We'll make some nice strong tea."

She shook her head.

He was definitely too old for this. "Well, if you don't want some, I do. I always think better with a good hot cup of tea inside me." Pretending nonchalance, he scuffed to the kitchen and put on the kettle. Before he'd finished setting two cups on their saucers, Mary trailed in.

"Does your mother know you're here?"

She shook her head and went to the window. Her hair was uncombed and she wore her pink parka over faded jeans and a wrinkled green sweatshirt.

"Don't you think we should let her know so she doesn't worry?"

"She doesn't worry about me. Neither does Dad. All they care about is themselves."

"Mary McBride." He stood beside her at the window. "Mary, Mary, you know that's not true. I've never had much time for your father and you might as well know it. But he does care about you. And your mother, well, I don't have to tell you how she feels about you. It wasn't so long ago we had another talk. You were saying then that you didn't want to be part of a divorced family like so many people you know. Well, young lady, you've given that message to your poor mother in so many ways that she's put you first in everything, even though she was miserable."

"She's not going to anymore." Mary sniffed and searched her pockets. Thomas took a Kleenex box from the windowsill and held it in front of her.

When she'd blown her nose loudly, he said, "Caitlin needs a new start, Mary. She can't live only for you, not forever. One day, and that may not be so far away, but one day you'll be ready to strike out on your own, and then your mother should have more to look forward to than loneliness." He knew all about loneliness and didn't want it for his niece.

"I wouldn't leave Mom alone. I'll never leave her."

"That's what most youngsters say. Then things change and they find out they don't want to be children forever."

The kettle boiled and he heated the teapot with some of the water.

"I'm not going home."

He sighed, dumped the water from the pot, spooned in tea leaves and poured from the kettle again. "I'll call your mother while you have your tea. There's cereal in the cupboard, or you can have an egg. Then you can patch yourself up and go to school from here. A day with your friends will make you see things more clearly.'' She'd be better off with people her own age.

He filled the cups and went to call Caitlin. Persuading her not to rush right over took more diplomacy than he'd known he could exert. She hadn't even realized Mary was up. ''Leave the girl alone for a while, Caitlin,'' he told her. ''Let her be with the kids at school today and start to settle down a bit. If you try reasoning with her now, she won't listen anyway.''

''She must have overheard us arguing. I told David I'm divorcing him.''

''Good. Are you all right? Do you need me over there?''

''No, thanks, Thomas. David's no threat.''

He looked at the ceiling, thanking God this was finally happening. David McBride's unexpected appearance in Wales had rattled Thomas, but he'd known he mustn't interfere. ''We'll talk about it later. And don't worry about Mary. She'll be fine.'' He hung up, not at all convinced Mary would be fine.

An hour and a half later Mary left for school. She'd refused to go home for her books and he'd decided not to push the issue. He could call the school and make sure she didn't get into trouble.

Mary trudged along the cliffs, passing her own cottage without a glance. The school was on the other side of town, above South Beach, and she was glad of the time it would take to get there.

Maybe her mother would change her mind. She didn't understand everything that had been said by her parents that morning, and Uncle Thomas didn't seem the right one to ask about it all. Her father drank a lot, too much, but was he an alcoholic?

A sharp pain shot through her stomach. She pressed a fist into her middle, but it didn't help. Pulling herself more upright, she lengthened her stride, and by the time she reached the harbor the discomfort had dulled.

A whoop came from below, in the alley that skirted a sluice where boats were brought to the dock for repair. Then someone shouted, "There's American Mary." She stopped and leaned over a railing. Several students she recognized sauntered up a ramp toward her. She managed a smile before she walked on.

"Hey, Mary, how's it feel to be slumming?"

She hunched her shoulders, suddenly frightened. A boy and three girls caught up with her and fanned out as if they were walking with her. Threatened was what she felt.

"Lost your tongue, poor little rich girl?"

Mary looked into the face of the girl who spoke. She was Susan something, a nice-looking girl who worked hard at being a leader among the other kids.

"I haven't lost my tongue," Mary said carefully. "You're being rude."

The group hemmed her in more closely, and her heart seemed to rise into her throat.

"Think you're something, don't ya?" the same girl said. "Well, around here you're nothing but the kid of a rich slut."

Mary stopped, her mouth open. "What—"

"That's right." Now they formed a circle around her. The boy, beefy, dark haired and with a ruddy complexion, brought his face close to hers. "Your mother's loose. My dad told me that. My ma, too."

"I don't know what you're talking about. Leave me

alone.'' She tried to move on, but they closed ranks more tightly.

The boy continued, ''The fancy-shoe designer. People around here don't get shoes designed, they buy them from the store.''

Mary opened her mouth to retort that someone had to design their shoes, even mass-produced ones, but a second girl, small, dressed in a loose denim jacket trimmed with studs, poked a finger into her arm. ''My family says your mother thinks people here are simpleminded. She teased a local man, made him think she was in love with him. Then when her slick husband turned up she didn't want the Tenby man anymore. Having an affair with him, too, they say she was.''

Mary covered her ears. She wouldn't listen and she wouldn't cry. Blood pumped in her head, and she closed her eyes tightly.

She felt movement around her but kept her eyes shut.

''Buzz off, you lot. Scram, or I'll take you apart.''

Owen Trew's familiar voice registered, but only vaguely.

''Her mom's a tart—''

The next sound she heard was flesh on flesh, and she opened her eyes to see the small girl holding a reddened cheek. Constance Trew's hand was raised to strike again, but Owen caught her wrist.

''Save it, Connie. She's not worth it.''

The kids sidestepped, backed away and finally went on their way, muttering among themselves.

Constance touched Mary's shoulder awkwardly. ''You okay?''

Mary nodded. She wasn't.

''Want to sit down?'' Owen put an arm across her back

and led her to a bench. The three of them sat facing the harbor, with Mary in the middle.

"Life can be a bummer," Owen remarked, staring straight ahead.

"What did they say to you?" Constance asked. "We only heard the last bit about—"

"Stow it, Connie," Owen interrupted. "It doesn't matter what they said. *They* don't matter."

"That's right," Constance agreed. She pulled a roll of candy from her pocket, peeled back the paper and offered it to Mary.

"No, thanks." Mary gave her a quick smile and felt her mouth quiver.

Constance stuffed the roll away. "There're always kids who feel big when they can put someone else down. That bunch are nothings."

The wind picked up, gusting, carrying sand up from the beach. Mary gathered her hair into one hand and held it. She needed an anchor. Everything was shifting around her.

Owen sat, silent, his hands hanging between his knees. Mary glanced at him and away again. He was kind, but he probably didn't want to get involved in a situation that could make his friends laugh at him.

"We'd better get going," Constance said. "We're going to be late for school."

"I'm not going today," Mary said softly. "Don't worry about me. I'll go home in a while. Thanks for helping out."

"Oh, Mary, do come." Constance twisted toward her, wringing her hands. "I'll stay right with you all day, I promise. I won't let anyone say rotten things to you."

Gratitude brought tears to Mary's eyes. "Please, I am okay, and I'll get over this. But I don't want to face them again today." She stood up, smiling through a blurry film. "See you. Maybe tomorrow."

Owen got up suddenly. Red patches stood out on his cheeks. "You carry on, Connie. I'll take Mary home... just in case there are any more smart mouths on the loose."

"No, Owen," Mary said, and started walking backward. "You should go to school, too. I'll be all right. Honestly I will." She couldn't stand thinking that he was making her his good-deed project.

He fell into step beside her as if she hadn't spoken. "My first class is math, Connie," he called to his sister. "Forge a note for me from Mom or something. I'm at the dentist, so I'll be late. Okay?"

After a short pause Constance shouted, "Okay," and carried on her way.

The entire length of North Walk neither of them said a word. When they reached the Norton, Owen pointed at the White Knight. "You like Mr. Morgan, don't you?"

She didn't answer.

Owen bent over to look into her face. When she met his eyes, he grinned. "You don't have to talk if you don't want to."

"I don't know if I like Mr. Morgan or not."

He jigged in place until she stopped and faced him.

"What do you mean, you don't know if you like him? I thought he was a friend of yours and your—" He turned red and bowed his head. "Oh, I see. I only got the tail end of our friends' comments. Were they suggesting— Was Trevor Morgan the man they meant?"

She turned and ran. It couldn't be true. Her mother wouldn't do that.

Owen was abreast of her in seconds and not even

breathing heavily. "Sorry, okay. Dumb. I'm a dummy. Forget I said anything."

Mary didn't trust herself to speak, but she let Owen hold her hand and lead her when they reached the cliff path. He picked his way, looking for level spots, checking to make sure he wasn't moving too fast. And each time he turned toward her she forced a smile, until there was no more need for effort. She wanted to smile at Owen.

The cottage came into sight. "Almost home," Owen said.

"I'm not going there," Mary said and sucked in her bottom lip. Where was she going? She couldn't stay away for ever and Uncle Thomas wasn't well enough at the moment to have a moping teenager around.

Owen hadn't answered. He marched on, pulling Mary with him.

"Where are you taking me?" Soon they'd be at Uncle Thomas's.

"I know a place where we can get under the wind and just hang out. You don't have to say a word if you don't want to."

He did like her, she thought. No way would he go to this much trouble for someone he didn't care about—a little bit anyway.

"How does that sound?"

"Great. But you shouldn't be playing hooky."

"Neither should you. Let's live dangerously." He hopped down into a depression below the path, tossed his book bag aside, then lifted her beside him. She could have gotten down as easily on her own. Owen kept his hands at her waist. "I like being with you."

Mary brushed her hair out of her eyes. Heat roared into her face. "I like being with you, too."

He sat down and patted the sand beside him. As soon

as Mary joined him he put an arm loosely around her shoulders.

"Mary," Owen said when the silence had become a peaceful place and his arm spread warmth and strength through her mind and body. "It's not just what the kids said that's got you upset, is it?"

"No. But I can't talk about it." She stiffened up again.

"Okay. I wondered, that's all. Anytime you want, you can talk to me."

She hugged her shins, rested her chin on her knees. "I expect you've heard the stories about my mother, too."

"My folks don't go in for gossip," Owen said. Then, after some hesitation, "But some of the boys on the team have said things about Mr. Morgan having a girlfriend. They seemed to think that was good. We all know he does things right. I knew you and your mother were friendly with him, but I didn't work it out that there was something between Mr. Morgan and your mom…something…well, you know what I mean."

"There isn't," Mary said, but she didn't believe it anymore. All those times Trevor had come to their cottage late at night and stayed talking after she'd gone to bed…. And then Uncle Thomas had taken Mom to the pub, and Trevor had brought her home. Mary looked at the gray sky. She'd thought Trevor liked her, but he probably only wanted her to think that so she wouldn't guess what was going on.

Owen touched her arm. "Your father's here now?"

"Yes. He's visiting between jobs. He writes movies."

"Oh." Owen's voice dropped and when Mary glanced at him he looked impressed.

She laughed, leaned toward him. "I know. That's supposed to be glamorous, right? Well, it's not, not if you've grown up around it. It's ordinary, just a job." She waggled her head. "Maybe all the people aren't so ordinary. Mom doesn't like a lot of them. She says they're phony and that's why she loves it here so much. Most people are real here and they're the same each day—" Embarrassed, she halted in midsentence.

"I only met your mom once, but I thought I liked her. Now I know I do. My mom's that way too, honest. Will you have to go back to America when your parents leave?" He held her hand again.

She squeezed his fingers hard and stared into his face. "I don't know. I don't know what's going to happen to me. I think my mother's going to stay here, for now anyway, and that means I'll stay, too, I guess." Blinking wouldn't stop tears from coming. "I feel so selfish, but I'm scared. My mom says she's going to divorce my dad, and I don't want that."

Gently, Owen took her by the shoulders and moved until he held her in his arms, cradled to his chest. He settled his chin on top of her head. Mary's tummy jumped around but she slowly put her arms under his and held him tightly.

"We can't make other people do what we want them to do," Owen said very quietly. "My parents have their troubles, but interfering wouldn't help and usually things straighten out pretty quickly."

"I guess you're right, about the interfering." But it didn't make her feel better. "I don't want my mom to be unhappy. What went wrong with them?" She raised her face. "We used to be so happy."

Owen looked down at her. "Whatever went wrong is their business. Maybe this is how our parents feel when we say we want to live our own lives—kind of helpless, huh?"

She nodded. And she felt, inexplicably, a little happier.

And…she wished she never had to go away from this place or away from Owen.

"How do you feel now?" His dark eyes were anxious. The breeze whipped his black curly hair this way and that. He was *the* best-looking boy she'd ever seen, and the nicest.

"I feel good," she said.

Owen touched her face. "Don't go away, Mary. Find a way to stay here."

"I…I want to."

"Do it. And…" He bowed his head so that his forehead met hers lightly. "We could do some things together if you'd like. Go out."

The jumpiness became a steady quaking in every muscle. "You want to do some things with me?" He was asking her to be his girlfriend. That had never happened before. In school back home she was treated like an outsider because she was quiet.

"If you'd like to," Owen said.

Mary put her arms around his neck and nestled her cheek against his neck. "I'd like that very much."

This had been the longest morning of her life. After checking on Thomas's health and hearing his report on Mary's visit, Caitlin left Thomas's in his ancient Morris, cursing herself for not having bought her own car by now. She'd put that right in the next few days.

Her target was Trevor. Never had she been so certain of what she needed to do, who she needed to be with. David had finally left, spewing threats with every piece of clothing he stuffed into his Aspetti luggage. She'd even called a taxi herself and paid in advance for the horrendously expensive fare the canny driver demanded for driving to London.

But David was gone, for now.

Speeding in the Morris was an impossibility, but she kept her foot to the floor all the way into town. Later there would be Mary to deal with. Not going to Thomas's as soon as he'd called this morning had taken control, but his suggestion that she wait made sense.

The White Knight was open. Caitlin parked in the forecourt and got out of the car. Suddenly she wasn't as sure of herself.

What if he didn't want to see her and said as much in front of a gaggle of customers?

Trevor wouldn't do that. Unlike David, he was a gentleman.

She went into the bar and walked straight to the counter. Nip Lymer stood there, wiping glasses and talking to three men who held tankards of beer.

When Nip noticed her, he smiled. "Hello, there, Caitlin. What can I get you?"

The three men rotated their heads in her direction as if pulled by a single string and she was treated to a joint assessment. They made her glad she wore her heavy raincoat with a silk scarf over her hair.

"Uh, nothing thanks, Nip. Is Trevor around?"

"No," Nip replied promptly. The men rolled to rest their elbows on the bar where they could watch her openly. Nip continued, "Trevor's not working till tonight. I think he said something about dropping in on his mom and dad. But I'm not sure. Then he'll be working with the team for an hour or so."

"Busy man, our Trevor," one of the men, tall and skinny with stooped shoulders, said and immediately tilted his glass to his lips.

Caitlin took a step backward. "I'm sure he is."

"Ray Best, I am," the man announced. "My boy

Robin is on the team. That team's the most important thing in Trevor's life." His comment brought a chorus of mumbled agreement from his cohorts.

"Yes, I'm sure." These people didn't like her. "Nip, where do Mr. and Mrs. Morgan live?" It was time she confronted all the demons, Trevor's parents included.

Nip gave her the Morgans' address and she escaped into the thin wintry sunshine outside, feeling like a dunked nonswimmer bursting into fresh air.

She left the car where it was and walked, following Nip's directions to a house some blocks away on the Esplanade. This was a part of town she hadn't explored since her return, but today wasn't the time to take in much of the scenery. When she'd cut across the town's streets to pass through a remaining section of the old Norman Wall, now incorporated into the outside of several structures, she emerged on the side of Castle Hill where she had a clear view of Caldy Island. Low, blue-gray against an indistinct sky. The island held the mystery she remembered from childhood, when stories of the monks who lived there in seclusion had fascinated her.

She glanced at the paper in her hand, checking the number Nip had written down for her. Crossing from the ocean side, she scanned the buildings and quickly located the surprisingly large house where the Morgans lived.

Not allowing herself to reconsider her decision, she ran up the steps and lifted a brass knocker shaped like a bulldog's head. A thunderous noise echoed inside the house, and she retreated a pace.

There was no sound of footsteps before the door swung open and she was confronted by Sam Morgan.

His distinguished features, at first bland, became pinched. "Good morning, Mrs. McBride." If he could have brought himself to close the door without speaking, she believed he would have done so.

"Good morning." She turned the corners of her mouth up. "I'm sorry to disturb you, but I'm looking for Trevor, and at the White Knight they said he'd come here."

"He did. He's left."

Caitlin clenched her hands in her pockets. "Oh, dear. I missed him." With a breath that didn't help a thing, she pressed on, "But I'm glad to have a chance to see you. I did meet you and Mrs. Morgan when I was a teenager, but that was a long time ago."

"Yes, it was."

A woman joined Sam Morgan, and Caitlin recognized her as Trevor's mother. She was of average height and build, her short graying hair well cut and swept back in a becoming style. It was her eyes that held Caitlin's attention—bright blue and large. If she were happy they'd be beautiful, but Mrs. Morgan wasn't happy.

"Hello, Mrs. Morgan," Caitlin said. "I'm Caitlin McBride."

"Yes."

She didn't need this, not today—or ever. "I was looking for Trevor, but Mr. Morgan says he's already left."

The woman stepped past her husband and onto the step where she could look squarely at Caitlin. "Mrs. McBride," she said, her voice soft and well modulated. "We wouldn't want to be rude to you. I'm sure you are a good person and well-meaning, but there are things that need to be said."

Caitlin glanced awkwardly around. Clearly the Morgans had no intention of asking her into their home for their little discussion.

"If Trevor isn't here," she said, hoping they'd drop

whatever was on their minds if she didn't react, "perhaps you can tell me where he went when he left you."

"I don't think so," Mrs. Morgan said. "But I can tell you that you're no good for our Trevor. He's a Welshman through and through, and this town is where he belongs. You don't belong here. All you'll do if you keep after him is make him miserable."

"Keep after him?" Caitlin, indignant, stood straighter. "I'm not keeping after Trevor, as you put it. We're friends, old friends. And I need to talk to him." Her heart beat wildly.

"There's one thing I want to tell you, Mrs. McBride and only one. Trevor listens to us. He grew up in a place where sons and daughters respect their parents. And we've warned him that you're trouble. Leave Trevor alone, Mrs. McBride."

Sam Morgan stood aside to let his wife pass. Before he closed the door he looked calmly at Caitlin and said, "Take notice of what Livie's told you. Leave Trevor alone or you'll wish you had."

11

By the time she reached the town's outskirts, every breath Caitlin took seared her throat. She couldn't believe it, not of Trevor's parents. They were treating him like a child and her like a scarlet woman. And they didn't even know her.

The school was on a flat area of land raised behind the westerlymost part of South Beach. Caitlin quickly located the big playing field beyond and began walking rapidly toward it, narrowing her eyes to make out which of the running figures might be Trevor. She'd already noted that, as was the case with Owen Trew, many of the players were as tall, if not as maturely built, as their coach.

Drawing near, she slowed down, then stopped and leaned against a tree where she could watch without being obvious.

Groups of boys worked out all over the field. Some were going through series of exercises she recognized as limbering and stretching, while others were busy with complicated movement patterns that involved the jostling and grunting and thumping she remembered from years ago. She'd hated this rough game even then.

"Hit him!"

Trevor's voice, raised and grating, snapped Caitlin's head around. Dressed in a black sweat suit, he stood, leaning forward, hands braced on knees, beside a circle of straining players who seemed bent on strangling each other.

"Go at it, you powder puffs. This isn't netball. There aren't any girls on the team, are there? Or are you all girls? You might as well be. Stop! Stand up and look at me!"

The boys did as he asked, and even at a distance Caitlin could see their red and sweating faces.

"You're useless. The whole lot of you." Trevor strode around the group like a snarling sheepdog working a wayward herd. "If you put half the effort into your game that you put into your other *activities*, you might get to look less like little boys trying to fill men's shoes."

The attack went on. Caitlin drew farther back. With each shouted abuse, she turned a little colder and weaker. This was what mattered most to him, the man at the pub had said. Trevor was different here, different from anything she'd known him capable of being. There was violence in the way his head jutted, in his raised fists, in the relentless hammering quality of his voice.

She tugged her belt tighter, wanting to look away yet rooted in place. She had always known there was a basic disparity between them. But she'd told herself it was just their backgrounds. Had she sensed but ignored a roughness beneath Trevor's gentle surface? Culturally they were definitely opposites; his absorption in these boys and their wild game proved that.

"Two hundred push-ups you little fools," Trevor yelled. The boys dropped to the muddy ground, and he continued to stride around them, flapping his arms across his broad chest.

Was Ray Best right? Was this the most important thing in Trevor's life? Caitlin tied her scarf more securely under her chin. To her, he looked like a man on an ego trip, pursuing some kind of glory game intended to bring him out a hero. They'd discussed his life in London very little. But he had mentioned the exhilaration he'd felt there, the fascination he'd experienced in the battle for the top. Trevor insisted he'd grown tired of it all and had been glad to return to a quiet life. Watching him now, Caitlin wondered if he was so satisfied with his lot here, or if, with these boys, he was searching for another outlet for a power complex.

Whatever the truth was, she didn't like what she saw. She broke from her cover, running toward the beach. The Morgans were right. She and Trevor had nothing in common.

Her scarf tore free of her hair, slipping to flap behind her neck. There was no one to turn to. The only person she wanted had materialized as a puzzle the moment she'd needed him, really needed him.

"Caitlin! Wait!"

She heard Trevor's voice over the thud of her Reeboks but didn't check her pace or turn back.

"Wait! Caitlin, wait for me!"

This was ridiculous. She should stop and talk to him, then go on her way. But she couldn't stop. If she did, she might say things she'd regret later.

The thought that she couldn't outrun Trevor came as he drew level with her. "Why are you running away from me?" He caught her arm but she pulled free.

They'd reached the slope to the beach and Caitlin dashed down, gathering momentum, her heels making troughs in the damp sand that squelched under the hems of her jeans. At the bottom she pitched forward, caught herself on her hands and bounced upright again.

"Are you mad?" Trevor skidded to a stop beside her. Despite the cold, he unzipped his sweat jacket. Under a tight red T-shirt his chest rose and fell rapidly. "The minute I catch sight of you, you run away. Why would you do a thing like that?"

"You were busy." She unknotted the scarf with shaky fingers. "And I didn't know you'd seen me."

"And you didn't hear me calling you?"

"I've got to get home."

"Don't do this to me." Trevor said. Before she could turn away, he trapped her by the waist. "You came here to see me. There's no other reason for you to be by the playing field."

"Let me go."

"I won't. Not until you start to make sense. And maybe not then, either."

"Trevor, I'm not up to this." How could she love the way it felt to be close to him yet be afraid of giving in to that feeling at the same time?

"*Did* you come to see me?"

She stared into his gray eyes. They'd always taken on a steely glint when he was angry. There had been too much anger in this day.

He jerked her closer. "*Did* you?"

"Yes." She took in the sheen of sweat on his brow, the hint of stubble along his sharp jaw. A pulse beat hard in his neck.

"And then you ran away?"

Dark hair at the neck of the T-shirt made a focal point—that and the hard pressure of his arm around her body. "I changed my mind." Damn, why couldn't she sound assertive and *be* assertive?

"Why?"

He wasn't angry. Caitlin opened her mouth but wasn't sure what to say. Trevor was hurt, not angry. They hadn't as much as spoken since the night David arrived when she'd more or less said she didn't want to see this man again.

"So help me, Caitlin. I've taken about as much as I can from you. So you changed your mind about wanting to see me. That doesn't explain why you ignored me when I called your name."

"I don't know what I want." Her forehead came down hard on his chest. "I don't know anything anymore. You're different. I'm different, and wanting something doesn't make it so."

She felt the beat of his heart against her face. His body remained rigid, but he put his other arm around her and held the back of her head. "You're talking in riddles," he said after a while. "Different from what?"

"From the way we were, from each other."

"We can't stay the same, Caitlin. We're both a lot older. And what's wrong with two people being different from each other?"

Being held by Trevor felt totally natural. She wished it didn't. "Let me go," Caitlin whispered.

Trevor bent his head over hers. She felt him kiss her hair. "You don't want me to."

Her hands were fists on his chest. She flattened them, spread her fingers. "I do." Coming after him without thinking first had been a mistake. Anything she did or said was bound to be colored by confusion over what had happened this morning...and by what had been obvious from the first time she saw Trevor after her return to Wales: physically, they mesmerized each other.

Trevor eased up her chin. "What made you come to me?"

The man, the wind, the sea that could always whip her soul into a wild free thing—the moment was potent. Caitlin managed not to look into his eyes. His mouth, slightly parted as he waited for her answer, did even less for her objectivity.

His mouth came fractionally closer. She felt his breath on her lips.

"I thought I wanted to tell you something," she said.

"What was it?" His voice was distracted now, the words reflexive. It would be so easy, so very easy to forget everything, for a little while…a little while.

"I changed my mind." Her own answer felt disjointed.

Trevor straightened. "Changed your mind? If you wanted to tell me something and you came all the way across town to do it, what could make you change your mind?"

That cutting edge was there again, the merest hint of what she'd heard minutes before when he was with the boys. "We shouldn't talk about this now," she told him, trying to move way. He held her fast.

"Tell me, damn it. I can see it in your eyes. I can feel it, Caitlin. Something's happened that I should know about. *Tell* me."

"Don't…don't talk like that. I won't be bullied like those boys." The accord, the sense of merging together, was gone.

Trevor shifted his grip to her arms. "What are you talking about?"

"You're violent with them."

"With the team?" He was incredulous. "I…I'm not violent with anyone. Caitlin, I coach them. I do what has to be done. And that has nothing to do with us, or this."

"You're shouting." A trembling rippled beneath her skin.

"I am not!" His fingers dug into her flesh.

"I can't stand shouting." Tears sprang into her eyes. Everything had gone wrong. "I've had too much…." She wouldn't say anymore, must not say anymore, at least until she was calm.

"Go on." His lips barely moved as he spoke. "You've had too much shouting? Is that what you were going to say?"

"I just don't like it."

"Okay," he said, stretching out the word. "I'm not shouting. Now will you talk to me?"

This was hateful. She couldn't open up now. "We've been talking."

"Sure." He nodded. "In circles, and so far I haven't heard anything that makes sense."

Caitlin shoved at Trevor with both hands, and he let her go. She brushed past him and felt him turn after her. "Forget me," she yelled. "That's what I came to say. Forget me."

Trevor took one more step and stopped. Caitlin was running again, stumbling, clawing her way up the bank.

"Go ahead." He lowered his voice, speaking to himself now, "Go ahead, if that's the way you want it."

He waited until she was out of sight and retraced his own steps slowly. By the time he got back to the field, the boys were standing around in clusters, muttering, glancing in his direction as he approached.

Looking at them, at their flushed young faces, his energy seeped away, stolen by the frustration that had taken its place. She was right though, dammit, he did lose his temper more easily these days...because of her. Not that he should take his disappointment and confusion out on the team, even if they had turned into more trouble than he wanted to shoulder.

"Gather around," he ordered.

They shuffled closer, arms crossed almost to a man.

And they were men, in size. What he wanted, desperately, was to help them mature emotionally.

"First—and this doesn't come easily—I'm sorry. Not for being mad at some of you. You've deserved it. But I am sorry if I've driven you too hard and if I've failed to give you whatever reinforcement you need to let you know your value. You're all worth too much to let yourselves down with bad behavior."

The only response was shifting of weight, bowing of heads.

"Do you know what I'm talking about?" He barked it out and closed his eyes for an instant. The rage had to go. "I'd like a response from some of you," he added more evenly.

"May I go, Mr. Morgan?" This from Will Colly.

Trevor opened his mouth to say no, before he noticed the kid's expression. The same kind of distress he'd shown the night at the police station. Some people couldn't take confrontation, and young Colly was obviously one of them.

"Mr. Morgan—"

"Go, Will. But think about what I've said, huh?"

"Yeah, I'll do that."

"We all will," Owen Trew put in, sidestepping after Will. "I'm sorry, too, Mr. Morgan. We all know how much you do for us. May I go, too?"

A murmured chorus of regret followed.

"You can all go."

Owen was sorry for what? Typical. A straight-arrow kid was the first to apologize. And Owen wasn't the only good apple in this barrel. He had to remember that.

"We through with workout?" Robin Best called.

"Yeah. That's it for today," he told them, making eye contact with no one as he set off in the direction of his car. "See if you can get your acts together by next practice." Violent, Caitlin had called him. Maybe he had overdone it today. But Caitlin didn't know a thing about coaching a group of unruly kids who thought they were minigods.

At the car he changed his mind and skirted the school buildings instead, headed toward the ocean again and found a spot where he could sit and look out toward Caldy Island.

He heard harsh breathing seconds before he saw Mary McBride pause a few yards away and bend over, clutching her sides as if she were winded.

"Mary?" he leaped up and hurried toward her.

Her body jerked and she stared at him, her face turning white.

He laughed. "Didn't you see me?"

She shook her head.

"I'm sorry. I didn't mean to shock you. Why aren't you in school?"

She glanced up at the buildings. "I'm not, that's all."

He looked at his hands, unsure how to go on.

"And it's none of your business. Nothing about us is any of your business."

First Caitlin, now Mary. This was his lucky day with women. "I didn't mean to pry," he said gently. "But if you're staying away from school for no good reason, then you'd probably do better not to be seen in this area." Terrific. Now he was helping the girl play truant.

"I'm meeting…I don't need your advice."

"Good." Enough was enough. He gave her a mock salute and started back toward the parking area.

"You stay right here, Trevor Morgan."

She couldn't have said that. The wind had distorted her voice. He shook his head and carried on.

"Trevor! Come back here."

"Mary, are you talking to me?" He checked his stride to look at her and immediately stopped. "Mary, oh, Mary, what is it?" He moved quickly toward her until he stood in front of her once more. Tears drenched her face.

"Nothing." She sobbed.

"Yes there is." He wasn't taking no for an answer again. "Spill it."

"Okay, okay." She sat down suddenly and covered her ears, her elbows resting on raised knees. "It's you. It's all your fault. My dad says...he says there's something that's wrong with him that's my mother's fault. I don't understand what they were saying. But Mom's going to divorce Daddy, and it's your fault."

"Whoa." Trevor dropped to sit on his haunches. He touched her hands, but she jerked away. One word sang in his brain, *divorce*. He forced himself to concentrate. "Why is it supposed to be my fault that your mother wants to divorce your father?" Oh, glory days. It was happening. Caitlin hadn't exactly thrown herself at him today, but he'd work that out later. She was probably upset and confused....

"You don't understand," Mary said, interrupting Trevor's thoughts. He raised his eyes to the sky. It seemed he was hearing an instant replay of earlier accusations.

Mary dropped her hands and leveled a red-eyed glare at him. "My dad likes parties. My mom doesn't. Daddy loves lots of people around and Mom likes quiet. Mom made Dad leave our house. She got a lawyer to write up papers to make him move."

"Mary," Trevor said, trying to keep his voice steady. "Sometimes people don't get along, and sometimes that means they aren't meant to live together."

"You sound like Uncle Thomas." A white line formed

around her mouth, and he felt her anger bubbling up. "I'm not a kid. I know all that and maybe I can get used to it. Owen says I should. He says you people have a right to your own—" She closed her mouth firmly, a faint flush sweeping over her pale face.

Trevor blessed Owen Trew. That kid had promise in lots of areas. "You should listen to Owen," Trevor told her. "He's got a good head on his shoulders."

"Yes, he has. He's...he's my friend," she said with a note of defiance. "And so's Constance and one or two other people, but not many. The kids are saying things about you."

He raised his face slowly. "Like what?"

"Like you—" She swallowed and passed her tongue over her lips. "They say you and my mother are friends."

"We are." A feeling of claustrophobia began closing in around him.

"Not *that* kind of friends."

"Oh." He studied the sky again, feeling more and more out of his depth.

"Are you?"

He couldn't think of the right way to respond.

"Trevor." Her slender hands, unexpectedly snaking around his wrists, startled him. "Are you and Mom...are you lovers?" She turned scarlet.

Poor little kid. "Mary—"

"I know you probably are. But what will that mean? What's going to happen?"

"Mary—"

"I'm not afraid. I'm not. I'm not." She bowed her head and cried afresh.

All he could do was take her stiff body into his arms and hold her tightly.

"What will happen to me?" she said indistinctly

against his shoulder. "If Mom stays here for good, will I get to see Dad anymore?"

She was pouring out all the questions in her heart, asking them out of her hopelessness rather than because she expected answers from him.

When she lifted her face his heart slammed. She was devastated—too devastated for what was happening, but Caitlin had already warned him that this was a fragile girl. His hand felt big and awkward as he wound a long tangle of blond hair behind her ear.

"Listen to me. And let me finish before you say anything else."

She tilted her head to one side, rubbing the heels of her hands over her eyes.

"I didn't know your mother had decided to divorce your father. Not for sure," he added rapidly. "She did tell me they were legally separated and that she'd come here to find out if the time was right for divorce."

"She didn't tell me—"

"Mary. Please allow me to have my say," he told her, and she took the handkerchief he found in his sweat-jacket pocket. "What I've already told you is all I know. I can't tell you what will happen in the future. And no, your mother and I are not lovers."

A huge sigh lifted her shoulders. "The kids said—"

"The kids said things that aren't true. Don't blame them too much. They probably heard rumors from their families. It doesn't take much to start a rumor, and this is a small town where news travels fast—what little news there is."

"Then you don't care about Mom, not...not that way?"

There were times when truth should be suspended, weren't there? "Your mom and I are friends, good friends. I hope we always will be. Now, I'm taking you home. Your mother needs you. You can talk to Owen tomorrow.''

With his help, Mary got up and stood blowing her nose. She ran her fingers through her hair and gave him a watery smile. "I guess you think I'm a hysterical kid."

"Wrong." He fashioned a bright grin that felt as phony as hell. "I think you're a great kid who loves her parents. And I'm a bit jealous I don't have a daughter who cares that much about me." That was true, he realized, surprised. And there was a smile hanging around, a genuine one, deep inside.

Caitlin was going to divorce David McBride.

12

"I'm your mother. I want what's best for you—and for Mary," Eileen insisted.

Caitlin's brain jammed. Almost idly, she smoothed the white satin boot resting on her knees. Her hand holding the phone tingled. Her mother had been talking a long time.

"You're being selfish. David was in tears when he called from Heathrow. He said he's tried everything he can think of but you're set on divorce. Why would you do this? It was bad enough when you insisted on the separation, but I thought you'd come to your senses in time."

"Mother," Caitlin said, "you know David ruined our marriage. You know the stories that circulated about his behavior. They're still circulating. He came here to beg for money, a lot of it, and I wouldn't give it to him. That's why he's crying."

"He's calling me back in an hour. I said I'd try to talk you into changing your mind. Let him come back to you, Caitlin. Give him another chance. He knows he's been bad, and he's ready to straighten out."

Caitlin held the cool satin of the thigh-high boot against her warm cheek. "Bad? I can't believe you said that. And I hate it when you let David manipulate you into his corner. End of conversation. I'll call in a few days."

"Wait! Are you sure—"

"I'm sure. I'm divorcing David."

"Is it because of that boy?"

Boy? How would her mother know about Owen…? No, not Owen. Caitlin's teeth came together hard before she could speak. "Are you talking about Trevor Morgan, Mother?"

"Well…yes, I think that was his name."

"Trevor isn't a boy. He's thirty-seven." David must have mentioned Trevor, and her mother still felt safe about her deception of all those years ago.

"You are seeing him again, though?"

"Goodbye, Mother." The time to discuss tampering with her mail would come later. Now there was work to do on these boots, and a pile of other problems to cope with.

"I'd like to come and stay."

Caitlin fell back in the hard wooden chair and rested her head against a stair rail. This was all—no, it was *more* than all she could take.

"Are you there? I said I'd like to come and stay. Things aren't easy for a woman alone who's trying to get her life back together. I need to spend some time with you, darling. We could talk and I could help…."

"No. No, Mother. I'm sorry, but I'm a woman alone who's trying to get her life together, too. And I *want* to do it alone." She hated denying her mother anything, but she suspected her mother's real motive for the trip would be to make more attempts to talk a way out of the divorce.

The phone line went dead. Slowly, Caitlin let the receiver drop into its cradle. Good old mother. Eileen Allen was nothing if not a dramatic actress, and she knew how to time an exit.

On legs that felt like lead, Caitlin trailed from the hall into the sitting room. She'd rigged a sheet of plywood on top of two trestles. A thick length of plastic, spread over the plywood and tacked under the rim, made a smooth clean surface. The mate to the boot she carried lay on top.

Caitlin looked at a list of specifications, checked several open boxes of seed pearls and rhinestones, counted a heap of white satin rosettes. Then she threw one boot on top of the other and flopped into a chair. Who was she kidding? She couldn't finish the boots in time. They were due for a TV Christmas special slated for live shooting at the end of November, three weeks from now. She couldn't do anything. Except lose her mind.

The low growl of an engine did no more than cause her to close her eyes. A car door slammed, then the front door, and the engine noise receded.

"Mom? Dad?"

Caitlin flinched. "In the sitting room."

Mary came in looking rumpled, tearstained and damp. "Hi," she said and hunched her shoulders. "Where's Dad?"

Caitlin almost tripped in her hurry to get out of the chair and go to Mary. She gathered her close. "Sweetheart, I didn't want you to hear your father and me arguing this morning. Why did you run off?"

"I'm here now. Where's Dad?"

"On his way back to Los Angeles."

Mary became rigid.

"We decided it would be best if he left immediately. Mary, everything's going to be okay. There will be a divorce, but you'll continue to see your father regularly. Both of us will want that."

"Why didn't he at least say goodbye to me?"

Caitlin's grip slackened. She'd expected tears, raging. "You'd already gone, remember. And I insisted he leave at once. So blame me, not him."

"I've been pretty hard on you, haven't I, Mom?"

She held Mary away. "You didn't mean to be. You wanted your family together. I understood that."

"I still want it." Mary's eyelids drooped. "But I guess you don't always get what you want."

Unease stabbed Caitlin. This wasn't as simple as it sounded. Mary was making some sort of compromise with her own feelings, or trying to. And it didn't seem believable that she'd come to this new point without talking to someone else.

"Is that what your Uncle Thomas told you?"

"Sort of."

"Why didn't he come in with you?"

Mary looked blank. "I haven't seen him since this morning."

"Who picked you up from school and brought you home?"

"I didn't go to school. And I wouldn't be out yet if I had." Mary's pursed lips warned Caitlin not to make the subject an issue. "Trevor drove me home. I met him while I was walking."

"I see." Anything else, any added pressure, threatened to burst Caitlin's head. She would not think of Trevor now. "Mary, can we discuss your father later?"

"I don't want to discuss him. I'm tired."

Fine, but they had other things that must be dealt with. "Whatever you say. But we've got trouble and it's going to affect both of us. Mrs. Johnson quit today."

"Why?" Mary, already taking off her parka, let it trail from one wrist. "She likes us. She likes it here."

"'Other considerations' was the reason she gave."

Mary's coat hit a chair and slithered to the floor.

"Don't do that," Caitlin said, startled. "Pick—"

"Are other considerations like we aren't good enough for Mrs. Johnson?"

Now her head ached. "I don't know. How…of course not. That's ridiculous."

"So we'll find another housekeeper, and until we do we can manage."

"I can't manage. Sauvage's boots for her Christmas special arrived from Paris today." She pointed at the makeshift workbench. "All the finish work on them has to be hand done by me, and the final specs for my collection must be in the Paris atelier within ten days."

"The boots are gorgeous." Mary picked up a rosette. "I love Sauvage. She's fantastic."

"If you're into rock stars," Caitlin said, distracted. "She's wearing them over silver lamé tights, which doesn't thrill me. But she's paying the bill and the boots *will* be something. Anyway, I haven't got time to clean this place and cook and go into town for groceries or do the garden or take time out to buy the car I'd need to do all the running around if I did decide to try being Super-woman."

"The groceries are delivered. And the milk. And Mr. Briggs does the garden."

Caitlin attempted a smile. "Not anymore. The grocery store no longer wants to make a trip out of the way to bring our order. Same story with the milkman. And Andrew Briggs says he's decided to take it easy for a few months. Oh, yes, and the plumber who was going to replace the bathroom pipes already has too much to do. Evidently October's a big month for plumbers."

"Other considerations?" Mary said.

The rhythmic chatter of raindrops on the window was the only sound for several seconds.

"Damn all of them," Caitlin said through her teeth.

"What did we do to any of them?" She didn't say that only this afternoon she'd been warned by Trevor's parents that she wasn't welcome here. They must know everyone in town, and she had no doubt that this was an attempt to let her know they could make her life uncomfortable if they chose.

"Mom, don't get upset. Not all the people here are gossips. Some of them are nice."

"What do you know about gossip?"

Mary sat down and rested her chin on her chest. "Nothing."

"Yes, you do. Who's said something to you...besides Thomas? Trevor?"

"No. He was nice. He told me not to let the stories upset me because they aren't true and he tried to make me feel better about you and Dad."

"You talked to Trevor about your father and me?"

"Only after I told him what the kids said about you and him."

Her scalp prickled. "What did they say?"

She listened while Mary talked. After she'd finished they both sat in silence for a long time. So that's what had happened. The whole town was buzzing with stories about an affair that didn't exist, and the small-minded way the town had chosen to deal with her supposed transgression was through ostracizing her—and Mary. It was like something out of the Middle Ages.

"Trevor said not to take any notice of the kids. He said they'd forget all about it in a few days and move on to something else."

And he'd brought Mary home but made no attempt to come in himself. Caitlin grimaced. There wasn't any question of Trevor staying away from her because he was afraid of public opinion. He was bigger than that. If he hadn't felt he could come in, it was because of the way she'd treated him on the beach. She'd overreacted to his behavior with the boys. David, and too much stress, were as much to blame for that as she was.

"Mom, I don't want to leave Tenby."

Caitlin frowned at the top of Mary's bowed head. "I thought you weren't particularly happy here. And with—" She stopped herself from saying she'd expected Mary to want to be near her father as soon as possible. "Why don't you want to leave?"

Mary gave the familiar shrug. "I just don't. People shouldn't be allowed to make other people unhappy. If we go away, that's doing what some of them want us to do, and I'm not going to."

Her own faint smile felt good to Caitlin. "That's my girl." She had no intention of being chased away—by the Morgans or anyone else—but it was wonderful to have Mary's determination on her side. "Maybe we should fix some dinner. Then I'd better get going with these boots."

"I think you should talk to Trevor."

"Did he say he wanted to talk to me?"

"No, but he said he's always going to be your friend, and I bet if you asked him, he'd help us find some different people to help us." Mary got up but sat down again quickly, a hand pushed into her stomach.

"What is it?" Caitlin's heart turned.

"Oh, nothing. I got uptight today and I guess I feel a bit funny. I think I'll go to bed."

"I'll take you up. You should eat, though."

"I already ate," Mary said. "Owen gave me one of his sandwiches."

The name was quickly dropped but Caitlin didn't miss it. "You saw Owen today?"

Imaginary lint on Mary's jeans needed immediate attention. "He stuck up for me when the others said those things."

Caitlin's eyes smarted. She thought of another special boy she'd once known. "I think I like Owen Trew and I'll tell him so."

"Mom!"

"Okay, okay." Caitlin held up her palms. "I won't tell him so. I wasn't thinking. Now, let's get you to bed."

"Then you'll go and talk to Trevor? You can borrow Uncle Thomas's car if you don't want to walk."

"Now? I don't think—"

"They're saying the rotten stuff about him as well. Maybe people are being mean to him, too. It isn't his fault."

No, it wasn't Trevor's fault. And she owed him her support and an apology and an explanation of what she intended to do about her marriage and a detail or two about her last years with David that she hadn't revealed yet, to anyone.

Knowing that what she was about to do was right didn't make her less anxious when she left the cottage an hour later. What did she expect of Trevor? What would he think she expected of him? In the weeks when they'd spent so much time together there'd been a tacit understanding that they were at a sexual stalemate until she made a decision about a final break from David. Now she'd made that decision. She'd opted for freedom.

Thomas had gladly loaned her his car again, and too quickly she arrived at the White Knight.

There was at least an hour before evening opening time, but light showed inside the pub and Caitlin went into the small vestibule.

Raised voices reached her as she opened the bar door.

"You don't own me. My dad says you need me more than I need you."

Caitlin hesitated.

"I own your free time, Best, because you owe me, remember? You owe money, and you owe me for what I've done for you." Trevor's voice came in the staccato bursts she'd heard this afternoon. "And don't think you've got anything so special that I can't replace you on the Knights any day of the week."

"Just because—" The boy who faced Trevor across the counter, cutting her view of him, stopped talking and looked over his shoulder.

She must have made a noise. Caitlin cleared her throat and Trevor leaned forward to see who it was. He smiled, but not quickly enough to stop her getting a clear impression of the way rage changed his face.

"I'll come back," she said hurriedly. Maybe she would. Maybe she wouldn't.

"No." Trevor came from behind the bar. "We're finished here." That part of him was there, the part she didn't understand, the part that liked power and made him so hard, even manipulative, if she'd understood what he'd implied to the boy.

"We'll carry on with this later, Robin," he told the teenager whose sullen eyes glimmered with curiosity before he sloped past her and slammed the door.

Trevor faced Caitlin. She returned his smile and they stood for seconds looking at each other.

"Sorry you had to walk in on another of my team lectures." He narrowed his eyes fractionally as if gauging her reaction. "You have to be tough with them sometimes."

"I guess." She could be too sensitive. And he was the one who knew what he was doing.

Trevor stuffed his hands in his jeans pockets and rolled from his heels to his toes.

Caitlin's smile dissolved in time with his.

"I haven't lit the fire yet."

She nodded. The dress she'd changed into was of rust-colored raw silk and not warm enough, even under her camel hair coat, but she said, "I'm not cold."

"Sure?" He made as if to touch her face, checked himself, touched her anyway. "You are cold. And damp."

He kept his fingers on her cheek, splayed them and rubbed gently, and Caitlin couldn't move, couldn't feel anything but him.

"Thank you for bringing Mary home."

"She's a sweetheart."

"I know." Hedging couldn't go on for ever. "I'm sorry I gave you a bad time this afternoon. This has been a tough day and—" She didn't want to continue with this. Voicing all the sordid little details of her life was more than she could handle. Gently, she removed his hand from her face. "That's all I wanted to say, Trevor. Please accept my apology. I've got to get home."

"Uh-uh."

Caitlin watched, breathless, while he undid the tie belt on her coat and leaned to slip it from her shoulders.

"You aren't running away this time. We both know why you're here and it isn't to say sorry for a few angry words." He draped the coat over a chair. "Upstairs, *cari*. There is a fire there and it's comfortable."

There was no brooking his determination. A firm hand at her waist marshaled her through a door at one side of the bar and upstairs to Trevor's elegantly comfortable flat with its eclectic coalition of period and modern pieces. Though she'd seen it several times in the past weeks, Trevor's flat still surprised Caitlin in its artistry.

Trevor pulled a rose-brown corduroy chair close to the coal fire and shepherded Caitlin to sit down. He lifted her feet onto an ottoman and slipped off her pumps, which were wet from the walk to Thomas's house.

Caitlin laughed. "You don't have to baby me, Trevor."

He gave her a measured look that took in everything down to her soggy hose. "Babying you has nothing to do with it. Any excuse to touch you is better than none at all."

If he had stroked her with his hands rather than his eyes she couldn't have felt the effect more strongly. There wasn't an appropriate answer but then she knew he didn't expect one.

"Don't move from that spot."

He left the low-ceilinged room with its dark exposed beams, its groupings of abstracts, landscapes and an occasional Chinese modern painting. The walls were stark white, the floors marvelous mahogany aged to a silken patina and broken only by two large Wilton rugs in softened hues of umber and earthy red. Trevor Morgan had matured into an interesting, many-faceted man. Caitlin dug her nails into the chair arms. Why did she feel so sad here, among the possessions that had been collected over his years? Because she regretted not having been a part of those years?

"Drink this." Trevor came back, a towel in one hand, a brandy snifter in the other. The glass he gave to Caitlin.

She sniffed the cognac, swirled it around. "What's all this about? Why the royal treatment?"

"Because I'm happy, that's why. Happy you're here, okay?" He sat on the ottoman and pulled her feet onto his lap.

"I'm going to say what I intended to say this afternoon.

Then I'm going home.'' Already she felt as if she shouldn't have come.

Trevor held one ankle and rubbed the foot hard enough to make her yelp.

He grinned. ''Can't take it, huh? When I dry feet, I dry feet. My mother brought me up properly. Keep your head and your feet dry if you don't want pneumonia.''

His mother brought him up properly. *In this town sons and daughters were brought up to respect their parents' opinions.* Caitlin looked into the fire. Much as she longed to tell him everything in her heart she must omit the part about his mother and father.

''Nothing to say about that?'' He took her other foot but dried it more gently.

''I feel like a fool.''

Trevor stopped rubbing. ''Because we're here like this? Why?''

''Because I've come crying to you like a little kid who needs a grown-up to pat her head and say everything's going to be okay.''

He held her ankles and slowly massaged circles with his thumbs. ''You mean you came to me for comfort? Because you're unhappy, maybe, and I was the person you wanted to come to? Or am I only dreaming up the reasons I like?''

The pressure on her skin, steady, insistent, distracted and stimulated her at the same time. ''Mary told me what the kids said about...about us. Trevor, I'm sorry if I've caused you difficulty with your own people. I'm really sorry.'' Tears were the last thing she expected. Stupid, damn tears. She gulped the cognac and coughed.

''Hey, what's this about?'' A large hand removed the glass but she wouldn't meet his eyes. ''Difficulty with my people?''

"This is your town, Trevor, and the people here respect you. It isn't fair that you get undermined because of me."

"I don't give a—"

"No. Don't interrupt me. I've got to get all this out while I've got the guts. I already said I came to Wales to decide if I was ready to go ahead with a divorce. That wasn't true, really. At least I don't think it was, but I didn't know that." Her nose was going to run. Oh, God. She fumbled for her pocket and realized she didn't have one.

Silently, Trevor gave her a handkerchief.

"If I'd been honest with myself, I'd have admitted that I'd come here to run away. I couldn't cope with the hell David was putting me through in L.A. Trevor, he showed up all the time. The restraining order didn't mean a thing, and he knew it. He knew I wouldn't have him forcibly removed. Mary was his insurance there. So he kept coming and staying and getting drunk and sleeping on the couch. And Mary thought that meant he wanted to be with us, so she went on hoping we'd get back together again."

"She didn't see him drunk?"

"Yes. But I don't think she ever realized how drunk he was. He was careful around her."

"But he did want you." The flat tone of his voice forced Caitlin to look at him. In his eyes she saw apprehension.

"Hold my hand, Trevor. He doesn't want us and I don't want him. All I am to David McBride is a meal ticket. Only I'm not going to be that anymore, either."

He clasped both of her hands in his, wound the fingers together.

"Mary told you I'm going to divorce David?"

Trevor nodded, bringing her fingertips to his lips.

Caitlin let out a shuddering sigh. "He'd like to try to make it hard but he won't."

"Are you sure?" Now he kissed her palms.

"We haven't been man and wife for a long time."

"Three years."

"Longer than that. He...he couldn't...he stopped wanting to sleep with me almost two years before the separation."

Trevor raised his chin, frowning. He gave a half laugh, shaking his head. "I don't get it. Did he...was there someone else even then?"

She'd never tried to verbalize this. "Not really."

"Either there was or there wasn't."

"He wanted me to think there was." The pain of those days and months came back. "He pretended, made sure he was seen with other women."

"Plural?"

"Yes. That was his cover. He couldn't afford to get too involved with one woman."

Trevor raised his brows. "You're going to have to spell that one out for me."

How could she expect him to relate to David's behavior? It had been bizarre, beyond anything a normal man would comprehend. Heat started up her neck. "David needed to make me believe the reason he didn't sleep with me was because he'd lost interest in me. He paraded women in places where our friends would be sure to see him and tell me."

He let out a hissing breath. "The bastard."

"He was...he is sick. Trevor, David's impotent."

In the silence that followed Caitlin's face throbbed. Trevor glanced down at their joined hands. She'd embarrassed him.

"I'm sorry. I shouldn't talk about—"

"Yes, you should." He interrupted her and his face, when he looked at her, was tense. After setting her feet on the floor, he pulled her from the chair and onto his lap. "This is awful to say, *cari*, but I'm glad...for me. I'm sorry for the poor bastard in a way, and sad for what you've been through, but, God, Caitlin, I've sweated through hours of thinking about you with him. When I saw him there, in your cottage, I wanted to kill him. Ever since that night I've imagined him making love to you and...hell, I don't think I knew what hate felt like before."

He held her tightly to him and she closed her eyes. His hand was in her hair, caressing her neck, her back.

"Look at me."

She did.

"It's all over now. We can go on from here. We—" His lips remained parted while he looked at her. Softly he brushed the backs of his fingers down the side of her neck, traced her skin beneath the lapels of her dress to the point where they met in a V.

Caitlin watched his mouth. In seconds, minutes, this sweet thing building between them would reach its inevitable conclusion if she didn't exert some restraint. When they made love for the first time—if they did—it mustn't be to assuage any underlying inadequacy she feared in herself, or because Trevor was acting out of pity or out of loneliness.

"There was something else I came to tell you." Think, she must keep thinking logically.

"Can't it wait?" His lips met the space between her brows and passed across her eyelid to her temple.

Her breasts ached, and she opened her eyes, breathing through her mouth. Sensations remembered, fantasized about, were all coming too fast and too real. "My house-keeper quit," she told him, and felt ridiculous.

"She did?" Her ear, her jaw, the corner of her mouth received minute attention.

"Trevor, this is serious. You need to know what's going on. The gardener quit, too."

"Briggs? Lazy devil." Collarbones were Trevor's latest fascination.

"And the grocer won't deliver anymore or the milkman, and the plumber doesn't want to work for me."

Trevor raised his head, his eyes narrowed. "What are you telling me?" His voice was gravelly.

She held his shoulders to stop him from trying to kiss her again. "It means that the folks in this town don't like me. And from what Mary's said, it's because they think I led you astray." Her laugh sounded awkward.

"You mean you think you're being punished over some assumptions made by a bunch of people with not enough to do? I don't believe it."

Now she laughed easily.

"What's so funny?" He looked wounded.

"You can't blame them for making the assumptions. If circumstances had been different, they could have been right."

Trevor's grin was sheepish, then devilish. "How true. I'll deal with the local yokels. But first I think I should deal with you."

"It's got to be about five minutes to opening time." Ignoring his protests, Caitlin slipped free of his grasp and stood up. She put on her shoes.

"Nip'll take care of things till I get there."

"He won't have to. We aren't going to make any false moves from here on, Trevor. There have been enough of those, for both of us. I think we should back off for a while and digest what's happened. You may decide I'm more of a hazard than you need, and I need some time, too.''

"Oh, no you don't, my love." Trevor positioned himself between Caitlin and the door. "You're not running out on me again. We'll take all the time we need—together."

She took a sideways step and so did Trevor. What was he telling her? That they'd miraculously become free of all obstacles?

"We can't brush everything under the rug," she told him. "I have to divorce a man and help my daughter through the bad times she's going to have. And we don't have any guarantees that we won't hurt each other if we do get more involved."

He rolled his eyes. "We aren't going to hurt each other. You came here because you want to be with me, isn't that the truth?"

"Yes."

"And I want to be with you. So we don't have a problem."

"We *do* have a problem," she said, exasperated. "We have a lot of problems."

Trevor took hold of her waist. "Okay, if that's the way you want to look at it. So this is what we'll do. First, stop chewing your fingernails over public opinion. It means nothing to me and it shouldn't to you. Last, we'll decide to be happy because you've decided to get rid of David."

"Mary—"

"We'll work together with Mary. We'll give her what she needs, a solid home life. Now, since you insist upon going home, go, while I can still control myself. And I'll go to work. But I'll be on your doorstep in the morning because we've got a lot of catching up to do and I want to get started.''

Before she could respond he reached back to open the door and started downstairs. Any protest she might have voiced was squelched when she saw Nip wheeling a dolly of beer crates from a storage room into the bar.

Minutes later she sat in the Morris. Trevor had bent to kiss her, closed the door with a thud and retreated into the pub without another word or glance.

Caitlin started the engine.

Had she just received a proposal of marriage?

13

Damn Andrew Briggs anyway. Trevor drove the spade into the slimy mud around a clump of pale weeds. Damn the lot of them. He gave a thought to his parents. In the week since Caitlin had come to him he'd tried several times to enlist their help with the locals who were boycotting her. His mother and father had refused to even discuss the subject. The less he dwelled on their attitude, the better.

With a sucking sound, the spade popped free of the ground, splattering grainy clots of soil on his pants. He'd never had a garden and didn't know the first thing about one, but this overgrown mess was bothering Caitlin, so he'd learn as best he could.

"Trevor Morgan, stop!"

He shot upright. Caitlin struggled through the gate, her arms full of boxes. A new, bright red Ford Escort was parked behind his Jag.

"I didn't hear you coming. Where did you get that?" He pointed a grimy finger at the Escort.

"From a car dealer. What do you think you're doing?"

He scratched his forehead before remembering the mud on his hands. "You weren't around when I got here and I needed something to keep me busy. Since the spade and boots were in the shed, I thought I'd do a bit of this for you." And he made himself smile and expand his chest in what he hoped was a picture of delight in his efforts. "Nothing like digging in the dirt to bring you close to nature."

Caitlin hid her face on the top box, and he heard muffled chuckling.

"What?" Squelching the rubber boots in a path toward her he jutted his chin. "What's so darned funny?"

"My alyssum," came between giggles.

"Your—" He looked back at the pile of withered shoots he'd dug up. "Oh, no. You mean that stuff was supposed to be there? I thought they were weeds."

Caitlin raised her face, coughed and set her mouth in a straight line. "They are to me," she said. "Can't stand the things. Never could. I was going to dig them up anyway, so you saved me the trouble. Thank you."

He leaned on the spade and sucked in one corner of his mouth. "Yeah. You're welcome. Isn't that what I'm supposed to say?"

She lost her fragile hold on sincerity and staggered, laughing wildly, to the door. "Get the boots off," she managed between gulps, "and come in. I need coffee and I've got to work my tail off for the rest of the day to start getting my shipment ready for Paris."

Trevor put the spade back in the musty, cobweb-strewn shed, retrieved his loafers and trod cautiously along a row of mossy stepping stones to reach the cottage. He cast a final glare at the doleful pile of uprooted plants before going inside. They'd be okay for a while, and he'd get them back in the ground later.

"Where are you?"

"Kitchen," Caitlin called.

Coffee was already dripping into the pot. She'd turned on the oven and opened the door to help warm up the room quickly. Rivulets of condensation wound down steamy windows.

He stood in the doorway, rubbing his hands and watching her. The boxes were piled on the floor, and she'd taken off her coat. "Are you ready to send off your collection?"

"Yep. I put a spurt on this week. Muffins with your coffee, or cookies? There's a pie, too."

"Yes."

She turned to him, a mug in each hand. The gray light from the window shone through her hair, such wonderful red hair, full, long, riotously disheveled by the weather and the way she had of pushing at it.

"Trevor?"

"Mmm." How many women could manage to look elegant and sexy at the same time? The kind of sexy that made him want to rumple the white Oxford cloth shirt she wore tucked into jeans. Her waist was tiny, her hips small but rounded and her legs very, very long. Without Caitlin inside them, those jeans would probably be just jeans. With Caitlin in them...

"Don't do that, Trevor."

He took in a quick breath and brought his glance to her eyes, her face. She was flushed, her eyes brilliant. "What was I doing?"

"You know perfectly well. Wash your hands—and your face. You're covered with mud."

"I'd rather stand here."

"And stare at me?"

"That's what I had in mind. Any objections?"

The rise and fall of her breasts caught his attention. "This isn't the time or place," she said and poured **coffee**.

He walked soundlessly to stand behind her. "When **will** there be a right time and place?" Pushing her wouldn't help, but he couldn't stop himself, damn it. The waiting was killing him.

"Soon." She'd felt his proximity and slid sideways along the counter.

He reached for her, saw his dirty hand and withdrew. "Soon, like when?" The old faucet was stiff and when he yanked it on, water splashed ferociously, sending drops over the window, the counters and his parka. "Damn. Look at this. All the pipes in this place need replacing."

"I know that. The plumber quit before he began, remember? And I haven't had time to find another one."

He leaned over the sink and sluiced his face and hands with cold water. A cold shower would have been a better idea. Caitlin was right. This wasn't the moment for him to let go of sexual restraint.

When he'd dried his face he gave her a sheepish smile and held out a still-damp hand.

She shook it. "What's this for?"

"Truce," he said. "Sorry for the slip. But it gets tough, and I think you're a big enough girl to understand that."

"I'm big enough." Her fingers at the collar of his parka were cool. She unzipped and worked the coat off, standing toe-to-toe with him until she could toss it on a chair. "Do you think I don't feel the same things you feel?"

"Sometimes I wonder."

"Did you think that as soon as I called the lawyer about the divorce I'd rush back and haul you off to bed?"

His belly contracted, and the muscles in his buttocks and thighs. "I could dream, couldn't I? Of course I didn't think that. When will you hear more from the lawyer?" She hadn't retreated. Her hands rested on his shoulders, rubbed lightly over his chest and under his arms. This close her eyes were navy blue. The little lines at the corners and between her brows, fascinated him. When she laughed she used all of herself and these lines were her badge of laughter.

The kiss she placed, so carefully, on the side of his neck did something to him that she'd be aware of in about a second if she stayed where she was.

"I'll hear from L.A. in a few days. I already told you the lawyer doesn't expect complications. David's signed his own walking papers." She raised her face, ran her fingers into his hair and kissed him fully on the mouth.

God, he was losing it. He closed his eyes and stood very still, letting her part his lips with hers, pass her tongue just inside. With only their cotton shirts separating skin from skin, he felt her breasts, firm against him, her nipples tensing.

"Caitlin." He framed her face, trying to lean away. Their hips met and she moved her pelvis. "Caitlin, you're right. This is no good. Someone's likely to walk in on us and if we don't stop—now—I won't be able to."

He heard a low noise in her throat. She opened her eyes and the raw desire he read there sent his blood hammering into his ears. "Coffee, do you think, *cari*?" he asked in a stranger's voice. Her nod was in slow motion. Deliberately, without taking her gaze from his, she moved his hands from her face to her breasts, pressed his fingers into her flesh.

Then she sighed but turned away. "Coffee. And then we both have to get to work. It must be time for you to go home."

The warmth of her body was imprinted on his, the picture of how she would look naked burned into his brain. With difficulty he made his legs move. As he passed her he kissed her shoulder but no more, he dare not do anything more.

She put two mugs on the table and a plate in front of

him. Trevor looked at the plate askance. "Are you trying to fatten me up for something...like a heart attack?" Two bran muffins, a pile of sugar biscuits and a wedge of some sort of berry pie crowded each other on a dinner-sized plate.

"You said you wanted them," she said with a smirk. But when her eyes flickered to his, they made contact for the merest instant. She was as ruffled as he. "I offered you your choice and you asked for all three."

"Very funny," he said, hoping he sounded as flip as he intended.

"Mind if I start packing these boxes while you eat? A courier's coming in the morning."

He shook his head. The tension was still there but blessedly ebbing. Nothing was going to be easy for them for a long time. Not the strong sexual drive building or the way they'd deal with the inhibitions that were bound to be there when they did come together as lovers. Anticipating that moment sent a fresh dart of heat into every vital part of him.

"Tell me about shoes," he said, swallowing some of his coffee.

She looked surprised. "Are you serious?" Piles of sketches separated by tissue sheets were rapidly filling a large box.

"Yes, I'm serious. I'm interested in what you do." And he didn't want to be left alone with thoughts that only wanted to go in one direction.

Shrugging, she flipped over leather and fabric swatches, checking numbers she'd written on the backs in ink. "They're practical for some people, a fetish for others. They can be as simple or exotic as you want. I'm crazy about them. I see them in my sleep."

"And I hoped you saw me in your sleep." He grimaced

when she raised her brows at him. "Forget I said that. Go on about the shoes. I want the trivia. And I want to know the serious stuff that you know."

"You start with this. The last." She picked up what looked like a metal-jointed wooden foot and started tapping one spot after another. "Vamp, or top. Cone, this part that goes up the front toward the ankle. Instep, that's obvious. Waist, not so obvious—it's the part from the top of the cone to the shank."

"Slow down. Shank?"

"Stretch between heel and sole. And the front of the opening's the throat, the rest behind the waist is the quarter, the heel curve is here and this—" she turned the last around on the table "—where the toe doesn't sit quite flat, that's the toe spring."

"Got it," Trevor said. In a pig's eye. "Now I'll know."

Caitlin laughed. "Sure you will. But you asked, remember?" Several covered and decorated heels were carefully wrapped and packed in a small box. "The last is made as a mold. There are about thirty-five different measurements used to make a last. Then the same measurements are used in the pattern-making. For mass-produced shoes, the system is different from what happens to mine. With these—" she tapped the box of drawings "—the leather, or whatever is chosen, will be hand cut and assembled into samples. I'll look at those samples when I get to Paris. Then the final products will be made for showing to the couturiers."

"And that's all there is to it?"

The measured look she gave him made him wince.

"That's all you'll be able to take in at one sitting, Trevor. I went to school for years to learn how to do what I do. What do you think the most famous shoes in the world were?''

Blackberry pie was his favorite. ''You're asking me?'' he said around a mouthful of sugar-covered crust.

''No. I just want to show off. Dorothy's ruby slippers from *The Wizard of Oz*. Guess how many pairs of them there really were.''

He groaned. ''Is this a test?''

''Six. They only found one pair when MGM held a wardrobe auction in 1970. They brought a price of $15,000.''

''What happened to the other five pairs?''

''Oh, they show up here and there. Get stolen now and again. There's one pair on display in the Smithsonian now. Did you know Fred Astaire always had a stand-in break in new dancing shoes for him? And Princess Diana's wedding slippers had 134 pearls and 542 mother-of-pearl sequins?''

Just as he was wondering how to stem this flow of information he'd sort of asked for, a small silence caused him to pause with a muffin on the way to his mouth. Caitlin, hands on hips, grinned at him. ''I know you'd like me to tell you *everything* I know about shoes but I have to save something.''

''Oh, don't hold back.'' He felt his own small beginning smile.

''You fraud, you're bored out of your skull and making conversation. And what you just sat through serves you right.'' She plopped on his lap and hugged him fiercely. ''Trevor, tell me it's going to be all right for us. I'm finally feeling that I could be happy and I'm scared to death.''

''I know.'' Hugging her back, he rested his chin on her

head. "But that's called superstition and I'm not giving in to it. What can go wrong?"

"Nothing." She gave him a short hard kiss and eluded his reaching hands. "I needed to hear you say it, that's all."

He heard Thomas's unmistakable heavy tread in the hall. The kitchen door swung open. "Who owns that horrible red monstrosity outside?"

Trevor made faces at Thomas, frowned a warning...and met Caitlin's amused eyes.

"It's mine," she said. "And I don't like it that much, either, although it does do more than twenty miles an hour and it's comfortable. More than I can say for some 'monstrosities.' In fact, I think I do like it, except for the color. I clash with tomato red, but it was the best I could do with only an hour to look."

Thomas made a harrumphing noise and appeared not at all disquieted by his own rudeness. "You won't have the thing in twenty years, I'll tell you that, girl. These modern vehicles fall apart. Planned obsolescence, they call it." He directed his attention at Trevor. "I came in because I saw your car outside. Wondered if we could have a few words." He inclined his head significantly at Caitlin, then at the door. "Can't hang around. I'm expecting company and there's a few things to do."

"Company?" Caitlin straightened, winced as she rotated her shoulders. "Like who?"

"Nosy, women are, Trevor. You noticed that?"

"I've noticed." He was already carrying his mug and plate to the sink.

"Mary's visiting if you must know," Thomas continued. "That's the other reason I stopped. I wanted to tell you she's coming by after school so I can meet her Owen."

Caitlin sighed. "*Her* Owen. He's a friend, that's all. They're only children."

"We were all only children once," Trevor remarked before he could censor himself. "But Thomas didn't mean that the way it sounded," he added quickly.

"No, not at all. A friend, that's all I meant. She's bringing her friend to meet me."

"Okay, you two. Get out of here and let me work. Uncle Thomas, please don't let Mary stay too late. And Trevor—"

He picked up his parka. "Yes, *cari*?"

She colored faintly. "Nothing. Thanks for coming over and working in the garden. See you soon, huh?"

"Soon," he agreed, following Thomas into the hall. How much longer would they have to play this waiting game?

"All right," Thomas said, all business once they were outside with the front door closed. "What progress have you made with the pea brains in this town?"

The frontal attack startled Trevor although he should have expected Thomas to be furious at the treatment Caitlin was receiving. "No progress to speak of. The excuses that were given Caitlin just get repeated. No one budges from his story. They're all too busy to come up here."

"And the gossip goes on. All that talk about her being... Curse their hides! Our girl shouldn't have to put up with that filth. She's one of the best, Trevor."

"You don't have to convince me. But there are always those who like to hang onto a little spice, especially the ones who have dull lives."

Absently, Thomas reached into a sagging jacket pocket and produced his pipe. He stuck it, empty, between his teeth and chewed on the stem. "This Owen is helping a lot with Mary. His sister, too. Mary seems not to care what anyone says as long as the boy stands by her.''

"He'll keep on standing by her," Trevor said. The way Owen felt about Mary was so obvious as to be palpable.

Thomas waved Trevor ahead of him toward the gate. "I've got to ask you something and you're not going to like it."

Trevor swung around. "Let's have it."

"I'd forgotten something, but now it's come back."

"What?"

"Snowy Williams was your father-in-law."

Trevor frowned. "Yes. And he's still a good friend. So is Bronwyn."

"And they're good friends of your parents."

"What does this have to do with anything?"

"How do Sam and Livie feel about Caitlin?" Thomas removed the pipe and stared into the bowl. "Like her, do they? Ready for you to get involved with someone again?"

This old codger was smart. "Ready for me to get involved, but not with someone from the other side of the world who doesn't fit in with their idea of the nice Welsh wife I should have."

"Makes sense that Bronwyn and Snowy would feel the same then, doesn't it?"

They did, but Trevor couldn't bring himself to say so.

"Okay, that's all I wanted to ask you. You on your way now?"

Trevor nodded. He hadn't missed Thomas's inference. "Got to take over from Nip."

"How's business?"

"Fair." Not as good as usual, actually, but he wasn't worrying yet.

Thomas sniffed thoughtfully. "I'll follow you out. Got

an errand to run in town, and I'd better make it quick if I'm going to beat Mary and Owen back.''

He waited for Trevor to drive past the frightful red thing Caitlin had bought before getting into his faithful old Morris and slushing down the lane to the Croft. The Jaguar was out of sight by the time he turned onto the main road. These young people were always in too much of a hurry. Shame they didn't know what he knew about the value of taking life a bit slower.

As he drove he formulated what he intended to say to Sam and Livie, and to the Williamses. Trouble was, he'd become too much of a hermit in recent years. He'd let old friendships wither. It might have been easier to approach the subject at hand if he were on closer terms with the people concerned. Although, if his assumptions were correct and they didn't come around fast, not being on better terms would be fine with him. Thomas drove through town to reach the Esplanade. They would come around, all of them, he'd see to that…nicely if possible, not so nicely if necessary.

The Morgans weren't at home. Grunting, Thomas climbed into his car again and charted his course for the Williamses' house.

Bronwyn opened the door and, before she could settle her usual cheery smile on her pretty face, Thomas caught her little indrawn breath and quick frown.

"Good day to you, Bronwyn. I was wondering if you and Snowy could spare me a few minutes."

Seconds later he was ushered into a comfortable parlor much like his own and filled with solid furniture of the kind he approved. Finding Sam and Livie Morgan ensconced on the couch temporarily unsettled him, but only temporarily. Might as well kill a few birds with one stone.

"Hello there, Livie…Sam." He sat on the chair Bronwyn indicated and ran his hand appreciatively over the brown chrysanthemums embroidered on a plump cushion. He liked the way lace antimacassars were draped over the couch back where heads might touch the fabric. Sensible stuff.

The Morgans mumbled and nodded in unison with Snowy Williams, who stood beside a bulbous oak sideboard, an open bottle of sherry poised over a glass.

"Don't mind if I do," Thomas said as Snowy waved the bottle in his direction.

The comfortable ceremony of pouring and passing took a few silent minutes that Thomas sensed were less pleasant for everyone else in the room than for him. The uncertainty he felt here fueled his confidence, and he began to enjoy himself.

"Nothing like a little Harvey's Bristol," he said, tasting the sherry Snowy gave him. "This is convenient I must say."

"Convenient?" Sam Morgan set his glass down on a small table.

"Finding you all here together. Saves me a trip."

Bronwyn Williams positioned herself on a straight-backed chair near the door as if ready to throw it open for anyone wishing to escape. "You said there was something you wanted to talk about," she said.

"Snowy—" Thomas said after a brief smile at Bronwyn "—you and I used to get along well."

Snowy's ruddy complexion turned a little ruddier. "That's true. We haven't seen enough of you lately."

"No, an old man on his own can go inside himself a bit. My mistake, probably. But I liked you. I always thought you were an honest man."

There was no reply. Thomas didn't expect one. "I've liked all of you."

"What are you getting at?" Sam Morgan stood up suddenly, slopping sherry on his blue pullover.

"I think you know."

Livie found a handkerchief, and Sam didn't seem to notice her dabbing at the spilled sherry. "I don't think we do know," he said.

"Snowy," Thomas turned away from Sam, "do you still own Quality Goods?"

The man's gusty breath sounded like a gale in a tunnel. "The Turners run Quality now. I'm too old to heft groceries these days."

"Yes, but did you sell, or are they managing for you?"

Bronwyn left her post by the door and went to her husband's side. "The Turners are buying the shop from us," she told Thomas, a note of defiance in her voice. "We like them and wanted to give them a chance. One day they might be able to buy us out completely, but they don't have the money yet and we aren't in a hurry."

"So you carry their contract." Thomas turned his attention on Livie Morgan. "Whose idea was it to tell the Turners to stop delivering to Caitlin?"

She looked at Sam.

"I don't think I like what you're suggesting," Snowy said. "The Turners run things their own way. Who they do or don't choose to serve is their affair."

Thomas kept his eyes on Livie who had become shades paler. "I wonder what Trevor would say if he knew his parents had persuaded their old friends, his ex-in-laws, to help make a nice woman's life miserable."

"Don't—"

"That's enough." Sam cut Livie off. "You're making a guess, Thomas Rhys. And it won't stick."

"You're denying that's the way it went?"

Bronwyn held up a hand for attention. "I think there's

already been more than enough said here today. Thomas, we all think a lot of you. Why not leave well enough alone?''

"You did put pressure on the Turners to boycott Caitlin, didn't you?"

"Thanks for coming to see us," Snowy said, and approached the door.

"And it was your idea," Thomas remarked in passing the Morgans.

"I'm not admitting or denying anything," Sam said, "but I will tell you that there are those of us who know how to stick up for our own."

Back on the street, Thomas screwed his eyes up against thickening drizzle. "They stick up for their own, no matter what the cost," he said aloud. "And I stick up for my own. I do believe my memory's getting better and better." He headed for Johnson's Bakery. Time for a word or two with Colin-crust.

"Trevor, where have you been? I just got in myself. I've been looking for you."

"Why? I told you I'd be in Cardiff on business all morning." He blew into his hands as he came through the kitchen door.

Caitlin ignored what he said, grabbed his hand and rushed him back outside and to the cliff path. He'd guess where she was taking him. They'd been to their old hollow many times in the past few weeks.

"Why were you trying to find me?" he asked when she tugged him behind her into the sandy bowl.

Excitement, relief, nervousness muddled her. She'd planned what to say but now it was all a jumble. When she tried to sit down Trevor stopped her. "The sand's too wet."

"So what. We won't melt." And she took off her woolen jacket and spread it out.

"What are you doing, Caitlin? That'll get wet and you'll freeze."

He had to choose this moment to become logical. "You wouldn't have said that when you were eighteen. You'd have shut up and kept me warm inside your parka."

His smile had its usual bone-melting effect. "In other words you think I'm an old fogy. Which I am." But he sat down and unzipped his jacket.

Caitlin huddled beside him, her arms around his warm body and her cheek pressed to his chest.

"Are you going to keep me in suspense much longer?" The parka made a tight cocoon for two.

"I got some news this morning."

Trevor eased up her chin. His eyes were clear, clear gray, his lashes a startlingly dark contrast.

"My lawyer called from L.A. He had good news." The statement was accompanied by a broad grin.

"Unbelievably good. David's actually making things easy. Evidently he's as concerned about Mary as I am and wants to get this over with as quickly as possible so she can see her life won't be changed much. Trevor, I'll be completely free in a matter of weeks."

"Thank God." He stared past her at the sea. "I was so afraid he'd keep you tied up for as long as possible."

"Me, too, and that could have been pretty long. Trevor, I leave for Paris in four days. I'll be there a week. When I get back I have one project to finish, then I'll put things in order and Mary can stay here while I go to L.A. to do whatever I have to do there."

They'd never made any formal declarations, no statements about how they intended to go forward. Was she moving too fast, assuming too much?

Trevor glanced down at her but she couldn't read his solemn expression.

"Anyway," she said, pulling away and wrapping her arms around her knees. "I thought you'd like to know. But right now I'll have to concentrate on Paris."

When he rubbed her back Caitlin closed her eyes. Please let them be meant to stay together.

"Can I come to Paris with you?"

Breath rushed from her lungs. It was going to happen.

His hand became still on her neck. "As far as I'm concerned there's no reason to consider propriety anymore, but we'll do it any way you want if you'll just let me be with you." The words came hurriedly. "Opposite ends of the hotel, different hotels. Let me come. I promise I won't get in the way as long as you wave at me from time to time."

Tears sprang free and trickled down her cheeks.

Trevor massaged her neck. "You aren't saying anything. Was I wrong to ask?"

Caitlin turned her head and smiled at him through the tears. "I was afraid you wouldn't."

14

Watching Trevor watch Paris was more fun than looking at the sights herself. Caitlin leaned across the round, marble-topped table at the sidewalk café where, despite the cold, they'd stopped for coffee. "You like it here, don't you?" she asked.

They'd eaten dinner at Maxim's and afterward walked and walked through the glittering night. "I can't take it all in fast enough," he said.

"Am I wearing you out? With my business, I mean?"

"Not a chance. I was the one who wanted to be a part of everything, remember? I'm so proud of you."

"And I'm proud of you. Although I don't like the way these glamorous French females ogle you."

Trevor smirked. "Well, if you've got it, you've got it." He returned the smile of a passing woman smothered in shiny black furs.

"Keep your eyes on the Arc," Caitlin ordered.

He complied, still smiling. The café was near the Arc de Triomphe. Car headlights streamed in neon lines along the Champs Élysées, illuminating the facade of the great carved arch. Gray by day, it appeared built of gold at night.

"Tenby seems a long way away." The cup Trevor raised sent up puffs of vapor. "I wonder how Thomas is holding up as guardian to a teenager."

"They'll be fine. Only four more days and we'll be home."

His hand covered hers on the table. "I didn't have any idea how successful you are, Caitlin, or how respected. All those people asking your advice. And the show today, you must feel fantastic when you see your shoes modeled and hear the couturiers applaud."

Caitlin looked at their hands and laced her fingers in his. "You applauded, too, I saw you. And you don't know one shoe from another. Maybe they don't, either."

"Rubbish. They do know and I was applauding you for being so wonderful. What happens tomorrow?"

"Photography sessions. Models wearing my shoes will be photographed in different locations. We're using *L'Opéra* for the evening collection."

"The opera house?"

"Yes. And I need to visit my atelier. There are a few modification requests I must talk to my people about."

"Another full day."

"Yes."

They drank coffee, silent for a while.

"You don't have to come if you don't want to, Trevor. Explore. Buy yourself some expensive French clothes."

That brought his laughter. The only panic before they'd left Wales had been over Trevor's wardrobe or lack of one. He'd gone, grumbling, to Cardiff and returned at the end of the day with a passable array of outfits. Tonight he wore a navy suit, pale gray shirt and red tie. And he did turn heads, Caitlin thought with satisfaction.

Once more there seemed nothing to say. She drained her cup and so did Trevor. He paid the waiter.

"Well, my girl, we'd better get you back to the hotel. You'll need rest if you're going to be ready for tomorrow."

The awkwardness had started again as it had on their first two nights here. In the taxi Trevor hailed, they sat far apart on the shiny leather seat. Caitlin already had her hand on the door as the car neared their hotel on elegant Rue de Rivoli. As soon as they stopped, she got out and stood facing the building.

Trevor walked with her over red Persian carpet to the desk in the vast marble and gilt foyer. He claimed two keys and Caitlin started toward the elevator.

"Here."

She turned and Trevor put her key into her hand. "Thank you." This hadn't been what she'd hoped for, this tension so strong it paralyzed her...and made Trevor remote.

"I think I'll have a drink in the bar," he told her. "What time in the morning?"

"Seven." The key was dull in her palm. "Trevor—"

"Yes?"

"Nothing. See you at seven."

He didn't reply or attempt to follow her.

Caitlin reached her room and shut herself inside without putting on a light. She passed the gloomy shapes of massive furniture to lift a sheer drapery and look over the twinkling city. From her window, as must be the case in Trevor's adjoining room, there was a perfect view of the Louvre and the beautiful Tuileries, the gardens that, during the day, teemed with Parisian children taking donkey rides and watching Punch and Judy shows or sailing brightly colored boats on a circular pond. Shivering inside her black cashmere coat, she let the curtain fall. At this time of night, the room, with its high frescoed ceiling, was uninvitingly cool.

Then she heard it, the gentle clicking open and shut of Trevor's door. Hugging herself, she went to sit on the foot of her bed. So much for going to the bar. He'd had time only to make sure she'd gone up in the elevator before coming upstairs himself.

They were both teetering, afraid to go on, desperate at the possibility of moving further away from each other, yet the gap between them seemed too wide to bridge. They had waited too long to be together…too long.

The decision to take two rooms, even if only separated by a door, had been hers. In case they were called from Wales she'd wanted to be certain there was a Mrs. McBride's room, not just a Mr. Morgan's. After all, she'd rationalized to herself, walking through a door wouldn't take any effort. But it had. This all felt so contrived, a setup so that they could sleep together. Trevor was also inhibited by the falseness. She felt that in him.

Caitlin scooted around to turn on a single lamp beside the bed, found her nightgown and robe and went into the gold-and white-tiled bathroom.

Tonight she'd worn her hair up. Trevor had said he liked it that way—but only for a change—and there'd been that self-conscious laugh of his as he'd stepped into personal territory where he so often seemed uncomfortable now.

A quick, cool shower left her glowing. Her hair was still pinned up but the escaping wisps sprang into dark ringlets. The nightie was plain, floor-length peach-colored satin. Broad straps topped a tight, front-buttoned camisole bodice. The robe matched except for the lace insert that ran from mandarin collar to hem.

Rest was exactly what she needed. In fact, rest was mandatory if she was to perform at peak tomorrow.

In bed, she snuggled down, pulled the duvet high over her head and willed her brain into neutral.

Rain clattered in spurts against the window. The first

rain since they'd arrived in Paris. November would be almost over before they left the city. There could even be snow.

The next sound she heard was music, soft, indistinguishable chords. Trevor had turned on his radio. Was he reading? Or lying in the dark as she was, trying to sleep?

Caitlin turned, turned again and sat upright. A faint glow came from the long narrow window. He wasn't making open moves because he'd promised there would be no strings to his being here. The decisions were in her court. He'd made that clear too. Early on she'd been the one with all the restrictions, now it was her turn to wonder what came next—if anything.

Cautiously, careful not to make any sound, she left the bed, pulled on her robe and tiptoed to the door between their rooms. At first the music was all she heard, but then a creak came, and another. Trevor twisted in his bed as she had in hers.

The door in front of her opened smoothly and she was confronted by another. She could knock. He'd come. The small knob glinted. Caitlin touched it, and the second door swung inward. Her heart stopped. She'd swear it stopped completely.

Several lights shone in Trevor's room. She narrowed her eyes, adjusting to the glare. Rather than lying in bed, he sat, fully dressed, in a chair near his window. Hearing the swishing of the door over the carpet, he leaned forward, his eyes fixed on her, both hands gripping the chair arms.

"I—" Her throat closed. His hair was tousled, his tie askew, and his connection to her felt as tangible as if his arms had surrounded her. "The door wasn't locked."

"I know."

She wouldn't pursue that. "Trevor, we've got a problem."

He laughed, a short, mirthless laugh before he buried his face in his hands.

"Could I come and sit with you, please?"

His head rocked and she heard his muffled "yes" before he looked at her fully. "If I have to lie in that bed one more night thinking of you on the other side of the wall, I'm going to go nuts. I'm a strong man, but not that strong."

"I know." She sat gingerly on the side of his bed. "We should have known this was going to be difficult. We're two people who were...we were little more than children together. Then we had separate lifetimes before we came together again. But it seemed like we'd never lost touch. It almost feels like...you're almost a relative. Does that sound sick, or do you understand?"

"Perfectly, sweet lady. It's the old friends-to-lovers routine. Or at least, in my limited understanding that's what it's like. Plus, I feel we set out deliberately on an assignation, which we did. Only I didn't expect it to bother me."

"Same for me. So what do we do?"

He ran his hands into his hair and looked at the ceiling. "We take things very, very, slowly. But we do move forward. Climb into my bed. I want to see you there. I'll just sit here and we'll try to talk. Maybe we can get used to the idea that we both belong in the same bed."

"You are such a darling—"

"Don't...don't say that, please. I'm no darling. What I really want is to explore that, that whatever that fantastic thing you're wearing is and get rid of it as soon as possible."

Heat, cold, goose bumps, a luxurious softening—one

sensation after another chased through Caitlin. "In other words, the hang-ups are all on my side?" She hadn't moved from the side of the bed, but now she did. Smoothly, the satin she wore swishing, she went to her knees between his.

"Uh-uh." He shook his head and averted his face.

The muscles in his thighs sprang, rock hard, beneath her fingers. A passing stroke across his groins brought a muffled groan and pressure on his belly broke his attempt at detachment.

"Don't do that."

"Why? Don't you like it?"

He held her wrists loosely while she pressed again, undid the waist of his pants and pulled his shirt free. With a sigh, she kissed his navel, his ribs, pushing the shirt up higher and higher to reach first one and then the other flat nipple.

He stopped her. "Not so fast, *cari*. Love is a two-way street, they say."

"They?"

"I say." He took off his jacket and his shirt and tie.

Caitlin sat on her heels. She and Trevor weren't the same as they'd been the last time she'd seen him partly naked. Then his body had been rangy, waiting for the maturity she saw now. She'd thrilled at the sight of him in a swimsuit at eighteen. At thirty-seven, tonight, looking at him was a purely sexual delight. But she was older, too. He'd never seen her in less than a one-piece swimsuit before, but the differences were there and he'd surely notice them.

"That bad?" he said when she'd lost track of time. "Is the old body a shock?"

Her answer came with the wandering of her hands over

him, the following kisses that explored inch by inch until his uneven breathing punctured her concentration.

"I'd like to make love to you, Caitlin. Are you ready for that?"

She disengaged gently and got up. "It's what I want."

Trevor rose too and stood beside her. Softly, he smoothed her hair, her cheek. She couldn't seem to move.

"May I take this off?" His fingers rested on the collar of the robe she hadn't bothered to fasten.

"Yes."

It parted from the gown with a sigh and fell noiselessly on the bed.

"Relax, *cari*. We've both got to relax." He must have felt her tense. The skin on her bare arms, her neck, the tops of her breasts, tingled.

His arm went around her waist, and he rested his lips on her shoulder. Then he moved behind her, hugged her carefully to him, crossing powerful forearms across her chest, and she shuddered. She felt his big body drawing her in, the textures of him: roughness of hair, smoothness of skin, tensing of muscle beneath that skin.

Trevor released her. "Don't..." She stopped speaking when she saw him throwing back the quilt and sheet.

"Don't what?" He sat and beckoned.

"Don't let go of me," Caitlin said as he pulled her onto his lap.

"I don't want to.... You're trembling." While he spoke he closed his eyes and brought his lips to hers, just to barely touch and brush and lift away again. "Cold?"

"Scared."

His eyes, when they opened, were dark. The rise and fall of his chest was rapid. "Don't be, please. We can stop this right now. Lie with me. Let me hold you. I'm not a threat, Caitlin. Never think of me as a threat."

With odd fascination she looked at his mouth. He'd paused, waiting for her response. Next she met his eyes. A black band rimmed dark gray. "It's not that. I'm scared I'll disappoint you. I want to be beautiful for you, exciting. But I'm not young anymore, except in here." She put a fist over her heart.

Trevor made a small noise and held her tight. His cheek on hers was rough. "You are absolutely beautiful, dammit." Then he held her face away and she saw his sweet, hesitant smile. "We're a couple of fools, you know that? From the day you got back to Tenby I've been checking my paunch."

Caitlin laughed, incredulous. "You don't have a paunch. You're…you're sexy." She grimaced with the word. "I don't say things like that but it's true, and…and I don't want to talk anymore."

He kissed her again, fully, parting her lips wide, leaning until she clung to him. When he lifted his head they were both breathless. "I want to look at you," he whispered.

She felt absurdly awkward as she stood up in front of him and fumbled with the buttons on her bodice.

"Let me do it." He pulled her between his legs and, concentrating fiercely, worked the tiny pearl buttons from their satin bound holes.

Gradually the pressure across her chest relaxed, to be replaced by Trevor's caressing hands inside the gaping fabric. His lips touched her, then kissed her breasts carefully, repeatedly. Caitlin stared down at his rumpled hair, his moving head, his large hands that seemed tanned against her pale skin. She felt small, disappearing, under those hands.

Without ceasing in the persistent pressure of kiss after kiss, he slid the straps from her shoulders and let her gown fall about her feet.

"You're so fair. You always were." He did glance up into her face then, and he was flushed.

Caitlin didn't move. Her skin was electric, transparent, made up of a million raw and aching nerve ends. He brushed his mouth across her belly, passed his tongue into the hollows in front of her hips.

Instinctively, she put a hand over her side.

Trevor paused. "Sensitive?" He smiled and pushed his fingers under hers to clasp her bottom.

"Stretch marks," she muttered, embarrassed. "I forgot them."

He frowned up at her. "Oh." The puckering of his brow softened and he bit his lip as if smothering a laugh. "You mean Mary marks. So what, my love. Badges of honor, aren't they?"

Caitlin put her hands over her eyes. "You always say the right things."

He covered her breasts again, and she started. When she looked down, it was at the back of his neck and her knees weakened. His mouth, his tongue, worked and a shudder of impatience gathered under her skin, grew before her head fell back. She didn't protest, hardly thought of his giving, her receiving. The stirring quickly became wonderful, searing release and he caught her as she slipped down against him.

After a few seconds while she clung to him, gasping, he lifted her onto the bed. The sheet felt blessedly cool and slightly rough now. Doubt had gone. She watched, confident, languid, while he shed the rest of his clothes. The broad patch of dark hair on his chest narrowed to a slender line over his stomach and then widened again. He was fully erect and there was an instant of hesitation in her. It had been so long.

"I'm not as beautiful as you," he said, catching her look.

"Yes, you are." She held out her arms.

He lay down and pressed close, the friction of hair, the solidness of muscle urgent now. Covering her uncertainty Caitlin said, "It's good one of us can take charge."

Trevor raised his face from her shoulder. "If you mean me, I'll be glad to oblige. Now, be quiet and just let it happen…and trust, sweet, trust."

He rolled over her and saying anything would have been impossible. His tongue searched hers out and her hips raised to meet his. Rigid hardness nudged her belly.

Reaching between them, she closed her fingers around him. Pulsing heat responded. She stroked, long, smooth, and his face left hers. Thrilled, her own heart hammering, she watched tense lines deepen around his eyes and mouth. When his head fell back she forced herself up to kiss the pulse in his throat.

"Enough," he said and took her hand away. Sweat gleamed on his skin.

He paused long enough to kiss her lips and she wound her arms around his neck. But he shifted again, pushed his knees between hers until he knelt over her. With his hands under her hips he eased her up. She felt the first tentative pressure, and, almost not soon enough, the thrust. She came close to crying out, squeezed her eyes shut instead and moved with him. Looking down she saw their mingled hair, hers only slightly lighter than Trevor's. Incredibly she had to stop a laugh of pure joy. The length of him was buried inside her at last.

This was right. She ranged her hands over his slick shoulders while he withdrew almost free of her then entered again, longer, stronger, deeper each time until sensations fused: rough linen on sensitive skin, slipping, openness, waiting, fullness.

A cry came, and another. Surely not hers? Not Trevor's? Strangers moaned wildly in the night and Caitlin could no longer think. Feeling was all. She lay very still, heavy, slid away into soft darkness.

Afterward, when her mind cleared, she slowly became aware of the lights that had never been dimmed or turned off, of the cooling dampness on her skin, on Trevor's skin.

"You are lovely, *cari.*"

His voice forced her almost back to reality. Propped on an elbow, he stared down at her.

"So are you," she said.

"Hmm." He kissed her. "Lovely am I? I didn't know that. I do know I'm in love."

There might never be another moment like this. She couldn't believe she'd be allowed to feel so explosively happy more than once. "I'm glad you said that," she scooted to lie on top of him, fitting her hips over his, "because I'd hate to be the only one of us in that incurable condition."

"We've got a reception committee."

Caitlin looked through the windshield of the Jag and saw Thomas hovering in the doorway of his house. "Thank goodness we're home on time," she told Trevor as he put on the emergency brake. "I'm glad to see him, but I'm not ready for reality. I guess that sounds selfish."

He switched off the ignition and pulled her into his arms. "Sounds the way I feel," he said and kissed her slowly. "I'd like to be alone with you forever, but we have to come down to earth sometime—partly anyway."

She smiled, rested her cheek on his. "Ready?"

"Let's do it."

Caitlin got out of the car. "Hi, Thomas," she called, pushing open the gate. "The wanderers return. Are you still in one piece?"

He wore his saggy overcoat and worn cap. "Don't I look as if I am?" he said.

Caitlin glanced at Trevor who was at her shoulder. Thomas's comment was in character but the tone was wrong, subdued.

"You look as feisty as ever." Trevor put down a suitcase and shook Thomas's hand. "We were afraid looking after a teenager for a week might finally break you."

"Where is Mary?" Caitlin looked past him. "She's home from school, isn't she?"

Thomas's cap came off. He rolled it, unrolled it. "She's fine now. Doctors only kept her a few hours. Out in less than a day, she was."

Caitlin opened her mouth. No air went in or out. "Mary's ill?" She felt Trevor's arm go around her.

"Now, now," Thomas said, sounding tetchy. "I told you Mary's all right. The doctors said she's got an ulcer, and they've given her some pills. It was like you said, Caitlin, she didn't eat properly for too long. Then with her father and—"

"What about her father? She was okay when I left. I thought she was happier."

Thomas closed the door behind him. "She was. She is. David called her after you left, and she got upset. Then he called again. Seems he wants her to understand he's not the one who decided on the divorce." He jammed the cap back on.

"Bastard," Trevor muttered. "He made her ill."

"It's my fault," Caitlin said. "I shouldn't have gone away at a time like this."

"You had to." Trevor sounded close to rage. "You

had a job to do. The man knew you were going. That's why he phoned when he did—to victimize Mary when you weren't around to protect her. He's still going to be a problem."

Caitlin couldn't put one thought behind another properly. "Please, don't talk like that about Mary's father. He didn't mean to hurt her."

Thomas coughed. "Mary's at the hospital now. She went down to wait with Owen."

"What?" Caitlin turned on him. "You said she was fine. Why is she at the hospital?"

Thomas didn't look at her. Awkwardly, he took hold of Trevor's upper arm. "You're not to listen to anything they say, boy."

This was mad. "Please," Caitlin interrupted, "why did Mary have to go back to the hospital?"

"It happened after practice yesterday afternoon."

She looked from Thomas to Trevor who frowned before he gritted his teeth. "An injury. One of the boys got hurt. Who? How bad is it?"

"Didn't get hurt." For the first time Thomas looked old to Caitlin.

"Trouble. Someone's in trouble again?" Color began returning to Trevor's face.

"You'll want to go," Thomas said quietly. "There's a couple in trouble but that's nothing. It's young Will Colly. He had a heart attack."

15

Caitlin couldn't stay in a chair. She paced, passing Trevor at each turn. Mary sat between Owen and Thomas in front of Will Colly's glass cage in the intensive care unit of Pembroke Infirmary.

Beyond the glass, Len Colly stood at the foot of his son's bed, clutching the rail while a nurse checked monitors and several leads running from Will's still form to a phalanx of hanging bags.

The nurse said something to Len and the man nodded before coming into the hall. His flaccid face was pasty, scored with gray lines of fatigue.

Owen was the first to move. "How is he, Mr. Colly?"

Caitlin was struck afresh by the boy's maturity. Mary got up and he held her hand. "Is Will going to be okay?" she asked.

Colly sat in one of the chairs the teenagers had vacated. He didn't answer Mary or Owen.

Mary's pallor was more noticeable than usual, but Caitlin had spoken with a doctor who assured her that careful diet, rest and control of stress in the girl's life would bring her full health. Anorexia had been mentioned, and the man had explained that Caitlin's concern had been well-founded, that anorexia often arose in children caught in destructive home situations, but that Mary had been fortunate and hadn't succumbed to the disease. Caitlin hated listening to the suggestion that because of her and David their child had come close to what might have been a fatal illness.

"Len." Trevor stood in front of Colly. "How is he?"

The man looked up, recognition dawning slowly in his dull eyes. "You." He lumbered to his feet. "This is your fault. You're going to suffer for this. Every one of us parents is going after your neck, Morgan."

Instinctively, Caitlin went to Trevor. He held an arm in front of her. "What are you saying, Len?"

"My boy's going to live. But no thanks to you and your damned pushing. And he's not going to be the same for a long time. What am I going to do? You tell me that. How am I going to look after a boy the way he'll need it?"

"Mr. Colly," Caitlin said, shaken. "I'm so sorry."

He brushed her aside, and Thomas moved more rapidly than Caitlin had ever seen him move. "That'll do Len. You're upset, but don't stop thinking, man."

Colly didn't appear to hear Thomas. He moved closer to Trevor. "It's all coming out, Morgan. How you drove them. Winning was everything to you, right? Trevor Morgan the big hero with the winning team. And now my boy's lying in there." He pointed through the glass. "And young Best and one of the others are being kept by the coppers."

"Hold on. Just hold up." Trevor's nostrils flared. "We'll deal with accusations against me later. What did Robin do this time?"

"Smashed up a couple of phone booths," Len Colly said distractedly. "More of your influence. You've got them all so high on themselves they don't know how to cope."

"Sh." The nurse bustled from Will's room, her shoes

squishing on rubber tile. "I'll have to ask you all to leave."

Len subsided into a chair and Trevor spread his hands helplessly.

"You go," Thomas said. "There's nothing you can do here, any of you. I'll wait with Len."

"I can't leave," Trevor said.

"You can and you will." Thomas gave him a significant look. "This isn't the place for you."

Len bowed his head. Limp wrists rested on his knee.

Without another word, Trevor swung around and strode to the elevator with Caitlin close behind. Owen and Mary caught up with them before the doors closed. Nothing was said on the way to the ground floor or as they walked outside into a freezing November day.

"Mrs. McBride," Owen put an arm around Mary's shoulders. "Mary and I came on the bus. There isn't much room in Mr. Morgan's car. Would it be all right if we went back to Tenby by bus? We'd like to try to visit Will and they said we might be able to later in the day."

"Good idea," Trevor said before Caitlin could respond.

She controlled the urge to say she didn't agree, that he'd better see to his own problems before he told her daughter what she could or couldn't do. "That'll be fine, Owen. But Mary shouldn't be out too long. She needs extra rest for a while."

"I'll get her back early." Owen smiled down on Mary and Caitlin's heart did something funny. Watching these two was like watching an old and familiar movie.

Trevor took her elbow and they walked toward the car park, leaving Owen and Mary to go back inside the hospital.

In the car, Trevor rested his head back and closed his eyes. Caitlin stared straight ahead at the impressive bulk of Pembroke Castle, its wonderfully preserved turrets and towers stark against the gray sky. There was only a cottage hospital in Tenby and emergencies were brought here to Pembroke, a larger town some miles farther west.

Finally Caitlin said, "It isn't your fault, you know. Not all of it."

"I know that. I— What do you mean, 'not all of it'?"

Now she was going to have to confront him honestly, hold back none of her misgivings. "What does winning mean to you?"

He jerked upright and turned toward her. "I don't understand you."

"I think you do. When you're out there with those boys winning is everything, and your intensity is bound to be transmitted to the team. You hound them, Trevor, yell and hound them. You call them names and drive them when they're already exhausted."

"What…"

"I know, I know. What am I talking about? You haven't thought about it, have you, Trevor? I've seen you and it frightens me. I think you've made them afraid to disappoint you. It scares me. That side of you makes me feel we're strangers."

"Hey." He caught her wrist and his fingers hurt. "How can you say you feel we're strangers, on any level, after what we've shared?"

Caitlin's stomach rolled unpleasantly. "I'm not explaining very well."

"Aren't you? You think I am to blame for Will's heart attack and for some of the kids getting into trouble with the police."

"I didn't say that."

"Yes, you did. God, I feel like you kicked me."

With a deliberate motion, she wrenched her wrist away.

"You're going to have to deal with this any way you can. I love you. Nothing's going to change that. But I want to be sure we don't rush on without knowing everything about each other, so think about it, huh? That's all I ask."

The drive back to Tenby was tense. Neither of them spoke, but Trevor thought a great deal. After he dropped Caitlin at the cottage, he returned to the White Knight. The warmth, the unspoiled joy of a few hours ago seemed a remembered hallucination.

Nip met him at the door, uneasiness in every line of his body, in the rapid sliding away of his eyes every time they caught Trevor's.

Two hours later, after he'd dealt with lists of business questions and fielded a dozen angry calls from parents, he took the phone off the hook, asked Nip to take over and went up to his flat.

With a large Scotch in hand, he set light to the fire in the sitting room and stretched out on the couch. He'd been threatened with everything, from a boycott of the pub to litigation and veiled hints of bodily harm.

An insistent thought kept hammering at his brain. There had been more than one occasion when Will Colly hadn't looked well, but he, Trevor, had chosen to ignore the symptoms. Hell. He wasn't a doctor. Why would he even imagine that a great strapping boy like Will had a weak heart? Damn, but he wished he had imagined it. The poor kid.

Exhausted, he closed his eyes and drifted. Caitlin thought he'd been too hard on the team. Had he? Was he an ambitious man in disguise? Could the ruthlessly competitive spirit he'd once accepted and enjoyed still be lurking inside the shell known as Trevor Morgan, gentle man?

He wished the tapping in his head would go away. He

rolled his face toward the back of the couch and his eyes flew open. The tapping was coming from the door.

"Come in." He swung his feet to the floor, remembering the Scotch in time not to slosh it. Pushing his hair back, he set down the glass and stood up.

"Trevor, can we talk to you? Nip said to come up and ask."

He stayed where he was, head bowed. "Hello, Caitlin." When he looked up, not just Caitlin, but Owen Trew and Mary waited, watching him anxiously.

"Sit down, sit down." He cleared his throat and made another attempt to bring order to his hair.

Mary approached him. "Are you all right, Trevor?"

Her narrow face was so sweet, her dark eyes perfectly innocent. No wonder Owen's heart was lost at the grand old age of seventeen. "I'm all right, Mary. What brings me all this good company?"

"Owen's got something to tell you," Caitlin said. Their eyes locked over Mary's head and Trevor felt his lips part as if they'd touched hers.

"Will made me promise I never would," Owen said, "but I've got to."

Trevor sank back onto the couch. He sighed when Caitlin sat beside him and rubbed his thigh. Owen took up a position with his back to the fire while Mary continued to hover.

"Mr. Morgan, you do work us hard, but not too hard—most of the time."

Trevor grunted. He was tired.

"Will's a special case. He's never felt worth much. His mom left when he was a little kid and his dad's never kept a job. That's why he put on the tough act, because he was covering up. He always said he was going to make it with rugger, be someone."

Owen's eyes glistened. "You know what I'm saying? He never felt like *anything*."

"I understand." Damn it, how could he have been so insensitive?

"Tell him the rest," Caitlin said. Trevor put his hand on hers. He wanted her in his arms. And he didn't want to think.

Owen looked at the toes of his sneakers. "He never wanted anyone to know he felt ill because it might have stopped him playing. He only told me."

Trevor shifted to the edge of the couch. "How long ago was this?"

"It happened a lot. Mostly after practice. He'd break out in a sweat and sit down. Once he told me he felt faint, and he held his chest. But I never guessed. Kids don't have heart attacks."

"Don't worry," Trevor said. "You weren't to know. If anyone should have noticed, it was me. I did wonder if he was feeling okay a couple of times, but he always covered up so well—and quickly now that I think about it. Poor kid. Someone had better let them know at the hospital how long this has been going on."

"They know. After you left, Mary and I went back up to the unit, and old man Colly was letting Mr. Rhys have it."

Trevor leaned farther forward. "So you let him have it?"

"Yeah. Drunken windbag. He's given Will a hell of a life. Now the doctors know he's probably been ill a long time."

"It wasn't anything to do with you, Trevor," Caitlin said in a low voice, rubbing his back.

"Not directly," he agreed, "but I played my part. I thought about what you said earlier. I hated it, but there's some truth in there, *cari*, and I'm going to have to do something about it.''

Mary touched his shoulder. ''Mom and I were wondering if you could come back to the cottage for dinner. Owen's going to be there, and Uncle Thomas said he'd come by afterward. You must be tired and hungry.''

Olive branches in all directions. And he was going to grab them, dammit. ''I am tired and hungry,'' she said, pulling Caitlin with him as he stood up. ''And if I hang around here I'm going to be lonely, too.''

Thomas followed Bronwyn Williams into her familiar parlor. The cast was as it had been on his last visit, even the positions were the same, except for Snowy, who stood with his back to the room, staring through the window.

''Afternoon.'' Thomas checked his watch. ''Almost evening.''

No one laughed. And no one offered him sherry.

''Been busy, have you?'' Snowy said, continuing to overlook the shadowed street. ''Asking lots of questions all over town, they tell me?''

''Who are 'they,' Snowy? Colin-crust, perhaps—and Andrew Briggs and one or two others you've got in your pocket?''

That brought Snowy swinging to face him. ''You're still making guesses, Thomas Rhys. A disappointed old man, you are, with too little to take up his time. A meddler.''

Without being asked, Thomas sat down. ''I've hit a few nerves, though, haven't I?''

''I wish you would leave this alone.'' Livie Morgan's voice was thin and troubled. ''We all make mistakes. I've certainly made mine. Why not let—''

''Livie, don't—''

"Leave her alone, Sam." Thomas nodded at Snowy. "He's the one with the real problem. Not that it'll do him any harm as long as he stops what he's been doing now."

Bronwyn smacked a hand on the sideboard. "He's not doing anything. Nothing wrong."

"And you intend to stick to that story, Snowy?"

Sam Morgan stood up and looked as if he was considering walking out.

"Don't go, Sam," Thomas said. "You need to hear this, too, because I don't believe my first assumptions about you wanting to hurt Caitlin were right. Oh, you went along all right. But I think you did it because you love your son and you were convinced your friend here was right."

"All I did was advise Trevor to be careful. He's already had one disappointment because of outside influence."

Thomas sighed. "And Snowy had you believing Caitlin was a dangerous outside influence?"

"I didn't say that."

"Snowy," Thomas said, "you blame Trevor for Gwen's death, don't you?"

"No!"

"I think you do, even if you don't recognize it. You blame him and you can't stand the idea of him having a life without Gwen. That's why you set Sam and Livie against Caitlin."

"Get out of my house."

"Will you stop poisoning this town against my niece?"

"Get out, I tell you."

Silence raced in. Nobody moved.

"All right. I gave you your chance. Now we'll do it my way." Thomas fumbled for his pipe, needing something to hold. "There's a word for what I'm about to do.... Well, I'll trust the Lord to forgive me." He just hoped he could pull this off. What he was going to present had shaky foundations in the proof area.

"Please leave us alone."

He glanced with pity at Bronwyn. "I will soon. Snowy, I was talking to Colin-crust about his early days in Tenby."

A flat stare was Snowy's reply.

"I mentioned that you and I had had a chat, and he seemed to think you'd said more than you had."

That brought a "damn you" from Snowy.

Carefully, Thomas took an envelope from his inside jacket pocket and eased out several yellowed newspaper clippings. He put them on his knee and kept a hand over them.

"What have you got there?" Snowy's face turned ruddy.

"All in good time," Thomas told him. "Colin must have thought you were a white knight when you two met. He told me it was at the hospital in Pembroke after his only child had been stillborn. Bronwyn had just delivered Gwen."

A small noise from Bronwyn made him dislike what he was doing even more.

"Colin said you'd promised never to let anyone know the truth about his background."

Snowy smashed a fist into the other palm. "And I never did. If he talked about it to you, it was because you tricked him."

"That's as may be. But the truth is that Colin confided in you that he'd been in prison for robbery and that he considered himself responsible for his baby's death. He said the stress his wife was under because of him caused it. He was sure of that. And there he was with no job and

a sick, depressed wife. But you helped him out. That was good of you, Snowy."

"Yes, it was. I got my father to give him a job at the shop. Nobody else would have hired him. Jobs were hard to come by, for anyone."

Thomas snorted. "Your father hired him all right. For half what it would have cost to hire anyone else. And he worked him twice as hard...as a favor of course."

"So what?" Snowy puffed up his chest. "None of that's a crime."

"Threatening to ruin a man's reputation if he doesn't do what you want isn't a crime? Preying on the little bit of pride he and his wife have scraped together, isn't that a crime?"

"Not one that would hold up in court."

Thomas picked up the fragile clippings. "We're not talking about court. We're talking about reputations and money and how the two can be used against a man if they're too dear to him. My father—" he looked directly at Snowy "—my father always said that every man has a weakness. Find it and the man is yours. You found Colin's and used it, and I've found yours."

"What the hell do you mean?" The ruddiness had faded to be replaced by doughy pallor. The Morgans and Bronwyn seemed fixed in place and unable to speak.

"Colin's capable of revenge, too. He made a mistake because he was poor and he paid for his stupidity, but he doesn't like you, and I don't blame him. He found these for me. Seems he started collecting interesting little items about your family—particularly your father—shortly after he went to work at the shop."

"He couldn't have found out anything about my father," Snowy said and snapped his mouth shut.

"What is this? What is he suggesting?" Sam asked.

Snowy fidgeted with a jacket button. He wouldn't look at Sam.

Distaste rippled up Thomas's spine but the only thing to do was press on. "Your father came to Tenby from a mining town." He glanced at a clipping. "You would have been eleven. I remember when you showed up at school. That was a few months after this was printed. Your father's first name was James, wasn't it?" He read aloud:

> "After the contract settlement, Jim Williams, local miner and union representative, was unavailable for comment. It's said he's planning to move and isn't divulging where he and his family are going. Williams, so our informants tell us, will set up a business, probably in the south. There is speculation about how Williams, supposedly a man of very modest means, has accumulated enough money to make this move."

"I think you've said about enough." Snowy's chest expanded. "Point taken. Now leave."

"And let you weasel a way out with Trevor's people? Sorry. They deserve to know exactly what you're capable of. Colin explained that your father had a lot to do with a dispute between the miners and management. The dispute was settled—very unsatisfactorily for the workers. Afterward, your father came here and set himself up in a lucrative grocery business."

A shuffling sound came from Bronwyn who crumpled a crocheted apron in her hands.

"Getting the Turners to stop delivering Caitlin's groceries was easy. They owe you a lot of money. And by the way, don't think it isn't obvious that if the economy

were better you wouldn't have carried a contract for them. Colin was more of a challenge. He resisted asking his wife to leave her housekeeping job because they need the income, but the old threat of revealing his prison record worked. And at your *suggestion* Colin was able to keep Andrew Briggs away from Caitlin's, because Briggs owes him money he's probably never going to be able to pay back. Same old thing. Find the Achilles' heel.''

"Shut your mouth." Snowy fumed now, his eyes narrowed beneath shaggy brows. "You can't prove a thing."

"Oh, I think I could with these." He held up the clippings. "And with what Colin knows. Only there's no point. But I'm going to finish what I started. One minute your father was a union representative and a miner. The next he had enough money to come here and buy this house—" he looked around "—and set himself up with a nice business. Someone convinced those miners that management had their best interests at heart and they settled for a terribly inadequate contract. And that someone came out of it smelling financially like a rose. I don't suppose we want to talk about management payoffs...and selling out friends?"

Thomas's last impression as he left the room was of Livie Morgan's horrified face.

The Morris seemed to have found new life. On the way up the Croft he pressed his foot to the floor and the jerky speedometer hit thirty. He whistled. He hadn't whistled in a long time.

Caitlin's Ford was in front of the gate and he pulled close behind to park. Red wasn't such a bad color.

He hurried to the door and entered the cottage without knocking. Voices came from the sitting room and he went in that direction.

"Evening all."

Trevor was there, thank God. Finally they were going to get everything sorted out.

"Good evening, Thomas Rhys."

He frowned and peered to his right at a woman with short frosted hair and bright blue eyes.

She came forward, her hand extended. "Don't tell me you don't recognize me. That's not very flattering."

"Good Lord," he said before he could stop himself. "Eileen Allen in the flesh."

Trevor paused on the bottom step from his flat. He didn't have to go into the pub tonight. This had already been one of the worst days of his life.... Why add to the misery? Because it was now or later, and now would be easier on his blood pressure. Facing his friends and acquaintances couldn't be put off forever.

Nip came from the storeroom, carrying a box of packaged nuts. He saw Trevor and hesitated. "Busy night," he commented but the banal remark said much more. Trevor felt the man's tension.

"What's the mood like?"

Now Nip looked straight at him. "Like they're waiting for the big event. There's two sides in there, Trevor. It's early yet. I'm worried about what'll happen when they get more beer under their belts."

"We'll cope," Trevor said, more shortly than he knew he should have. "Business as usual." And he followed Nip into the bar.

At least working, regardless of the atmosphere, would help keep his mind off Caitlin and the way her mother had treated him. Mrs. Rhys had hoped he wouldn't be upset if she asked him not to stay for dinner. She needed time alone with her daughter. Caitlin had started to protest, but he'd insisted on leaving anyway, as had Thomas.

He and Thomas hadn't spoken before getting into their cars. But the look that passed between them said it all. They were both unnerved at the prospect of the effect Eileen Rhys might have on Caitlin.

His first impression upon approaching the counter was of a still and silent tabloid of players in the foreground against an obliviously animated backdrop.

Not bothering to attempt a smile, he surveyed glasses and tankards, spread his hands on the bar in his usual waiting attitude…and waited. Now he really blessed the stereo he'd installed. At least those patrons who weren't involved were less likely to notice the pending floor show.

"All right then, Trevor?" Colin-crust sniffed and shifted; squared his narrow shoulders. "Had a good trip, have you?"

"Fine, thanks." He could feel the subtle parting between friend and foe, the choosing of sides. Colin was a friend and Trevor was grateful.

Barry Thompson, already swaying, stood with feet spread. Ray Best was at his shoulder and Reggie Hearn, father of Michael Hearn, the best seventeen-year-old fly half Trevor had ever seen, slouched on Barry's other side. A silent ring surrounded them—all faces Trevor knew, more parents, friends of parents. He met each pair of eyes squarely, or tried to, before some of them darted away.

"Any empty glasses?" he asked.

Barry immediately slapped his down and Trevor pulled him a pint.

"I've never been to Paris," Colin said. "Don't think I'd like the food. All them snails and froggy legs."

No one laughed but Trevor smiled at Colin. "None of it holds a candle to one of your pasties, Colin."

Nip moved behind him, serving customers who were

forced to approach on either side of the entrenched group apparently poised for battle.

In Colin's corner, a foot or so separating them from the others, stood Andrew Briggs, Jon Ellis and, surprisingly, Jimmy Trew, Owen's dad. But the presence Trevor felt most strongly was that of Len Colly, seated on a stool a little apart from the others. He drank morosely, looking at no one, saying nothing.

"All right, then," Barry said, rolling onto his heels. "No more pussyfooting around. What have you got to say for yourself, Trevor Morgan?"

This was it. He crossed his arms but didn't respond.

"Yeah," Ray Best said, "and what are you gonna do about it? We aren't taking any more from you, Trevor Morgan. You've finally done a bit too much, boyo, gone too far. And we want satisfaction."

Still Trevor didn't respond. Some sense he hadn't known he possessed warned him to let them spit out their ire, mix it up between themselves first.

"Come on, Trevor," Barry said, pushing his beefy face over the counter, "let's have it. What are you going to do about it?"

Trevor took a breath but before he could break his self-imposed silence, Jon Ellis stepped in. "About what, Barry? What is Trevor supposed to do something about?"

Barry laughed and the effect wasn't pleasant. Saliva rimmed his stained teeth. "Thanks to him there's a boy lying in Pembroke Infirmary."

"That's right," Reggie Hearn echoed, pushing closer. "Will's never going to be the same. Isn't that right, Len?"

Len stared into his beer, raised his glass to drain it and didn't answer.

"Another one, Len?" Trevor asked automatically.

Len pushed the glass toward him.

"Man's in shock," Ray Best announced, and sucked in his lower lip over toothless gums. He usually discarded his dentures when he planned a hard night's drinking. "Plastic choppers" got in the way, he'd told Trevor.

Len's head was soon tipped back and the fresh beer steadily left the glass to run down his throat. He wiped his mouth with the back of his hand and waved for service.

Now Trevor fixed him with a worried eye. Silence wasn't Len's forte. Certainly the man must be upset, his presence here at all seemed odd, but that he wasn't blustering and adding his accusations to the others made no sense.

Barry Thompson pounded the counter. "There's men here who want retribution, for...for...trouble," he finished lamely. "Len there had a boy who was going somewhere. The man had things to look forward to. Now he's got an invalid on his hands and no way to pay for the kind of care he needs."

A chorused assent went up.

"Hold it," Jon Ellis said. "Just hold on. Why is it Trevor's fault Will got sick? And why is it his fault the boys got into trouble? That's what you're all suggesting, isn't it?"

"You're damn right." Ray Best approached Jon and shoved his face close. "If Trevor hadn't worked the lads so hard, Will would be all right today. And if he hadn't pushed the way he did, the whole team wouldn't be so pent up they had to run wild to let off steam. But he wanted to be the big man around town, didn't he now? Particularly in front of his fancy lady friend."

"That'll do it." Trevor made to open the counter flap but Colin-crust and Andrew Briggs moved as a man to hold it down. Frustrated, Trevor reached to grab Ray and missed. "Leave Caitlin out of this."

"I don't think you're going to be able to." Jimmy Trew, speaking low and clear, had the effect of a gunshot. No one moved, or spoke. "First, Trevor, you've got to recognize that there are people in this town who are too small-minded to accept what they call 'strangers.' They're suspicious of anything different or new and they love a good gossip."

Barry shifted toward Jimmy who stopped him with a hard stare. "Truth hurts, doesn't it, Barry? You don't even have a boy on the team but you're enjoying every minute of this, and mixing it up. The Knights' problems started long before Caitlin McBride ever came to Tenby. She's a good woman and deserves a bit of respect."

"I'll second that," Andrew Briggs said, and Colin nodded agreement.

Trevor hardly knew Jimmy, but looking at his solid body, the face that had been the pattern for Owen's, he decided he'd like to know him better.

"Len," Ray Best said, and put an arm around the seated Colly who was downing yet another beer. "What do you say, Len? We're all behind you in this. That's why we're here. You've got a problem, and he—" with this he pointed at Trevor "—he's the cause, man. He gave our boys big dreams and big opinions of themselves and now we're supposed to go on like nothing's happened."

"Stow it, Ray," Andrew said. "This isn't Trevor's fault. Leave Len—"

Before he could finish Barry Thompson grabbed his sleeve. "Shut your mouth, Briggs," he yelled. "Shut your damn mouth!" He hauled Andrew close an instant before Jimmy Trew went into action. His forearm came down beside Barry's bull neck, and the man howled...but he let Andrew go.

The counter flap hit wood with splintering force as Trevor shot between the three men. "That's it," he shouted. "Enough."

Now they had the attention of everyone in the bar. Smoke hung over them all, bluish and drifting and stinging when it hit the eyes and nose. The fire popped and fizzled. In his cage, Spot sidestepped scratchily back and forth on his perch.

"Enough," Len Colly muttered, and all eyes turned on him. He slid from the stool and reached for the counter, missed the first time but clasped its rim on a second attempt. His pallor was deathly, and what little hair he had stuck out from his head in grimy wisps. "Enough, enough, enough."

"Sit down," Trevor urged him, putting aside what he'd set out to do—to get Barry and friends out of the pub. "Come on, Len, sit down. You don't look well."

"You don't look well," Barry mimicked. "Tell him, Len. Tell him why you don't look well...since he doesn't seem to know. And tell him you're going to sue his ass for the trouble he's brought on you. A lot of people are going to sue him."

Len turned slowly, hanging onto his support with whitened fingers. He passed a hand over drooping eyes and swiveled his head a little as if to see Trevor more clearly. "I'm sorry, Trevor," he said.

"Tell him to—"

"Shut up." Someone gave Barry a shove.

"I'm sorry, Trevor." Len began to slide down. His elbows rested on the counter now. "I knew," he said. "I knew he wasn't good. When he was a little lad they told me his heart might be a problem. But my Mary had left, see. There was only Will and me, and...and he looked healthy, didn't he?'' His eyes found Trevor's.

"Yes, he did," Trevor said quietly.

"He was going to pull us both up out of it. I never amounted to much, but Will was going to do it for his dad. We were going places."

Trevor put an arm around Len's waist and grimaced with the man's slumping weight. "It's all right, Len. Let's get you home. Will's going to be fine. The doctors said so."

Jimmy Trew wordlessly held Len from the other side.

The crowd parted as they moved toward the door.

Len resisted, made an attempt to straighten. He turned his face to Trevor. "It wasn't you, it was me. I almost killed my boy."

16

Caitlin felt as if someone were running a razor blade up and down her spine. Her teeth locked together. But she kept smiling...until her mother kissed Mary and walked her to the front door when she left for school.

"That boy's out there," Eileen said as she returned to the kitchen. "I can't imagine what you're thinking of, Caitlin."

"Owen's a very nice young man, Mother, and he's good for Mary."

Eileen made a disdainful moue. "You didn't have a great track record for picking male winners at Mary's age, either."

Caitlin prayed for patience. "Okay. There wasn't time to talk last night, so let's have it. Why did you come to Wales when I asked you not to?"

"Oh, don't be hard on your poor old mother. You know I only want to see you."

The guilt Caitlin was supposed to feel didn't materialize. "You were rude to Trevor—and Thomas."

"Thomas always was difficult."

"Don't evade the subject. You were rude."

A gusty sigh accompanied her mother's graceful descent to a chair. "I've never like these dark, ominously Welsh men."

"Come on, Mother. You married a Welshman and you adored him."

"He had red hair."

Caitlin's patience was definitely cracking, no, fracturing completely. "Why are you here?"

"Because I need you. And you need me."

"You had no right to tell Trevor to leave and stay away."

"All I did was ask for a couple of days alone with my daughter and granddaughter. Was that so much to ask?"

Their conversations always went in circles. "It wasn't for you to suggest."

Eileen shuffled idly through the photographs Caitlin had brought back from Paris. "I was surprised you took him with you."

"I'm a big girl, Mother." She should bring up the letters her mother had intercepted.

"Maybe not as big as you think you are. You're gentle, Caitlin, too gentle. A persuasive man could charm you into almost anything. He is good-looking, though, in a Welsh way."

Caitlin seethed. "We have some things to discuss, Mother, like the letters I sent Trevor and he sent me after I came to Wales the first time."

"Don't be silly, dear." Eileen tossed down a photo. "I was naughty but I only wanted the best for you, and so did Red. We did the right thing."

Just like that. Not even a question as to how Caitlin knew what had happened. "And you thought David McBride was best for me?"

"I still do."

Her mother couldn't have meant that. "David is history as far as I'm concerned," Caitlin said. "He was a special man when I married him, or I thought he was. He changed and there's nothing left. Even he admits that."

"He's trying to make you happy, so he's going along with what you want."

"What?"

"David loves you and Mary. He's destroyed by all this."

"Mother, don't! How can you fall for anything he says?"

Eileen's eyes filled. The effect electrified Caitlin. Her mother never cried. "David's always been kind to me. I hate seeing him suffer."

Caitlin hadn't seen this side of her mother for a long time. She felt selfish. Preoccupation with herself had made it easy to ignore Eileen's vulnerability. "David can be kind," she agreed. "He used to be kind all the time. That's what made me fall in love with him. But the people he admired so much ruined him."

"We all make mistakes." Eileen sniffed. "But he wouldn't want me making you sorry for him. I came because I wanted you to know what I intended to do and why. There shouldn't be any distance between us, darling, no misunderstandings."

Foreboding raked Caitlin's fragile nerves.

"I had hoped I might be able to persuade you to bring Mary back to L.A. for a while. David's different, Caitlin, changed. If you'd give him another chance, I know you could work things out."

No, no, no. She pressed shaking fingers to her temple.

"I know you don't believe that," her mother said. "So be it. But think about this. You and Mary are out of place here. You belong in L.A. Mary was never hospitalized with an ulcer there. The girl's life is a roller coaster. Can't you see that? Can't you see how highly strung and overexcited she is? You may want to pretend she's happy. But she's not. She misses her father, and she's pretending to be all right for your sake.''

''Mother—''

''That's all I'm going to say on the subject.''

Caitlin got up and poured more coffee for both of them. ''You really think Mary—'' She shook her head.

''You haven't seen David the way I have lately. He's trying so hard to be brave that it breaks my heart.''

''Is David coming to the house a lot?'' Caitlin returned her entire attention to her mother.

''We've been out for dinner a few times. He's very lonely and worried. But we've worked that out.''

''What have you worked out?''

Eileen smiled and patted Caitlin's hand. ''You're not to worry, I can afford it.''

All she could do was stare. She knew what her mother was going to say.

''I'm going to help him get the money he needs for the movie. Actually, we'll more or less be partners, and I'm excited for him, Caitlin, genuinely excited. There might even be a part in it for me. The script's very strong.''

Oh, God! And her mother had talked about women who were pushovers in the hands of persuasive men. Caitlin bowed her face over her cup. She'd abdicated, left a woman who pretended to be selfish, but who was essentially sensitive—left her alone to be taken advantage of by a man who was Caitlin's responsibility.

''Well, darling. What do you think?''

Her mother's pride was at stake. ''It all sounds very interesting. Did you sign anything yet?''

''No. Like I said, I was determined to tell you what I was doing first.''

And that took a trip halfway around the world?

"We're getting together on Monday to hash out the details."

Monday, five days. "Mother—"

The phone rang. "Stay there, darling. I'll get it. You look worn-out."

And Eileen, clipping on her elegant high-heeled shoes, whipped into the hall before Caitlin could protest. She began to feel helpless. Trevor. She needed to talk to Trevor.

Eileen returned quickly. "That was a Mrs. Johnson. She said she was your housekeeper."

"Yes." Caitlin frowned. If she had her way, skirmishes with the locals wouldn't be aired in front of her mother.

"Something about being sorry. I gathered she's been off looking after a sick relative?"

"Mmm."

"Anyway, she said that if it's all right with you, she'll be in tomorrow morning. I said fine. Was that okay?"

"Fine." Caitlin wasn't at all sure she wanted Mrs. Johnson back.

"Are you feeling ill, dear?"

"I'm going out, Mother. You should probably rest after your trip. When I get back we'll...we'll talk."

"Why Castle Hill on a day like this?" Trevor pulled up his collar. Rain slashed their faces, driven diagonally by a steady wind.

"Because it is this kind of day. No one else is likely to come here."

"We could have been alone at my place."

And comfortable...too comfortable. "This is fine."

Trevor's hair was plastered to his head, drips fell into his eyes and he'd given up wiping them away. "Could we at least stand in the lee of the ruins?"

Without a word, she led the way until they stood looking down on the town with their backs to the crumbling castle walls.

Trevor squinted through moisture and smiled at her. "How can you look like that when you're soaking wet?" He lifted a handful of her sodden hair. And he kissed her, so suddenly she had no time to prepare. His mouth was wet from the rain—cool, firm, incredibly mobile. Her cold skin covered the start of shifting heat beneath. He'd locked her to him, and with her hands in her pockets she was incapable of pushing away, even if she'd wanted to.

"Thank God you came," he said against her lips. "I was afraid you'd stay away for days because your mother's here." The next kiss was harder. He ran the tip of his tongue along her bottom lip, then opened their mouths again.

When he raised his face they were both clinging. With his forefingers, he started between her brows, stroked to her temples and down along her jaw to meet at the tip of her chin. He bent to lick the rain from that spot.

With a full heart Caitlin looked down on his wet hair and closed her eyes. "Trevor," she said, then, more firmly, "Trevor, I've decided there's something I've got to do. I need your blessing."

His eyes, when she saw them, held the darkening that uncertainty brought. "Okay," he said, sounding uneasy. "But first, before I forget, my mother called this morning and my parents want you and your mother to come for dinner on Sunday."

Caitlin blinked against the rain. Rivulets found their way beneath her collar and she shivered. "I didn't think your parents approved of me."

He smiled and she looked away. "Well, evidently

they've come to their senses. They asked if six would be all right."

Her mother at the Morgans'? With a little shock wave, Caitlin saw the picture clearly, and felt her own response to the scene. Embarrassment. Through Eileen's eyes, the Morgans would seem anachronistic.

She made up her mind. "Trevor, I'm leaving for London on Sunday. I want to be in Los Angeles by Monday."

"That was fast. What did your lawyer say?"

"I haven't spoken to my lawyer. My mother needs me. That's why she came here."

"So help her here. The only reason to go back to L.A. is to deal with the divorce."

She needed his advice, but he wasn't going to be objective. "Mother's gotten herself into a business deal I'm not sure about."

"Isn't there someone else to help her?" A muscle twitched beneath his right eye. He was angry.

Caitlin drew herself up. "I've got responsibilities, and I intend to take care of them. I'm sure you understand."

"No, I don't understand."

"Look, I didn't want to say this, but David's dragging my mother into some movie venture, and I've got to watch out for her. I think I should go, don't you?" This hadn't been a good choice of a meeting place. The cold wasn't helping her already shaking limbs.

Trevor half turned away. "No, I don't think you should go. Not for the reasons you're giving."

"It would do Mary good to be near her father for a while, too. At least until her health is more stable."

His laugh grated. "You've got to be kidding. You're being manipulated."

"Maybe, but I can't ignore what I ought to do."

"It's always, you 'ought' to do something. You owe

everyone but me…and you." He gave her a narrow-eyed glare.

Caitlin's cramping calves hurt. "You're not being fair."

"I'm telling you not to go."

"You don't have the right!" All they needed was for her to lose her temper. "I came to you for advice."

"You came expecting me to say, fine, drop me again. But if you leave, I'll know how important I am to you."

A slow thudding started in her throat. "Don't do this."

"Each time a member of your family—even one you supposedly intend to divorce—crooks a finger, you run." He gnawed at his bottom lip. The rain made it hard to be sure she saw tears in his eyes.

"I thought you'd…I thought it would be all right."

"It's not. This is it, Caitlin, time to make up your mind what you really want."

Again she was being backed to the wall. "If we've got a strong relationship, it can stand an interruption."

The wind, the rain, the squalling of gulls receded. He stepped back. "And how long an interruption did you have in mind? Another nineteen years?"

She must hold herself together for just a little longer. "You're not being objective."

"If I'm not, it's because I'm sick of being used."

"You haven't been used. Not by me." She trembled all over. "I've made up my mind. I'm going home."

"Home?"

"Home. I come from Los Angeles. Maybe that's where I belong. I've got to find out. You told me once that we have very different roots. We do. Maybe I couldn't be happy living in a backwater like this."

As soon as it was said she knew the wound she'd inflicted. Trevor slowly pushed a hand through his hair.

"Trevor, I—"

"Go."

"It's for the best, at least for—"

He didn't give her time to finish. "Forget it. I'm not being dropped by you one more time. It hurts too much." Walking quickly, slipping on muddy turf, he went to the steps and leaped down to disappear behind a wall.

Red's fascination with Eileen hadn't been hard to understand. He'd been an exuberant man lacking in only one area: social standing from birth. Eileen had that and much more. And she'd adored Red. They'd made a dynamic couple, and looking at Eileen now, Thomas's wall of resistance weakened. She missed his brother, there was no doubt of that.

"Where is Caitlin?" he asked. He'd waited three days to hear something from her and had finally decided he couldn't stay away any longer.

Eileen had taken him into the sitting room and poured him a Scotch. "Picking up some tickets," she said, avoiding his eyes.

The Scotch lost its flavor. "Tickets to where?"

"The States. She's decided to bring Mary and come home with me for a while."

He smacked his glass down. "So you got your own way as usual."

"Oh, Thomas, don't be so hard on me." She looked up at him from beneath finely arched brows, her blue eyes shining. "You always did think I was a conniving female. You've had me stereotyped from the day we met."

"Don't try that act on me. Poor little helpless woman. Misunderstood and needing to be looked after."

Eileen drew herself up but he thought he saw something different in her eyes...uncertainty? "I'm not helpless,

Thomas. If Red were here he'd tell you as much. But I want my daughter to be happy and I don't think she will be here. Oh, it'll amuse her for a while—until she gets bored.''

Frustration overwhelmed him. Argument would get him nowhere. Not a thing had changed with this woman from the day Red had brought her home and she'd turned her nose up at everything Welsh.

"Thomas? Couldn't I be right?''

He lumbered to his feet. "I'm not going to argue with you. Caitlin has to make up her own mind about what she wants. But remember this, Eileen. And Red would agree with me. When you interfere in other lives you're on dangerous ground. Look at your motives, girl. Look carefully, because even if you believe you've got Caitlin's best interests at heart, you may end up hurting her more than you ever dreamed of. I'm going home.''

"Wait." She stepped between him and the door. "Wait, Thomas. I…I'm only doing what I think's best for Caitlin and Mary.''

"Are you? And you don't want to keep her near for yourself, because you're afraid of being alone?'' He bent to retrieve his muffler, pretending to dismiss her with the question.

"No more than you, Thomas,'' she said quietly. "I know Caitlin probably thinks I've been an aloof mother, but that's just my way. I couldn't love her more and I don't want her to make a mistake she'll regret later.''

He put on his coat. There was a ring of sincerity in her clear voice, and she looked at him for approval, he could sense as much. But he couldn't give that approval. "There's a time to let children go, Eileen. I was never lucky enough to have a family, but I've learned that from observation.''

Her sigh gave him hope. For an instant he thought she might agree with him, but then she shook her head. "You're wise, Thomas. But I think you're wrong in this case. Give me your blessing. Say I'm right to want Caitlin to give her marriage another chance."

Yes, he understood why Red had loved this woman. How old must she be now? Sixty? Yes, and she was still appealing with her hint of shielded vulnerability.

"I can't say what you want to hear, Eileen," he told her. "But I do wish you well. I hope you don't do more damage than can be fixed."

This time she made no move to stop him leaving.

Outside the door, on the path that had become his road to a second home, sadness swept over him, and helplessness. He didn't know what he could or should do. If he could dislike Eileen it would help. But he couldn't. She was a misguided mother scurrying to gather in her only child. Either the outcome would be all right or it wouldn't.

"Uncle Thomas!"

The gate swung open and Mary jogged through, followed by Owen and his sister, Constance.

Thomas forced a smile. "Hello, you lot."

"Come with us and hear what happened today," Mary said.

He shook his head. "Got to get on. Your grandmother's in the sitting room. I expect she'll want to hear your news."

Owen felt his own smile dissolve. Mr. Rhys sounded... angry? No, more tired, but angry, too. Connie and Mary had already gone ahead into the cottage. Owen followed more slowly, his growing uneasiness putting every nerve on alert.

When he entered the hall he heard Mary, already pouring out her story. He went into the sitting room and caught her grandmother's hard stare before she turned back to the girls.

"It was Owen who came up with the idea," Connie was saying.

Eileen Rhys's eyes moved back to him, then to Connie and on to Mary. The woman was comparing them and not finding Mary's friends to her liking.

"I'm going to paint the scenery for the school play," Mary said. "Not all of it, of course, but I'm going to do the designs and a lot of the painting. Owen suggested it to some of the other kids and they thought it was a great idea. He showed them some of my drawings."

The way her words tumbled out, the pinkness on her pale cheeks, the contrast between her blond hair and darkly glowing eyes, gripped at Owen. If he told an adult how he felt he'd be laughed at, told he was too young to know what he was talking about. But he and Mary knew they had something special.

"That's very nice, dear," Mrs. Rhys said.

Mary glanced back at him and he felt real fear. They were also considered too young to know what they wanted, and the adults in their lives could come between them.

"You're a very pretty girl." Mrs. Rhys was saying now, looking at Connie. "Dark and healthy. Very like your brother. I've always admired the strength of the Welsh, different...quite different from most of us."

They were different. He and Connie were from another race as far as this woman was concerned. He thought of his mother with her work-worn hands and plain clothes, his father dressed in a patched blue shirt and threadbare jeans on his way to work on a roof, the way he did every day. *Quite different.* She hadn't meant only in appearance.

"Where's Mom?" Mary asked. The pink had gone

from her cheeks. A fire glowed in the hearth, but the room was cold.

"She'll be home any minute. In fact, we'd better start getting organized."

"Organized for what?" Mary's white teeth pulled in her lower lip.

"Oh, just organized. Say goodbye to your, er, friends, Mary."

Consternation puckered Mary's brow. Owen's insides did horrible things.

He managed an "it's okay" signal and grinned. "Meet you in the morning."

"Not tomorrow," Mrs. Rhys said. Again she wasn't making eye contact. "Mary won't be at school tomorrow."

"Why?"

"Say goodbye, Mary. I'm sure you'll be in touch with Owen soon. But we're going to be busy for a few days."

Just like that. Mary treated like a little kid who shouldn't ask questions. But anything he said would only make things worse.

"Come on Connie." He led the way. "Don't come out, Mary. We'll talk soon."

Why did he feel, when he reached the lane, that it might be a long time before he spoke to Mary again?

17

"Why did you come to me with this?"

"Mr. Rhys said I should," Owen told him. "He said you'd know what to do."

Owen had given him a letter from Mary. Trevor smoothed it on his knee and read for a second time. The bleak feeling only increased. "I don't know what to do."

"Couldn't we help each other, Mr. Morgan?"

Trevor looked at the boy and, with an uncanny inner eye, saw himself as he'd once been. Owen was begging him to intervene so that history wouldn't be repeated.

"Mr. Morgan?"

"Let me think."

Three weeks had passed since Caitlin and Mary left. For a second time, Eileen Rhys had come between Trevor and her daughter. He tasted his own bitterness.

"She isn't happy."

"Hmm? Oh, you mean Mary." He glanced down again. "No. I hope her grandmother's satisfied."

"Mary's sick again, Mr. Morgan. It's awful there. Mrs. McBride must have wanted you to know because—"

"I can read, Owen. Mary wrote this while she was in bed, ill. So Caitlin probably mailed the letter, knowing you might show it to me."

Owen folded his big hands together in his lap. "Mary's dad comes to the house drunk. And her grandmother's angry with everyone." He fidgeted with the start of a hole in his worn jeans.

Trevor leaned back in the couch and stretched out his legs. He stared at the ceiling. From the moment Caitlin returned to Wales and they'd started their hesitant steps toward friendship, he'd been afraid of another disaster, that she'd somehow be snatched from him again. The weeks since she'd left had been the hardest in his life, other than when Gwen had died. He'd argued with himself that he must forget Caitlin, but she only filled more and more of his mind.

"If I could, I'd go there and get her back," Owen said in a small voice.

"In other words, you think I should go."

Owen chewed a fingernail.

"Do you understand all this?" Trevor tapped the letter. "Mary's mother is caught in the middle between her...her husband and her mother."

"Yes. Only she's divorcing him, isn't she?"

Trevor wished to hell he knew. "Mrs. McBride doesn't want her mother to lend money to Mr. McBride or to help him borrow even more. And her mother resents the interference."

"Mary's the one who's really in the middle."

"They both are."

Owen got jerkily to his feet. "Mary's dad's something. I'd take my dad over him any day. At least I know where I am."

"I've got to think about this, Owen, okay? I'll let you know if I decide there's anything I can, or should, do."

The hope in Owen's eyes squeezed at Trevor. "Thanks, Mr. Morgan. Things'll work out."

That seemed unlikely. "Did you go to see Will? He's home."

"Uh-huh. My mom's been taking food over." He hooked his thumbs in his jeans pockets. "I didn't think so at first, but you made a good decision when you disbanded the team for a year."

Trevor was distracted, but he managed a smile. "Maybe we'll give it another shot next year, after our little vandals have learned their lesson. Being reduced to mortal status should take the wind out of their sails." He got up and followed Owen downstairs to the bar.

The last person he expected to see at seven-thirty in the morning, hours before opening, was Thomas Rhys.

"Showed you the letter, did he?" he asked, leaning on the counter.

"He did." Trevor put an arm around Owen's shoulders and walked him to the door. "Keep your mind on schoolwork, boy. Things have a way of turning out the way they're supposed to." Trite. But what else did he have to offer? Slowly, he skirted tables to reach the fireplace where he gave Spot's cage an absentminded tap and received an affronted squawk for his efforts.

"What brings you here at this time of day, Thomas?" He went back behind the bar.

Thomas took out his pipe and a small knife to scrape the bowl. "Thought I'd drop in for a pint."

"At this hour of the morning?" Trevor laughed. "You'll have to do better than that, Thomas Rhys."

"Coffee, then?"

Trevor flipped a switch. "It'll be a few minutes."

They fell silent. Thomas finished cleaning his pipe and set it on the counter. He cleared his throat. Trevor hummed and slid clean glasses into their racks. Thomas was looking at him; he could feel it.

"Fridays are busy," Trevor remarked at last. "It's order day."

"Mmm. I had Colin-crust's wife go ahead and clean the cottage."

Trevor paused with a glass in his hand. "Why?"

Thomas made an airy gesture. "Oh, I just thought it was the thing to do. Andrew's done a bit of work in the garden, too. And there's plenty of groceries in."

"The Turners delivered?"

"Yes. Seems it was coincidence that everyone had to stop working for Caitlin at the same time. But they're all over whatever was wrong with them now."

"Do you know something I don't know?" Trevor eyed him closely.

Thomas's expression was cherubic. "Not a thing. Wouldn't worry about it if I were you. Won't happen again, I'm sure."

"You're sure, are you?" The glasses were endless. "Seems academic with the cottage empty."

"I thought you might want a place away from the pub if—"

Trevor shot him a warning look. "Why don't you just say what you came to say?"

"Coffee ready?"

"You're stalling."

"How are you feeling?" Their eyes met and Thomas shrugged. "Okay, so you've never felt worse. And whose fault is that?"

Blood came pounding into Trevor's temples. "Caitlin left because she wanted to. I asked her not to go."

"So get her back. You saw the letter. She went to try to protect that harebrained mother of hers. Caitlin's loyal and she feels responsible now her father's gone. What kind of man gives up on the woman he loves?"

"What the hell do you know about love?"

Thomas inclined his head. "I don't blame you for saying that. But each of us has a past. I know about love because I ended up a lonely old man. If I hadn't been too proud to go after a woman who meant a lot to me when I was your age, I wouldn't be alone...I might even have children.''

"I shouldn't have said that. I'm—''

"No, don't apologize. I'd have said the same in your place. Will you at least consider a bit of advice?''

"Of course.'' He felt a heel.

"Go to Los Angeles and bring her back...and Mary.''

"She probably won't come.''

"And you're too pigheaded to risk rejection?'' The pipe stem tapped as Thomas closed his teeth on it. "I'll have that coffee another time, Trevor.''

Beyond a stucco wall Trevor could see emerald lawns sweeping up to a low-lying Spanish style house. Sun glinted off tinted windows and glistened on the fronds of dumpy palms and jade trees. A security warning sign glared against white plaster next to the gate. The house was huge, elegant...intimidating. And this was Caitlin's house. That their roots were different went beyond understatement.

He looked for a bell but didn't find one. When he pushed against it, though, the heavy wrought-iron gate glided open easily, and he walked to steps flanked by twin stone planters aflame with begonias. Sprinklers sprayed rotating curtains of water that were transformed into rainbow prisms by the sun.

He climbed slowly upward. Now he was the foreigner, the interloper. Caitlin would be comfortable anywhere, but Trevor had never felt less comfortable than in this perfect, warmth-kissed place that reeked of money in amounts he'd never tried to calculate before. Caitlin must be a fantastically wealthy woman. Overcome by the enormity of what he'd done in coming here without warning, he turned around, disoriented.

"You looking for someone, sir?"

He jumped before he saw a small, wiry woman in a simple cotton shift emerge from tall metal gates that bisected the front of the house. "Caitlin... I'm a friend of Mrs. McBride's."

"She expecting you?" The woman's skin was weathered and scored with wrinkles. Her dark hair strained against a tight chignon.

"No," Trevor said, then, "Well, yes. She thought I might come." Not a complete lie. Caitlin must have expected him to react to Mary's letter.

"Mrs. McBride's by the pool." She inclined her head in the direction she'd come.

As simple as that. He'd expected more questions. Rather than ask where the pool was and run the risk of delay, he walked through the gates into the cool shade formed by walls on each side and entered an atrium. A square pool filled the center, with the house and lush plantings on all sides.

At first he didn't see Caitlin, until splashing noises guided him to the water where a slender body in a green suit plowed toward the side farthest from him. Her arms caused too much spray. Trevor smiled, moving closer. Caitlin was a strong swimmer, but she'd never be accused of having aquatic style. She started back and quickly approached.

"Hi ya, Shamu," Trevor called when her face came up for air.

Caitlin heard the voice through popping eardrums. She stopped in midstroke and trod water, scrubbing at her eyes and squinting. "Trevor?" Her mouth stayed open. "Trevor, it's you! Oh, my God, it's you.'' A single stroke brought her to the edge, and she shaded her face to look up at him.

She grasped his proffered hand, and he hauled her out. He didn't speak but told her of his love with his eyes. ''I've missed you so much,'' she said. Her arms slid around his neck and he nuzzled her brow, kissed her closed eyes. His hands, at her waist, gripping tight, lifted her to her toes.

When his mouth found hers it wasn't gentle. He sought and found her tongue. The kiss, and the next, was intimate, slow and heavy with restrained desire. He cupped her bottom, urging her against his taut hips. Caitlin responded as best she could. Part of her awoke, achingly aware and longing. Part of her slumped, weary, confused, wanting only his strength to hide her from reality, to offer her oblivion without strings.

He must have felt her exhaustion. ''It's been bad for you, *cari*.'' His breathing was labored but he relaxed his hold. ''I had to come. Did I do the right thing?''

''Yes.'' She didn't know how right it was, but she wanted and needed him. ''Where are your things?''

''At a hotel on...Wilshire?''

''Probably. Oh, Trevor!'' She leaped away. ''Look what I've done to you. You're soaked.''

He grinned, the grin that pulled in one corner of his mouth and turned Caitlin into a wobbly thing. ''Feels good. Cool. I'm not used to all this sun, remember. Particularly in midwinter.''

In the sun he looked wonderful, handsome. A short-sleeved black polo shirt and tan chinos would be counted out of uniform for him but he wore them beautifully. Not for the first time, Caitlin felt the power of his masculine strength.

"Owen showed me Mary's letter."

She bowed her head, massaging frown lines between her brows.

"I decided you were hoping he would and that I'd come."

Was she that transparent? "Yes."

"How is Mary?"

"Not good. She's at school today. I'm in a mess, Trevor. I did the wrong thing coming here, but I don't know how to get out of it."

The flexing of his fingers chilled her. "Is your mother at home?"

"No."

"What's the situation with the divorce?"

"I'm not married to David anymore." He made a move to hold her, but she shook her head. She must make it clear she wasn't free to walk away, not yet, nor for as far as she could see into the future.

"Leave it all behind and come back with me," Trevor said, and his voice broke.

"And leave him to milk my mother? Trevor, I've got to make sure he can't keep playing on her the way he does. He's got her thinking this damned flimflam notion of his is going to be her vehicle back to the limelight. Do you know what it costs to make a movie? Millions. She's talking about cosigning loans."

"There's no problem."

As always, Trevor the optimist. "There's a big problem."

"No. Think, Caitlin. The man wants money. Give him enough to get started and tell him you'll be the one to help him borrow the rest. If he's going to bomb, it'll start to happen before the loan stage, won't it?"

She gritted her teeth. "I've thought of that."

"Do it. Back him on the assurance that he'll never go near your mother again—or be a nuisance to you. Make him sign something in blood. Your lawyer can deal with that. Then bring Mary and come back to Wales with me. She's happier there. And she'll always be able to keep in touch with her father." He looked into the distance. "Not that he deserves her."

Oh, how she wanted to walk into his arms and hold on forever, to say yes, yes and do exactly what he suggested. "Trevor, I don't trust him to keep a bargain if I'm not around. He's perfectly capable of getting at my mother again. She's lonely and vulnerable."

His "Damn it all" startled her.

"Trevor—"

"It's all this, isn't it?" he said, sweeping wide a hand. "You're afraid to give it up. You said you might be. I can give you everything you need, but you know I can't give you all you've had...or all you might want again one day."

She jerked away from him and planted her hands on her hips. "That's not fair. Things have never mattered to me. Sure, it's easy for me to say that when I've never wanted for anything material." Acid tightness burned her throat. "But remember I have a stable career, and even if I do pay David off, I'm not going to be poor. I can live anywhere and provide very well for Mary and myself."

His mouth thinned to an angry line. "You don't need anyone, is that what you're telling me? Am I a diversion to you...something different because I'm not your social or financial equal?"

"No." She needed to sit down. "I'm telling you that money isn't an issue between us. I love Wales and I love you and I pray to God I can work things out so I can be there with you."

The hardness didn't fade from his features. "You're going to have to convince me of that. I've done my part."

"You've done so much. Please be patient."

"Caitlin..." In frustration, he wound his hand into his hair and tugged. "Caitlin, I've come halfway around the world to a place I *don't* want to be. Back in Tenby there's a business I've got to run. My father's filling in, but he can't keep that up for long. This is one of the busiest times of the year for me."

"What am I supposed to do?" She couldn't simply walk out.

"You're supposed to make up your mind, and quickly. Here's the address of the hotel." He took a card from his pocket and gave it to her. "Let me know what you decide." He turned and walked swiftly toward the atrium gates.

"Trevor, wait!"

"I'm going back to Wales on Thursday morning. That gives you three days."

18

The hotel room, big as it was, began to close in on him. From the balcony he could see buildings, pale with glittering glass, in every direction. And palm trees popping their crowns up here and there, and splashes of color where flowers he couldn't name flourished in planters.

At any other time, in any other circumstances, he'd have enjoyed the mystery of the place. But a day into his pronounced time limit on his stay, he considered Los Angeles hell. This wasn't going to work, this waiting around. He'd always been a doer, and he'd better figure out something to do about what was happening or he was going to go nuts.

Since his parting from Caitlin he'd eaten every meal in his room, warned the switchboard to hold calls each time he took a shower and slept no more than a few hours at a stretch.

"Finished, sir." The maid came from the bathroom, smiling brightly, and left with a pile of used towels.

When the latch clicked behind the woman, Trevor stopped pacing and flopped into a green satin chair. He stared at unlikely green tulips on clothlike wallpaper behind a vast bed covered in a spread bearing matching tulips. Not his taste. But the whole effect was fairly pleasing, and the cost of staying here was exorbitant enough, so he supposed it was his frayed nerves that made him critical.

A tapping came, so faint that he cocked his head to make sure he'd actually heard it.

The tap sounded again and he leaped to open the door.

"Mary!"

"Hi."

A large suitcase, the handle clutched in both her hands, pulled his attention from her pinched face. "What are you doing here?"

"Mom told me what you said. I'm coming back to Wales with you. I can't stay here anymore."

Trevor scratched his jaw. "Come in." He took the suitcase from her.

Even drained, as she obviously was, she was a lovely girl. He noted the blue streaks beneath her eyes, the huddled raising of her shoulders. Damn David McBride. He'd like to take the man apart.

Mary sat down abruptly on the nearest chair and closed her eyes.

"Are you okay?" Trevor asked, alarmed. He dropped the case.

"I will be when I get away from here." Her dark eyes opened and fixed on him. "I've got my passport and there's enough money in my savings account to buy a ticket. Uncle Thomas will let me stay with him once we get there."

"Mary—" he sank to his haunches beside her "—you can't run out on your mother and grandmother."

"I can," she responded fiercely. "I love them—Dad, too, when he's not being horrible—but I need a fresh start. If Mom would come, too, I'd like that best, but I'll go alone first if I have to. I'm going with you." She shut her eyes again and leaned back in the chair.

Wonderful. Now he had a fifteen-year-old runaway to cope with. Trevor got up and resumed pacing. If he turned her away, he couldn't even be sure she'd go home. He could take her home, but that didn't mean she'd stay there.

"All right, Mary," he said, striving to sound matter-of-fact. "I'll get you a room of your own here, and we'll work things out. How's that?"

Her small body, flying at him, almost knocked him over, and he smiled, holding her gently. Protectiveness, a kind he hadn't experienced before, welled up in him until his chest was tight. He wished this were his daughter.

Two hours later, Mary was sleeping in a room several doors down the hall from his and he'd called the McBride house, reaching not Caitlin, who was out, but Eileen Rhys who was surprisingly civil. She would do what was necessary.

When reception called announcing that Mrs. Eileen Allen Rhys had arrived, Trevor experienced his worst attack ever of what-the-hell-have-I-done?

His first and only exposure to Eileen had been brief and strained. Today, he wondered if he'd been too numbed by what had happened to Will Colly to see her clearly the evening they'd met. She came into the room, accepted his suggestion that they go onto the balcony and also his offer of a drink. She had white wine and sat, blue eyes staring across Beverly Hills, the picture of a subdued penitent. A beige linen suit showed off her trim figure and good skin. Short straight frosted hair was just right on her, the style deliberately simple to complement her fine facial bone structure.

Trevor decided he'd let her do the talking, and she took her time.

After a lengthy silence she said, "David McBride is no good. How can you be so wrong about something?"

He made a neutral noise.

"Oh, who am I fooling? I've known it for a long time, at some level. I chose to let him snow me because I needed all the strokes I could get, or thought I did. These last weeks since Caitlin came back have made me really face what the man's become. He's a useless leech...poor devil. You have to feel sorry for him, but my daughter and granddaughter come first and he's bad for both of them."

Trevor murmured again. Saying he heartily agreed wouldn't be appropriate.

"I went for an audition yesterday." Eileen brought her eyes to his. This wasn't an act. She felt remorse. "And I'm going to play a major character part in a movie called *The Lady*. My career is pulling back on track, only I can't be happy, not until Caitlin is.

"Thomas warned me. He said I could be causing a problem that would be tough to fix. And he told me Red would have said the same things...and he would have. But I've always been too sure of my first instincts to take anyone's advice until I've made a hash of things. I guess I haven't changed. I owe you an apology."

He tilted his head in question.

"For destroying your letters to Caitlin years ago. And hers to you. I'm sorry and embarrassed. Red never approved, but he went along because he let me persuade him it wasn't important."

"Forget it," Trevor said, suddenly uncomfortable with this woman's contrition. "We all do things because they seem right at the time."

Eileen set her glass on a green marble table and leaned urgently toward him. She laid her hands on his. "At close quarters, David is no good for Caitlin or for Mary. Please, will you convince Caitlin that she doesn't have to stay here to protect me? I know that's what she's doing. But she's the one who needs looking after. She loves you and you wouldn't be here if you didn't love her. Please, Trevor, make her go back to Wales with you. And don't let her worry about Mary, either. Mary wants to be in Tenby, that's why she came to you. She'll adjust very nicely.''

He traced the lines on his palms. "Caitlin is worried about you. She's worried about David McBride's influence on you. I'm not sure I can get her to leave Los Angeles until she's sure you're all right.''

"Make her go." Eileen moved forward in her chair. "Tell her. He called her again today, demanding,and—''

"Demanding what?''

"I don't know. He threatens and uses Mary to back up his threats. Caitlin was going to see him—''

"Now?" He shot from his chair. "Is she with him now?''

Eileen stood, too, her hands clasped together. "I think so. I try not to get excited, but he frightens me. He's never been violent, but—''

"Stay here." Caitlin pulled Eileen into the bedroom. "Stay here in case Mary wakes up before I get back.''

"Where are you going?''

"What's David McBride's address?''

The man was cool, he'd give him that.

McBride had looked Trevor over slowly, with no sign of surprise, before ushering him into an elegant studio apartment a few blocks from Caitlin's house.

"Drink?" McBride asked, waving toward a white leather chair shaped like a manta ray stretched over a chrome frame.

"No." Trevor took up position in the center of a room that was too modern and too smooth for his liking. White fur, white leather, glittery glass and senseless artwork. Not, Trevor acknowledged, that he'd like anything that belonged to David McBride.

The man was pouring himself a drink: Chivas Regal, straight up, in a water glass.

"Where's Caitlin?" Trevor hated having to ask Mc-Bride about her.

"How would I know?" The sweep of both arms was expansive, too expansive. Davey boy already had a start on getting drunk.

"She was coming here. Her mother told me."

McBride scowled. "That bag tells too much. Caitlin was here. She's left, but she'll be back. She always comes back to me." With this he lifted his arrogant dark head. The khaki bush shirt and slacks he wore suited him, made his tan more noticeable, accentuated his slimness...but did nothing for the ravaged lines on his face.

Caitlin had been here and left. Or so McBride said. Trevor looked around, glanced up at an open loft, half expecting to see her tied up somewhere.

"Look, Morgan, why don't you put your provincial self back on whatever plane you crawled from and return to wonderful Wales? Surely you feel out of your depth here. Better go where you belong."

Trevor stared at him. Pathetic bastard. But he had a hold on Caitlin and he used it. "I thought we'd have a chat, McBride."

"We don't have anything to 'chat' about."

"Oh, but we do. Caitlin."

"Caitlin's none of your damned business." Another sweep of his arm sent whiskey over the white rug, but McBride took no notice. "None of your business. She's my wife."

A slow boil started in unidentifiable parts of Trevor.

His every muscle tensed. *Easy,* he warned himself. "Caitlin isn't your wife anymore, McBride."

"Says who? Tell me that? Says who?" A hefty measure of whiskey made it into his mouth, and Trevor heard him swallow. "And what if some lawyer or judge or whatever did sign a paper? Mary's still my daughter. I told Caitlin she won't get away from me. She thinks she will but she won't. I'll...I'll... She owes me."

Trevor swallowed acid disgust. "Where did Caitlin go?" The man was changing before his eyes, losing control.

"To hell, I guess." Now he postured, minced across the rug in a parody of a two-step. "Undoubtedly she's somewhere worrying about what I may do next. And she should worry about that, because when I'm angry, I can do very, very nasty things."

"Do you ever threaten men...McBride?" The heat in his body grew, the desire to squash this man to the nothingness he really was.

McBride shuddered. "I hate violence. Anything physical. You sure you don't want that drink?" He sucked more whiskey, making a greedy sound. "No, no. Busman's holiday for you, right? Barmen probably don't drink off duty."

The creep wasn't worth what he made Trevor feel. "I've got a few things to say to you, then I'm gone."

"My dear—"

"*Let* me say what I came to say. Caitlin and I are in love. In a way, we have been for a very long time. Now we're going to do something about it."

The glass, catching light as McBride threw it, sent Trevor diving out of its path.

"Get out!" McBride's voice veered into a scream. "Get out! Go back to your miserable little country and your miserable little town. You don't belong here, and Caitlin wouldn't live where you do. Don't you see that, idiot? You're dreaming. And if you think you can get your hands on her money, dream on. It's mine. I earned it.''

Trevor's hands curled into fists. With difficulty he kept them at his sides. "How did you earn it, McBride?" What Trevor couldn't control was the menace in his words. "Did you earn it by being a sterling husband? Did you earn it by looking after Caitlin, by being around when she and Mary needed you, by being the gentle lover Caitlin deserves?"

"I married her, dammit. I married a dumb little girl and showed her how to live—or I tried to show her. She never did catch on to what life can be if you let go and enjoy it."

"You married her? That was doing Caitlin a favor? Damn it all…she did you the favor, and she wasted herself on you."

"You fool." McBride shook his head slowly, deliberately. "Who the hell cares what you think? As long as I can use Mary, Caitlin won't go…no matter how much she threatens. I know that. I know her too well. And I want her where I can get at her when I need something. For better, for worse, the old vows say, and I intend to go right on collecting."

The sound, skin on skin, bone on bone, came even before Trevor knew he was about to hit that arrogant face. But he knew exactly what he'd done when McBride tripped over one of his elegant chairs and blood sprayed from his nose onto the white leather.

"Don't!"

Trevor ignored the wail, fell on him and pinned McBride's thin shoulders to the floor with his own solid knees. "Damn you, McBride. I haven't hit a man since I was a teenager, but I'm not taking any more from you, and neither is Caitlin.''

"You won't get away with this. I'll have you arrested for assault and battery.''

"How about murder, McBride? Maybe you'll have me arrested for murder!''

For a second, McBride was shocked into silence. Blood oozed steadily from his nose. "You aren't that much of a fool,'' he said at last. "You want to be around to play with Caitlin, don't you?''

Trevor drew back his fist again, then stopped himself. In some quiet part of his mind, he realized that if he didn't move away, he might do something he wouldn't want to live with. He got up slowly, shaking with the effort of self-control and backed away to sit on the edge of a table. "Stay right there and listen, McBride. You won't tell anyone what happened here today. Got it?''

"The hell I won't.''

"You won't, because if you do, I'll tell a few things about you—things I think you'd rather no one knew.''

David had found a handkerchief and was dabbing his nose. "You hurt me, and you're going to pay. Caitlin, too.''

"Caitlin's always going to pay, huh? Wrong. And you aren't listening to me. The basic difference between you and me, the one that can't be seen, is that appearances are everything to you. You don't give a damn in hell what kind of a man you are. You only care about the way people see you. But I *know* who and what I am. That's the important stuff. What I don't care about is other people's opinions of me. Believe it, McBride, if I couldn't stop you victimizing Caitlin and Mary, I wouldn't rely on court orders that can't be enforced. I'd find some way to get rid of you, and to hell with the consequences. But you aren't like that, are you?"

"I want you out of here." He wobbled to his knees.

"As soon as possible, friend. I want out, too. McBride, don't ever bother Caitlin again or I'm going to tell the world you're impotent."

McBride stayed where he was, half-crouched, huddled, staring.

"I see you get my drift. Leave Caitlin and her mother alone, and be very, very careful around Mary, or one of those gossip rags this town is buried in will find out that David McBride can't get it up."

The man seemed to wither. He sat on his fur rug and scooted away until his back hit a wall. "She told you," he whispered. "She told you."

Trevor stood and made himself walk slowly to the door. "Do we have a deal? I want to hear you say you'll leave them alone or I go to the press. *Say it!*"

"I can't—"

"Say it."

The heaving of McBride's shoulders, the muffled sobbing, turned Trevor's stomach. He waited with a hand on the doorknob.

"Yeah," McBride said, raising a bloody and tear-stained face. "Yes, damn you, they're all yours. I hope you rot together."

Trevor left. He hadn't needed the words to prove he'd got the message across.... He'd just needed the words.

Where was she? Trevor picked up the phone to call her house again, then changed his mind and dropped the receiver back on the hook. Eileen Rhys said she'd contact him the minute she heard from Caitlin.

The phone, ringing under his hand, jolted him before he snatched up the receiver. "Caitlin?"

Reception informed him that Mrs. McBride was on her way up.

Trevor met her at the elevator. "Where have you been? I've been out of my mind."

"I went to a—"

"Get in here." He hustled her into his room, where he closed her inside and backed her to the wall with a hand braced each side of her head. "Listen," he said in a voice he hardly recognized. "Listen, I've had it with this. You think you have to take care of the whole world...with the exception of you and me. Well, you don't anymore. I've made sure of that. Your mother's told me she can look after herself. Your daughter hates this place and is in this hotel with her passport in hand ready to go back with me. And you're going back with me, too."

"I—"

"*Don't* interrupt me. You're headstrong, d'you know that? And sometimes you rush off in every direction, accomplishing absolutely nothing simply because you don't stop to think."

She'd flinched, and he didn't like that but occasionally a man had to do things he didn't like.

"So, whether you like it or not, we're going to Tenby, and you're going to think. If you decide you can't stand the place and can't stand me, we'll call it quits. But this time the decision's going to be made on the basis of our needs, yours and mine, not someone else's. I already know what Mary needs, and you'll have to come to terms with that." He wouldn't tell her what had passed between him and David. With luck she need never know.

"Trevor—"

"It's all fixed, and I'm right about this, I tell you."

"I know you are. I just saw a travel agent and we're coming with you. I hope."

Caitlin barely contained a laugh at the expressions that passed over his face. His Adam's apple moved sharply. "As soon as I got back from dealing with David, Mother gave me the rundown on what's happened with Mary. Mary's ticket, and mine, can be waiting for us at the airport the day after tomorrow."

"Dealing with David?" His arms dropped heavily to his sides. "He... How did you deal with him?"

Caitlin edged past him, moving toward the open balcony doors. She inhaled slowly as the sheer, celery-colored draperies billowed in the warm breeze. "This morning I had a showdown with David."

Trevor came to her side. He rubbed her neck beneath her hair, tipped her face up. "Do we have to talk about him right now?" His jaw was shadowed, his hair disheveled, undoubtedly from many distracted tuggings, and in his clear eyes the pupils were big and dark.

"We have to talk about David, and about other worries I have."

He was handsome and strong. Vulnerability, hope, gentleness animated his expression. Life without him wasn't a possibility she could consider. She kissed his chin and quickly put her fingertips to his lips to stop the kiss he was about to deliver.

"I told you that David's part of my history now. I guess he didn't realize that, or maybe he just didn't believe I meant it. He still may not believe I mean it, but I do. Mother told him she'd looked into his so-called venture and decided it was no more than a hole to pour money into. So he tried turning back to me.

"I went to him today, and he didn't even give me time to say what I intended to say, which was that I knew where Mother stood with him but I'd still give him some help."

Trevor removed her fingers from his mouth and brushed back her hair. "I don't like thinking of you dealing with that man."

She smiled at him, giving him her love in the smile. "I'm a pretty tough cookie, kid."

"Of course, I'd forgotten." He laughed and she had to hold him away as he tried to pull her close.

"David was Mr. Confidence personified. He was glad I was ready to shoulder my responsibilities to him, that I understood what a worthy project he is."

Trevor snorted.

"Sh. Let me finish. He was very magnanimous. Since I was supposedly ready to give him money and cosign for millions of dollars worth of loans, he wouldn't be coming to the house uninvited anymore, particularly since he'd be very busy. Of course, he would see Mary regularly—when he had time."

"Son of a... What did you say to him?"

"Get lost."

"That was it? Get lost?" An odd expression crossed his face, as if he were thinking of something else.

Caitlin shrugged. "Seemed to cover it. Not that I think I've heard the last of David on that score. He was raging and threatening all the way to my car. I thought he might throw himself on the hood. He was yelling something about how I'd never have the guts to leave for good."

"Was he now? Well, we'll just have to prove him wrong."

This time she didn't stop Trevor from kissing her—a soft, searing kiss that brought her, weak and clinging, into his arms.

"You're coming back with me, aren't you?" He whispered against her throat.

Her eyelids were heavy and she let them droop. "If we're sure it's the right thing to do?"

He became very still. "Look at me."

She did as he asked.

"I want you to marry me. That'll mean living in Tenby. Will you get bored there?"

Why did she always want to cry when he made her the happiest? "I couldn't be bored anywhere with you, Trevor. We've had the longest trial relationship in history and I know this is right. But I want to be fair to you. David's not going to give up easily. He's vengeful and he'll probably try to get at me through Mary. Why should you put up with specters creeping in from my past?"

Trevor shook his head. "Dumb question." He kissed her brow, her nose, each cheekbone and, finally, her mouth. Long, slow and moist, his kiss played her nerves to singed points. Then he kissed her again, his tongue grazing the sensitive parts inside her mouth over and over until she trembled and felt his answering shudder.

He paused long enough to lift her to the bed and stretch out beside her. Rolling to rest an elbow each side of her head, he smiled as he looked at her mouth. "Caitlin, would you, just for once, let go of the notion that you're solely responsible for everyone else? Trust me, please. I want you as you are, with whatever you bring with you. Mary's already begun to understand and accept her father's foibles. She'll be fine. And stop concerning yourself about what David might be able to do to us. He isn't going to bother us again, I'm sure of it. End of discussion."

"You make it sound so simple." She loved his weight, the solid mass of his body on hers. He intoxicated her.

"It is simple. But maybe there is something else we should look into."

Weakening heat in her limbs, her womb, scattered her concentration. She could only stare into his face, so close now.

"There are differences between us. And I can't completely change. Can you accept me as I am?"

Her laughter sounded far away. "Now who's asking dumb questions? I want you because you're who you are."

"So we'll go to Wales together?"

She pushed him onto his back and undid the buttons on his cotton shirt. "We'll go, and we'll get married there as quickly as we can if that's what you want." Her kiss stopped his attempted reply. She moved her lips down to his chest and spread her hands, sweeping circles over the hair before she rested her cheek on the beat of his heart. He worked the shirt all the way off.

"We'll build a house if you like." His breathing became irregular.

"We'll live in your flat," she told him. "If there's room."

"There's room, but it's not what you're used to." He pulled her thin white sweater over her head.

Words caught in her throat while he stroked his fingertips over her breasts. She held his hands to her. "I don't ever want to hear about what I am or am not used to again. Give me a year or so in Tenby and people will forget I haven't always lived there. You'll see. I'll even sound Welsh."

"That I'd like to hear," he said, his voice indistinct.

Caitlin could tell he wasn't really listening anymore.

_____ Epilogue _____

"*Dinbych-y-Pysgod.*" Mary tutted and tried again, "*Din—*"

Owen's laughter silenced her efforts. She twisted her hand in his but he held fast. "Give it up," he told her, "Welsh is hard for the Welsh if they aren't born speaking it. Yours is awful."

Mary stalked ahead along the cliffs with Owen dragging just enough to slow her down. "I don't want to be fluent, just to be able to say a few words here and there. The next time I write to Dad or my grandmother or a friend I'm going to print Tenby at the top in Welsh."

"Wonderful. And you already know how to spell the words, so why say them?"

"You're mean."

"No, only honest. You hurt my ears. Do you know what it means in Welsh even?"

She waited for him to climb beside her. "It means Tenby, I suppose."

"Little fort of the fishes."

He was always joking. "Don't be silly, Owen. That's senseless."

"Would I lie to you? It probably had something to do with this being a fort and a fishing town."

"Seems logical, I suppose," she admitted.

Owen had told her they had important things to discuss,

and she thought she knew what they were. She moved on, apprehensive, yet anxious to do what must be done.

April had arrived, bringing showers and a fresh spurt of life in the plants that struggled to live in sandy soil constantly bathed by salt mist. Mary breathed in, her senses sharp and pleased.

"Far enough," Owen announced, pulling her to sit on a flat rock beside the path. "Can you believe we've been going together for seven months?"

She bowed her head, hiding her smile with the forward swing of her hair. Owen always let her know she was important to him, that what he liked most in the world was being with her. "Sometimes it seems *so* much longer than seven months."

"You've got a wise mouth, do you know that?" he asked. "Ever since you got to be sixteen, you've been impossible."

"For two whole months? I guess I was okay before then?"

He hugged her, waited until she looked at him and kissed her. Mary closed her eyes, kissing him back and loving the feel of his mouth on hers and the tightening of his strong arms. He drew away to smile at her and settled her cheek against his neck.

"We've got to make plans."

Mary tried to raise her face but one big hand kept her head where it was.

"We've got a few more months, but I want to go to university in the autumn. That'll mean going away."

His scholarship made her proud, but being glad he had ambition wasn't always easy. "And I'll still be in school here." Her throat began to ache. "I don't want to think about it."

"I do. We've both seen what happens when people

want to be together but don't look into the future to find out how to go about it."

He was talking about her mother and Trevor. "Four years seems endless, Owen."

"It'll be more than that."

Her heart dropped. "Yes. I guess I haven't let myself think too much about how long you'll be gone." Owen intended to study medicine in Edinburgh. It would take forever, and Scotland was so far away from Wales. Even the slow rubbing of his fingers over her back didn't dull a wave of dejection.

"Hey, cheer up." Owen lifted her chin and kissed her lightly again. "That's why we're here now, to decide what's going to happen to us."

Mary sighed. "You're eighteen and I'm sixteen. Our folks wouldn't think too much of us making plans about our future."

"They don't have to know, because we aren't going to try anything stupid." He let her go and fumbled beneath his shirt collar. "This'll do for now...if you'll wear it."

The heavy gold medallion he wore around his neck had belonged to his grandfather for whom Owen was named. On one side the worn engraving was of a dove carrying an olive twig; the reverse bore the faint tracing, Owen Trew. Mary had never known him to take it off, until today.

"Will you wear it as a promise between us?"

She touched the smooth metal. "Won't you miss it?"

"No. If it's around your neck, it'll still be mine. It'll be our way of saying we're going to be married one day."

Mary didn't attempt to hide her tears. She nodded, lifted her hair and turned her back to him. The clasp snapped into place, and Owen planted a kiss on her nape.

"There," he said, turning her toward him. "You're wearing it for me until it's time to do things properly."

She still felt stalking sadness. "I hope the rest of the school year and the summer go very slowly."

"They won't. We'll enjoy ourselves and they'll go quickly, but Trevor says he'll help me get home at Christmas and in the spring, and then it'll be summer again."

"And then you'll leave again."

He shook her gently. "Will you stop looking on the black side? What will happen then is that you'll be ready for college yourself. And that's when we can be together."

Mary frowned. She hadn't really considered where she'd go to college. One of the London art schools had seemed the most likely. "Do you think I'd be allowed to go to Scotland?"

"Trevor didn't say you wouldn't."

She rubbed her fingertips along his jaw, touched the cleft in his chin. "And he didn't say I would. And he isn't my father, remember." Why did she have to be too young to do what felt right? "You and Trevor talk about a lot of things, don't you?"

"He understands."

"My mother probably would, too, now. Only she won't want me going to the other end of the country with you. She'd probably expect, well—" She felt hot blood rush into her face.

"Okay, okay, we're getting ahead of ourselves. How does this sound?" Owen's cheeks bore their own touch of red. "We will work things out—together—one step at a time. For today, we'll make one big decision."

With his fingers laced behind her neck he studied her seriously.

"Whatever you say," she told him.

"The decision is this. We're...well, we can know we're engaged in a way. Anyway, we'll marry one day. Agreed?"

Her smile felt wonderful. "Agreed."

"And one other thing."

"Anything."

"No way will we allow the kind of fuss Trevor and your mother made getting to be the way they are."

"No way!" Mary agreed.

The wind carried away their laughter, and when the rain came, it fell on the top of Owen's dark hair and Mary's upturned face.

BARBARA

DELINSKY

When Leah Gates arrives at a remote cabin in the woods,
all she is seeking is refuge from a vicious storm. But
instead she finds Garrick Rodenheiser, a man wary of
strangers and hiding from his past. He can't refuse Leah
shelter, but he's determined to protect his isolated life.
But somehow Leah and Garrick can't seem to resist each
other. Because sometimes love finds you, no matter how
well you hide....

Twelve Across

Available mid-April 2000 wherever paperbacks are sold!

Stella Cameron

| 66463 | MOONTIDE | ___ $5.50 U.S. ___ $6.50 CAN. |
| 66495 | UNDERCURRENTS | ___ $5.99 U.S. ___ $6.99 CAN. |

(limited quantities available)

TOTAL AMOUNT	$_____
POSTAGE & HANDLING	$_____
($1.00 for one book; 50¢ for each additional)	
APPLICABLE TAXES*	$_____
TOTAL PAYABLE	$_____
(check or money order—please do not send cash)	

To order, complete this form and send it, along with a check or money order for the total above, payable to MIRA Books®, to: **In the U.S.:** 3010 Walden Avenue, P.O. Box 9077, Buffalo, NY 14269-9077; **In Canada:** P.O. Box 636, Fort Erie, Ontario L2A 5X3.

Name:_____
Address:_____ City:_____
State/Prov.:_____ Zip/Postal Code:_____
Account Number (if applicable):_____
075 CSAS

*New York residents remit applicable sales taxes.
 Canadian residents remit applicable GST and provincial taxes.

MIRA

Visit us at www.mirabooks.com   MSC0500BL